MW00979944

PENGUIN BOOKS

Mother's Day

Mother's Day is the final novel in Laurence Fearnley's southern trilogy. The first was *Butler's Ringlet*, published in 2004. The second, *Edwin and Matilda*, was runner-up for the Montana Award for fiction in 2008. Laurence's earlier novel *Room* was shortlisted for the Montana Award in 2001. She has been awarded several fellowships, notably the 2004 Artists to Antarctica fellowship, the 2006 Island of Residences fellowship in Tasmania, and the 2007 Robert Burns fellowship at the University of Otago. Laurence lives in Dunedin.

Mother's Day

By Laurence Fearnley

PENGUIN BOOKS

PENGUIN BOOKS
Published by the Penguin Group
Penguin Group (NZ), 67 Apollo Drive, Rosedale,
North Shore 0632, New Zealand (a division of Pearson New Zealand Ltd)
Penguin Group (USA) Inc., 375 Hudson Street,
New York, New York 10014, USA
Penguin Group (Canada), 90 Eglinton Avenue East, Suite 700, Toronto,
Ontario, M4P 2Y3, Canada (a division of Pearson Penguin Canada Inc.)
Penguin Books Ltd, 80 Strand, London, WC2R 0RL, England
Penguin Ireland, 25 St Stephen's Green,
Dublin 2, Ireland (a division of Penguin Books Ltd)
Penguin Group (Australia), 250 Camberwell Road, Camberwell,
Victoria 3124, Australia (a division of Pearson Australia Group Pty Ltd)
Penguin Books India Pvt Ltd, 11, Community Centre,
Panchsheel Park, New Delhi – 110 017, India
Penguin Books (South Africa) (Pty) Ltd, 24 Sturdee Avenue,
Rosebank, Johannesburg 2196, South Africa
Penguin Books Ltd, Registered Offices: 80 Strand, London, WC2R 0RL, England

First published by Penguin Group (NZ), 2009
1 3 5 7 9 10 8 6 4 2

Designed by Mary Egan
Typeset by Pindar NZ
Printed in Australia by McPherson's Printing Group

ISBN: 978 0 14 301125 5

A catalogue record for this book is available
from the National Library of New Zealand.
www.penguin.co.nz

ARTS COUNCIL OF NEW ZEALAND TOI AOTEAROA

The assistance of Creative New Zealand towards the production of this book
is gratefully acknowledged by the Publisher.

For my mother

PART ONE

$\mathscr{A}$WAD OF TOILET paper floated on the surface of Mr Paxton's toilet bowl. When originally flushed, foam from a cleaning dispenser might have obscured the floating remains, but now it merely clung to it, like lacey frill. Maggie flushed the toilet and stepped away, reaching across to the cabinet where the cleaners were stored. As she did so, she caught sight of her reflection in the mirror. The dark lines beneath her eyes seemed, even to her, more pronounced than usual and despite her gaunt appearance, she was sure she was developing jowls – or at least a sagging jaw line. It was hard to believe she had only recently turned forty. From her face she'd guess forty-eight, fifty, maybe even fifty-five. Her gaze remained on her reflection as she raised her top lip with her fingertips. Her teeth were small, the spaces between them exaggerated as if baby, rather than permanent, teeth. More noticeable was the gap between her two front teeth. If she ever felt like it, she could slip a matchstick into the space.

'Matchstick' had been her nickname at school. The name had referred to her height and weight, rather than her teeth. Throughout her teenage years she had felt self-conscious about her body. She was unlucky to have inherited her father's scrawny frame rather than her mother's fuller figure. In her uniform she had felt freakish, all head and bones – like a chop sucked clean of meat. No matter how many layers she wore, she couldn't disguise the fact that she was skinny.

Her father's bone structure was not the only thing passed down from his side of the family. Maggie also inherited his talent for singing and, from a young age, she had embraced his religious beliefs. Not that she sang much now – except, once in a while, during Mass. From her mother she had picked up a sense of responsibility, a strong work ethic and an eye for a bargain. Plus the gappy teeth, of course. She had her mother's mouth.

Maggie squinted at her reflection, scrutinising the size of the pores on her nose, and then returning to the toilet, she started to clean.

Mr Paxton, her client, would be devastated to learn that she often encountered more than just paper floating in his toilet. An elderly man, both fastidiously neat and polite, he had been introduced to Maggie two years before when she had been assigned to him by her sister's care-giving agency. They got along well. But, having all but lost his sight, Mr Paxton believed he was little more than a friendly nuisance.

Once, several months before, Maggie had attempted to raise the subject of the toilet with him. She had remarked, as tactfully as possible, that the toilet was not flushing properly. He had listened attentively and nodded his head as she spoke but, despite her concern, had done nothing. He couldn't afford a plumber. It was that simple. Only if the situation got worse – if the bathroom flooded, for example – would he call for help.

Today, as Maggie finished wiping soap scum from the shower base, she prayed Mr Paxton would not try to keep her longer than her scheduled two hours. She had arranged to meet her teenage son, Bevan, at court and she couldn't afford to be late. Not today. She wanted her son to be present for his older friend Todd's appearance. Though nowhere near as bad as his companion, her son definitely lacked sense. He was at an age when he all but worshipped the ground Todd walked on. He was incapable of seeing him for what he was: a troublemaker. Aware she was fighting a losing battle, Maggie nevertheless felt she had to intervene. Bevan needed to understand where his life was heading. It was her responsibility to *make* him see.

Thinking about what had happened made her angry. Bevan swore he had nothing to do with it, but a group of his friends had ganged up on a man in a wheelchair and stolen his cellphone. From what she could gather, her son had remained in Todd's car, which was parked half a block away from where the incident took place. According to Bevan, he had been selecting new ring tones for his own mobile and had been completely unaware of what was taking place outside. He thought Todd and his mates were buying milkshakes from a nearby café. It had come as a complete shock to learn that they had snatched a phone and then upturned the victim's wheelchair, leaving the middle-aged man stranded on the pavement. Bevan stressed that he hadn't noticed a thing. But, when he thought about it, didn't people in wheelchairs live in halfway houses? And didn't they travel by minibus, ferried from one place to another by professional caregivers? Wasn't it a bit odd for someone disabled to be out like that? People like that wheelchair guy shouldn't be in Dee Street in the first place. It was kind of stupid really. Probably asking for trouble.

It was clear that Bevan couldn't understand why Maggie was upset. As far as he was concerned, she was making a huge fuss over something that had nothing to do with him. Didn't the fact that the police gave him a bit of a lecture about the company he was keeping – and nothing more – prove it? It wasn't his fault his friends hadn't got off so lightly. It was bad luck that they now had to attend family group conferences and court hearings, or whatever they were called. He bet none of them would end up in jail. It was hardly a big deal.

But now her son was going to apologise. Maggie was going to meet him at court and drag him inside if need be. He had to learn; he *must* understand that you couldn't get away with treating people like that. She would stand him in front of the victim and make him say sorry.

Maggie glanced into Mr Paxton's lounge and noticed he had begun to set up his chessboard. Watching him was excruciating. First he examined each piece through a magnifying glass held to his right eye – his 'good eye' – after which he bent low over the board, his nose almost scraping the pieces, as he arranged them on the squares. From where she stood, Maggie could see that he had confused the Queen for the King.

Once she had asked Mr Paxton to describe his vision to her. The question had appeared to flummox him at first, but after some thought he had responded by telling her that it was as if he were looking at images projected onto a faded, torn sheet. Rather than being crisp and bright, everything was dull and obscure. The area in the centre of the sheet was dullest of all. He couldn't really see that part, at all. He gave his condition a name – macular degeneration.

He also drew her attention to a small chart attached to his fridge. The chart, with the words Amsler Grid Eye Exam across its top, consisted of a simple grid with a black dot in its centre. The grid no longer served any purpose as far as he was concerned. It had been included in an information package describing his condition, given to him years before by his eye doctor. Once Maggie had learnt about the symptoms of macular degeneration she had found herself examining the grid from time to time, testing her eyes to see if the lines wavered or blurred, or if the dot in the centre disappeared. Her eyes were fine but she continued to look at the chart, anticipating the day when the grid would distort.

Never having been a chess player, Maggie had been taught the basics by Mr Paxton during the first months of her employment. Since then, he would often ask her for a quick game. In fact, there was no such thing as a *quick* game. She was too good an opponent to be beaten in anything under thirty minutes. And today she had only twenty minutes to spare. On top of which she had forgotten to wipe down the window sills. She was surprised Mr Paxton hadn't already noticed. Most days he amused himself by keeping track of her movements as she cleaned, politely teasing her about any changes in her familiar routine. He would be aware that she had missed the sills. What's more, with little else to occupy his day, he was prone to edging around each room, running his hand along the furniture and sills as he walked. He'd feel the dead flies and moths beneath his fingers.

But as she picked up the damp tea towel she used for dusting, Mr Paxton suddenly called, 'You can leave them for my niece. She may drop in later, I believe.'

Maggie smiled, automatically covering her mouth with her hand as she did so.

'You wouldn't care for a quick game of chess with your cup of tea?' he continued, though he knew her answer already. She wouldn't refuse him one of the few pleasures left in his life.

Maggie did not have time but she sat down, watching as Mr Paxton orientated himself in front of the board. 'You be white,' he said, indicating the board, before adding, 'I hope it's set up correctly.'

Without responding, Maggie quickly rearranged the misplaced pieces and then glanced at the time, grimacing as she did so.

Normally she tolerated these games of chess. She found the time spent in front of the board almost peaceful, and the game itself engaging. For half an hour she allowed her thoughts to focus on the board, as Mr Paxton prompted and talked her through the moves. But today she felt impatient with Mr Paxton and the time he was taking to move. At one point she reached out and took a knight from his hand as he placed it on a square, saying – rather more brusquely than she intended – 'That's the wrong square. You can't put it there.'

To her shame, Mr Paxton apologised. Because of that, she remained seated despite being conscious that time was ticking by. If only she had warned him that she was in a rush, she thought. Then she could have slipped away without feeling guilty. Instead, she jiggled in her seat, becoming more and more tense as Mr Paxton raised the subject of his wife. They had been married for fifty-two years and besides being his soulmate, his wife had been his chess-mate. In fact, they had met at a chess tournament. They had been opponents and she had beaten him, just. She had challenged him to a new game and had beaten him again – not once but five times in a single session. Rather than becoming annoyed, he had savoured his defeat, marvelling at her skill and, he smiled, her cunning. And, in time, he began to admire her not only for her skill in chess but for her character, her generosity of spirit and her wit. He had adored her. Right up until the time of their separation and her death.

Mr Paxton's eyes became misty as he recalled the day she had first begun to slip away from him. It happened, he recalled, as they were playing chess. His lips trembled as he described the moment she had attempted to corner him into checkmate by manoeuvring her rook diagonally. The slip-up had caught him by surprise. She had always been such a focussed player and he hadn't at first understood what her move meant. He had examined her face, searching it for some sign of playfulness – but her expression had remained impassive. She hadn't been aware of her mistake. At that moment, he recalled, he had felt gripped by fear.

'I couldn't bring myself to point out her error,' he told Maggie. 'She was always so quick to catch on that I believe she would have been frightened had she been made aware of her slip-up. So I let her continue with the game, but we were never to play properly again.'

'She never stopped playing chess,' he added. 'When she moved into the nursing home she packed our board, but by then she couldn't even lay out the pieces without making a mistake. It was best that she never found out.'

Beginning to shuffle, Maggie glanced at the clock. She'd heard Mr Paxton's story many times before, and each time the story had been more or less the same, as if he had learned it by rote and deviated only slightly from the formula with each retelling. There was more to come, she knew that. This was merely the intermission, and if she didn't make a move for the door now, she would be caught for another five minutes. What would follow was a tale of how, after so many years together, his wife would finally reach the point when she no longer recognised him. That while he sat at home, missing her company, feeling the emptiness and silence of the house, she would be sitting in a vinyl day-chair, yelling abuse at anyone who came too close or tried to make her eat. She had lashed out at him on more than one occasion, swiping the glasses from his face as she swatted him with the heel of her hand. She had told him to go away, to stop pestering her and leave her alone. Then, discontented, she had told him that her husband never visited — that he had abandoned her and that all she wanted was to go home. Snivelling, and then wailing, she had cried, 'I want to go home! Why won't they let me go home? Why won't you take me home?'

It was at this point that Mr Paxton's story stopped. His wife had passed away several years ago, before Maggie had made his acquaintance, but he could not bring himself to speak further. Traumatised by his wife's decline, Mr Paxton would not permit himself to finish the story.

The minute hand on the clock clicked forward and unwilling to remain any longer, Maggie abruptly stood to leave. Mr Paxton's face twitched and he turned his head in her direction. Yet, somehow he misjudged his movement and lost his balance, toppling onto one hand as he floundered to support himself.

'Is that the correct time on your oven clock?' asked Maggie, pointing to the stove, which was clearly visible through the open archway separating the living area from the kitchen.

Mr Paxton swivelled around in order to face what he thought was the stove and replied apologetically, 'I believe so, but I can't see the numbers myself. My niece takes care of that type of thing.'

He paused, as if considering more fully Maggie's question,

then added, 'I don't think there have been any power cuts which might affect—'

'It's all right,' Maggie cut him off and reached for her cell-phone, flipping it open to read the time. It wasn't all right. She was late. Bevan would be waiting for her. Even now, he would be sitting outside the courthouse, impatient for her to appear.

'Sorry, Mr Paxton, but I have to go. My son's waiting for me at the . . .'

She didn't finish. She didn't want the business concerning her son to become common knowledge. What went on in her home was private. Unlike some of her clients, who revealed all manner of personal information, she preferred to guard what was hers. She couldn't speak out in that casual, easy-going manner adopted by so many of her acquaintances.

'I have to go . . . It's important.'

Mr Paxton nodded, his expression one of concern, 'I hope nothing's wrong—'

'No,' interrupted Maggie, 'Everything's fine but I have to go.'

'I'm sorry if I've kept you,' responded Mr Paxton. Whereas some of her clients might say such a thing in a needy, whiny voice she knew Mr Paxton was genuine in his concern. She felt a pang of guilt as she hurried towards the door, calling back, 'I'll see you the day after tomorrow and I'll do the window sills . . .'

She was gone. Glancing back through the window as she passed, she caught sight of Mr Paxton with a chess piece held close to his nose. It was white, one of hers. From experience, she knew that he would finish the game and that, being the gentleman he was, he would let her win.

As she started her car, Maggie remembered it was rubbish day and that Mr Paxton's wheelie bin was on the kerb. Annoyed, she turned off the engine and flung the door open, snagging her pantyhose as she climbed from the driver's seat. A tear the size of a coin appeared above her left knee, her white flesh protruding through the nylon. Suddenly her decision that morning to dress for court rather than work struck her as stupid. How crazy to think that she could spend all day cleaning and yet appear neat and tidy by afternoon. She pulled the hem of her skirt, hoping she might be able to cover the hole. It was no use. She'd have to buy a new pair of pantyhose and change into them before meeting her son.

Reaching the kerb, she saw with increasing irritation that Mr Paxton's bin had blown away. In fact, all the bins from the neighbouring houses were scattered across the road, their wheels having taken them this way and that in the strong wind. I haven't got time for this, she wanted to yell but instead marched onto the road and grabbed the first bin she saw. Yanking it back to the garage, she glanced at her mobile. Seeing how late it was made her even more frustrated. 'That stupid boy,' she protested, 'Stupid, stupid boy.'

Ten minutes later she was pulling into the Pak'nSave car park. As she parked she noticed a large sign advertising bread for twenty-five cents a loaf. She smiled. At least something was going right today. She'd grab some pantyhose, stock up on bread and then make for the express counter. It would take no more than five minutes. Everything would be fine. Court would be running late, in any case.

Hurrying into the supermarket, she sensed immediately how busy it was. It wasn't that she had to jostle to get past the customers in the vegetable section but that there was an atmosphere of fatigue and hostility permeating the place. Must be dole day, she thought, as she skirted past family groups on her way towards the bread aisle. She scanned the shelves as she tried to locate the reduced loaves, but could find none. She took a step back into the main aisle and glanced around, catching sight of a young shelf-packer not far away. Quickly, she hurried towards him but was still a few feet away when he began to wander off, heading in the opposite direction. To her relief, she caught up with him as he reached the door leading out the back. 'The twenty-five-cent bread,' she puffed. 'Where is it?' The boy raised his hand slowly and gestured towards the bread aisle. Maggie saw immediately what she had missed only moments before – a large banner proclaiming the specially priced loaves. Feeling stupid, she half skipped, half ran back the way she had come, reaching the display stand within seconds. It was empty. A woman who had joined her grumbled, 'Must have sold out. Typical,' before pushing her trolley away.

Frustrated and pressed for time, Maggie looked around for a shelf-packer. It wasn't good enough. If they advertised cheap bread, she fumed, there ought to be cheap bread. The boy she had spoken to was nowhere to be seen. It wasn't good enough. She sped towards the shelves stocked with pantyhose. Aware of how much time she had already wasted in the supermarket, she decided, nevertheless, to complain. She would have to get a move on, but she couldn't let them get away with it.

Maggie dodged past a woman with three young children as she headed towards the service desk. Ahead of her were five or six other customers already waiting in line. She wondered what to do, but then one of the customers in front of her shrugged and moved off. Taking this as a sign that the queue would quickly shrink, Maggie took her place at the back and waited.

Where moments before there had been three assistants

attending the desk, there was suddenly only one. Like Maggie, the woman in front of her noticed the sudden disappearance and took it upon herself to complain, calling across to a girl at a nearby checkout, 'Can you get someone over here to help? We've been waiting for hours.' The operator hesitated. Gripping a bottle of Coca-Cola in her hand, she slowly turned her head, searching for her supervisor. Unable to locate her, the girl looked puzzled and then scanned the bottle, averting her eyes when the customer at the service desk tried once more to catch her attention.

Maggie could feel herself getting angrier. She caught the eye of the woman who had spoken and sighed, 'Where do they find them?' The woman shrugged and shook her head, saying, 'Don't you hate it? I come across from Stewart Island once a month and it's always such a relief when I finally finish my errands and get the ferry home.' Maggie blushed slightly; she'd never been to Stewart Island. She glanced at the service counter and noticed a clock above the main entrance. There was nothing for it, she would have to pay for the pantyhose and then come back later.

It took several more minutes before her turn in the express queue came around. She hadn't been able to take her eyes from the clock – fixating on the second hand, which stuttered from one mark to the next. It was all she could do not to push the man who was ahead of her when, to her right, an operator became free. His attention was focussed on his basket of groceries and he had not noticed the operator's signal. Maggie had noticed, however, and yet despite her repeated attempts to draw his attention to the empty line, nothing had happened. 'Get a move on,' she hissed under her breath, nudging the man gently. 'Checkout's free,' she said more clearly but even then the man refused to take notice. Finally, he turned his head and shuffled off, and moments later

Maggie's own turn came, allowing her to approach another operator with her single purchase.

The barcode refused to scan. Yet, despite telling the operator the cost of the pantyhose, Maggie was forced to wait while another staff member was summoned to track down the price. Maggie could feel the hostile glances of those waiting in the queue behind her. It's not my fault, she wanted to protest, but instead she stood mutely, glowering, as the operator attempted to make small talk to fill in time.

'Is it still windy outside?' asked the girl as Maggie shifted her weight from one foot to another. 'Looks like the washing might have a chance to dry, at last . . .' she continued when it became clear that her first question would remain unanswered. 'Busy day?' she smiled, glancing anxiously past Maggie towards the aisles.

Tight-lipped, Maggie nodded.

The operator looked down at the till as if engrossed in reading its keys. A second later another operator appeared behind her, a cash tray held in her hands. 'We're just changing over,' announced the new arrival, stepping forward.

Before she could think, Maggie snapped, 'No you're not.'

'It will only take a second to set up,' continued the new operator, insensitive to the tone of Maggie's voice.

'No,' repeated Maggie, speaking more firmly than before, 'You can wait.'

'But it will just take a second,' insisted the operator, her smile fixed. 'It's the rules.'

Maggie stared back, shaking her head as she said, 'Wait until I've gone.'

The new operator looked annoyed, but Maggie ignored her. She didn't care what the girl thought.

Finally, she was back in her car, heading down the road towards the court.

As she hurried towards the building, she noticed immediately that no one – least of all Bevan – was waiting outside. Pushing through the doors, she hoped he would be inside, but a quick glance confirmed what she already suspected – he wasn't there. Even as she thought, he might have gone in without me, she felt a surge of anger deep within her which surfaced as she quietly slipped into the courtroom. Todd was near the front, neatly dressed in a white shirt and dark trousers. Maggie barely recognised him. Only his poor posture struck a familiar chord. He picked his nails, raising his hand to his mouth as he tore at his cuticles with his teeth. Catching his eye, Maggie saw him smirk. Had she not been in court, she might have been tempted to give him a piece of her mind. Not that it would do any good.

Fuming over the absence of her own son, Maggie scanned the room, stopping when her eyes settled on a man in a wheelchair. Despite everything that had happened, she couldn't recall his name. He looked about forty-five years old. His hair was greying slightly, and he had pulled it back into a plait that hung below his shoulders. It was difficult to gauge, but he seemed to be of a normal build – neither fat nor thin, but not particularly muscular, which was hardly surprising given he was in a wheelchair. He wore a navy shirt and jeans, and his shoes, which were brown, appeared well worn. That surprised her. The majority of her wheelchair-bound clients had good shoes, shoes that showed little signs of wear and tear. For a second, the thought went through her head that he might be a phoney. Perhaps he only pretended to be disabled in order to claim ACC or some other benefit. She glanced back at the man's face, and tried to read his expression.

He looked hostile. She kept her gaze trained on him and as she watched she realised that she had been mistaken. His expression was not simply anger, but bitterness and humiliation too.

With her attention held by the man, it took a moment for her to register that her phone was ringing. In her haste to reach the court, she had forgotten to turn it off. She saw that the man in the wheelchair was frowning at her, and she could feel his eyes remain on her as she backtracked towards the door and left the room. Expecting the call to be from Bevan, or perhaps Lisa, her youngest daughter – who was at home babysitting Storm, Maggie's five-year-old grandson – she was surprised to recognise the number of her eldest daughter, Justine. For a brief moment she hesitated before answering. She wasn't sure she could handle Justine at the moment. Her daughter, who lived in Auckland, never called with good news; it was always some drama. Reluctantly Maggie took the call, her voice flat as she said, 'Hello, Justine.'

Her greeting was barely out of her mouth before Justine's icy voice cut in, 'I thought I should tell you that things aren't very good at the moment – not that I expect you to take an interest.' Maggie opened her mouth to respond but was interrupted. 'The twins haven't stopped crying all day, and I'm telling you, I've had enough of it. I'm going to put them into care. I'm sick of it.'

Maggie took a deep breath and rubbed the corners of her eyes. She ought to be used to these calls, but she could never listen to her daughter without feeling sick with anxiety. If only Justine hadn't gone to Auckland. As far as Maggie was concerned, the move, which had taken place a few years before, made no sense. On the spur of the moment Justine had announced that she was following some boyfriend north, and then, taking her son, Storm, had upped and left. A few months later she was pregnant, and the boyfriend, Aaron, had more or less vanished from the scene. Following the subsequent birth of her twins, Kayla and Mischa, Justine had then managed to persuade Maggie to take Storm. And so, still a pre-schooler, Storm had returned to Invercargill. He had been accompanied on the flight by a girl who described herself as 'Justine's best friend', a woman called Kelly, who handed over the child as if depositing a soiled nappy into a bin. Waiting for the boy's bag to appear at the baggage claim, Kelly's only attempt at conversation, Maggie recalled, was to say, 'Justine says to give me the money for the air tickets. She told me you would pay. My flight back to Auckland boards in a few minutes, so, you know . . . you might want to hurry.'

Incensed by the girl's behaviour, Maggie had responded that she would send the money by post. 'Yeah, whatever,' replied Kelly. Apparently unconcerned by Maggie's response, she then took out a packet of cigarettes and started towards the exit in search of a place to smoke. As she walked away, she turned back, calling for all to hear, 'He wets the bed, so you'd better buy some nappies.'

Despite being outraged by Kelly's manner, Maggie quickly discovered that she had been right about the bedwetting. Maggie had tried everything to solve the problem – taking Storm to the toilet twice in the night, and offering him both 'prizes' and bribes in order to encourage him to stop – but nothing worked. Her only hope had been that he would grow out of it one day. Now, a year-and-a-half later, he was almost there. He was prone to the occasional accident but they were becoming less and less frequent, and Maggie felt cautiously confident that things would improve.

The main problem facing Maggie was how to deal with

Justine. If only she could be persuaded to return to Invercargill. But as long as Aaron, the twins' father, remained in Auckland, Justine wouldn't budge. In Justine's mind, there was a chance that Aaron would 'come round' as she called it, that he would accept his responsibilities and be a proper 'dad' to the girls. Justine hoped, too, that he would return to *her*. Although she never admitted it, she was desperately lonely. She felt abandoned, and even though there was little chance of her boyfriend settling down, she couldn't bring herself to face the truth. It was from this position of powerlessness and unhappiness that she harangued her mother.

Maggie had a fair idea of what was going through Justine's head – of what she wanted – but could do nothing to help. There was no way she could take the twins. She already had Storm as well as her own children, plus her full-time job. She couldn't be responsible for the two girls as well. Night after night, she lay awake, as her brain struggled to work out a way in which she could make it all work. And even when she knew with certainty that there was nothing she could do, she continued to defend her position against the reproach that pounded in her head. Her hands were tied. Everyone knew that. She wasn't to blame.

Maggie sighed, 'Look Justine, I can't talk about this now. I'm at court. Why don't you phone back at dinnertime and then you can talk to Storm as well, if you want . . .'

Her daughter's voice came back, louder than before, 'Why do you say things like that?'

Maggie didn't understand what Justine was driving at, but before she could figure it out, Justine continued, 'Why do you assume I don't want to talk to him? He's my son – why wouldn't I want to talk to him? Why do you say that stuff to me all the time?'

Maggie hesitated before replying, 'That's not what I meant, Justine. Listen, I can't talk now. You'll have to call back—'

Justine cut her off. The phone went dead. Returning it to her bag, Maggie shook her head, worn out by the brief exchange that had taken place. 'You need to sort yourself out, Justine,' she murmured. 'This isn't helping.'

She could feel her heart racing. It was always the same. After talking to Justine she would always feel shaken, as if she had come close to being struck by a car while crossing the road. It would take several minutes for her pulse to return to normal and even then she would feel wrung out and drained. Occasionally, she would feel so sick after these conversations that she would pray to her Confirmation Saint, Theresa, for guidance. Prayer calmed her. It was the quiet room she retreated to whenever she had time.

Conscious of the dull ache in her head, Maggie searched her bag for an aspirin. She was tired. Every part of her body ached, and she wanted to stretch out and rest before going home and starting on dinner. Because Bevan had failed to turn up, it was her duty to introduce herself to the man in the wheelchair and apologise on her son's behalf. She wouldn't feel comfortable until she had tried to make things right. She needed to put an end to the unfortunate episode; it was the least she could do.

Taking a seat in the foyer, she allowed her mind to wander, reviewing her day and thinking how much like every other day it had been. She had got up at 6.30 and put out food for the children's breakfasts. After that she had made Storm's lunch – revitalising and reconstructing the sandwiches left uneaten from the previous day. She had then put out the washing, which she had put through the machine the night before, and then thrown Storm's sheets into the machine before making the beds and peeling the potatoes ready for that night's dinner. Once that was organised, she had phoned the agency to check her daily schedule and to remind them she was leaving early to go to court. Fortunately, everything had been agreed to with little fuss. She'd then made her own packed lunch and taken Storm to the bathroom, where she helped him brush his teeth and wash his face. She'd reminded Bevan to be at the courthouse, she'd reminded Lisa to collect Storm from school and look after him until she got home. Then she'd washed the breakfast dishes, watered the garden, put out food for the cat, taken the vegetable scraps out to the guinea pig, packed Storm's school bag, found Bevan's sports gear, scribbled a note excusing Bevan from his afternoon classes, picked up a pair of underpants lying on the hall floor, and taken them out to the washing machine and chucked them in. And that was about it.

By 9.15 she had been standing in the bathroom of her first client, a woman who was recovering from a hip replacement. Helping her onto a stool in the shower, Maggie had turned away and set about cleaning the bathroom sink as the woman washed herself. Her client, Mrs Young, had refused Maggie's offer to help. She was uncomfortable in Maggie's presence, preferring to take care of herself rather than being fussed over. Maggie respected her wishes but remained in the bathroom nevertheless, explaining that she ought to be on hand to assist. 'You don't want to slip,' she had reasoned, and Mrs Young had agreed.

Only now, she thought as she sat facing the courtroom door, had she really been able to take the weight off her feet. Under different circumstances she might have felt impatient, held up by waiting for the end of the session. But today, she didn't mind sitting quietly and thinking. Her thoughts drifted towards Justine but she tried to steer them away. With luck her daughter would calm down.

Although Maggie hadn't asked, she suspected that something had happened to stir up her eldest child. Most likely Justine had tried to contact the twins' father. That always got to her. His complete indifference caused Justine so much stress that she tended to take it out on Maggie. So regular were Justine's outbursts they seemed to Maggie to be something of a 'fact of life'. Nevertheless they hurt.

It was a terrible thing to admit, but sometimes Maggie thought it was lucky that Storm's father had played no role in his son's life. Justine was the only one in the family who even knew who Storm's father was. 'I'm all right the way I am!' her daughter had protested throughout her pregnancy, 'I can take care of myself. I don't need help. I'm not one of your stupid clients, eh.'

Maggie sighed. So much of her time and energy had been spent on sorting out Justine's problems that her other children had suffered. Lisa wasn't so bad. A sensible girl, she had got on with things, looking after herself for the most part. Bevan, on the other hand, was heading for trouble. He missed his father – missed all those things that boys are meant to do with men. Maggie rubbed her eyes with the heel of her hand, murmuring, 'That's something else I have to do. Get hold of Ross.'

Even now, after three years, she found it difficult to believe her husband had left her. 'All you ever do is work,' he had told her one morning. Unknown to her, this had been his way of informing her that he felt starved of attention, and that if she didn't start taking more notice of him, he would be forced to look elsewhere. But goodness knows what she could have done. He'd lost his job, and someone had to work. What else was she meant to do? The bills needed paying. It wasn't her fault the mill had closed.

Ross had been true to his word. He had left, but, as far as she knew, he had lived alone ever since. What he had achieved by moving out, she didn't know. He was probably as lonely now as he was before. Perhaps she was missing the point?

I'll get Ross to speak with Bevan, she thought. He's his father.

She stretched her legs, rubbing her calves with the heels of her hands and then rotated her ankles, first clockwise then anti-clockwise, as she watched the door, willing it to open so that she might get this thing with the wheelchair victim over and done with. She thought about how she had hurried away from Mr Paxton's house earlier and how, with the benefit of hindsight, she needn't have bothered. She could have wiped his window sills or finished the game of chess, after all.

Suddenly feeling thirsty, she stood up and walked across the foyer to where a large drink dispenser stood. Never having used such a machine, she read the instructions carefully before deciding on a bottle of water. Seeing the price, she changed her mind, arguing that it would be just as easy to find the ladies and scoop some water straight from the tap. As she stepped away from the dispenser, the doors to the courtroom opened and out swaggered Todd and two of his friends. Seeing Maggie he raised his hand, giving her a 'thumbs up' before leaving the building.

Knowing the man in the wheelchair must be on his way, Maggie began to feel nervous. It was one thing to imagine push-ing her son forward so that he might apologise, it was another trying to think of what to say herself. She hoped she wouldn't be lost for words, that she could make him understand that her son hadn't been directly involved in the incident but had been a hanger-on – not even an observer to what took place. She would apologise, assure the man that the matter had been dealt with – that she had taken it very seriously – and she would go.

The doors swung open once more, and were held back by two men in suits as the man in the wheelchair negotiated his way through. He paused for breath and then turned to thank the men, who nodded and disappeared back into the court, leaving him alone in the foyer with Maggie. He caught Maggie's eye and smiled briefly, then began patting his breast pocket – searching, Maggie guessed, for a packet of cigarettes. Stepping towards him, she said, 'I want to apologise to you – on behalf of my son.'

Instantly, the expression on the man's face hardened.

'That little shit back there is your son?'

Assuming he was referring to Todd, Maggie shook her head, before giving a brief outline of her son's whereabouts during the attack. She noticed that she chose her words carefully, and glossed over most facts. She also avoided mentioning her son by name, although she did make it clear that he hadn't joined in with Todd, and the others.

While she talked, the man turned his cigarette around in his fingers. The gesture distracted her; it made it increasingly difficult for her to get her thoughts in order and after a few moments her voice began to trail off, lost. She finally snapped, 'Can you stop doing that for a minute, please.'

The man looked up, genuinely surprised by Maggie's request. Offering no apology, he asked, 'What's your name?' His words, Maggie noticed, were slightly slurred, as if he had trouble speaking.

'Margaret,' Maggie responded, 'Margaret – Maggie.'

'And your son, where is he now, exactly?'

Maggie felt uneasy. She couldn't predict the direction in which the exchange was leading. 'I'm not sure,' she faltered. 'He was meant to meet me here. Something must have held him up. He promised he'd be here.'

The man nodded and as he did so a strand of grey hair fell to his shoulder, settling on his navy shirt like a length of spider's silk. Seeing the hair, the man brushed at it with his right hand, revealing as he did so a small tattoo of what looked like a guitar which had been obscured by the cuff of his shirt.

Resting his hands on the rims of his wheels, he began to roll slowly forward towards the main entrance. Unsure if he was finished with her, Maggie kept pace with him, reaching for the door as he approached. 'Where were you, Maggie, when your son was out playing teenage pranks?'

The way the man spat the words 'teenage pranks' made Maggie wince. She guessed the phrase had been used at some point during the court proceedings, probably by Todd's advocate.

'I was at work,' she said, her voice wavering. 'I'm a caregiver. I provide help around the home for people recovering from operations or for people with disa—' She stopped, her reply cut off by the expression on the man's face.

'Maybe your time would be better spent taking better care of your own kids,' he growled by way of reply.

Although she nodded, Maggie felt angry. The response, How dare you judge me, sprung to her lips, but instead she said, 'I do my best.'

The man held her gaze, then placed his cigarette in his mouth before reaching for his lighter and lighting it. He inhaled slowly, his eyes narrowing and then he shrugged, and exhaled, coughing.

Maggie had the impression that he was performing for her benefit. Something in his manner was so staged that she wanted to protest, Get over yourself. You're not the only one with problems. Look around. Do you think my life is easy? But, remembering why she was here, she repeated, 'Sorry again for what happened. I can assure you my son will never be involved in that kind of prank again' and walked away.

*T*HE BEDSIDE clock-radio cast a greenish tinge over the cover of Maggie's Bible. She had been given the volume by her father, not realising at the time that he had removed it from a motel during a trip to Christchurch. She had taken it from him, beaming with pride as he said, 'I got you this – your own personal copy.' He showed her the inscription on the inside cover and patted her on the head, adding, 'Yours is the only one like it. No one else will have one quite like this.' And she had believed him.

Maggie stirred in her bed, trying to recall in greater detail the pleasure she had felt when presented with the gift. She knew she had been so happy, ridiculously happy, but she could no longer conjure up a memory of what it felt like to be that happy.

Rolling over she turned on the radio, then lay quietly as a voice filled the room. She listened. A car sales-yard was running a competition – the winner would walk away with a 1992 Toyota Corolla in mint condition. She reached across to the radio, intending to change channels, but the advertisement abruptly finished and the presenter's voice came on, announcing a song. She recognised the singer and liked her voice, but then she liked all country music. The words made sense to her; she understood what was being said.

There was a time when she used to sing herself. Not often, but every now and again. She could barely remember what it was like to stand before a group of friends and strangers, open her mouth wide and feel her chest bursting with the anticipation of that first note. She had never sung solo – at least not in public. Being part of a choir was safer; as least the voices of the other singers could camouflage her mistakes.

She held onto that faint memory, trying not to allow her mind to be hijacked by competing thoughts involving Justine, the twins' future, or Bevan. She recalled the look on the face of the man in the wheelchair, his expression of bitterness. Clients like him were always the worst. Angry and resentful, they were difficult to please. Nothing would make them happy, so working for them was almost guaranteed to fail.

Pulling her gown around her shoulders, she walked quietly towards Storm's room. It had been Bevan's room, but now he preferred to sleep in the shed at the bottom of the garden. Built from rimu, the shed was small but solid and it retained its heat in winter. Inside, there was room for a single bed, a chair and a heater. The drawers containing all Bevan's clothes and junk remained in his old room, shoved up against the wall at the foot of Storm's bed.

Pausing at the door to Storm's room, Maggie listened. Her grandson's breathing was heavy, as if he might be coming down with a cold once more. While her own children had been for the most part healthy, Storm was asthmatic and tended to pick up any bug that was doing the rounds at school. His poor health often gave Maggie cause for concern. She had dreaded the approach of winter when the dampness of the house became more apparent. During the past few weeks every window had become moist with condensation and the bedroom walls had once more started to sprout mould.

Crouching next to Storm, she stroked his hair gently, whispering, 'Storm, wake up. It's time to go to the toilet.' She couldn't go to the child in the night without feeling sorry for him. To be dragged from a warm cosy bed, to be led down the hall to a cold bathroom was hardly fair on a child of five. Some nights he barely woke at all, and she would take him into the bathroom and support him, hold him upright as she eased his penis from his pyjamas and aimed it towards the toilet bowl. At times his legs would shake and she could feel them buckle as she tried to rouse him from sleep, saying, 'You have to pee. Please, pee . . .' Even so, it might take minutes before a thin trickle of urine would appear, and occasionally nothing would happen. No matter what she did to encourage him, he would remain too sleepy to perform and she would be forced to take him back to his room, knowing as she did so that he might wind up wetting the bed.

Tonight was one of those nights. He cried softly, his legs shaking and buckling as she supported his weight. Giving in to a moment's frustration, Maggie snapped, 'Wake up,' but the boy merely began to cry more loudly, and Maggie was forced to gather him into her arms and carry him back to his room.

Back in her own bed, she couldn't relax. In her mind, she anticipated the moment when Storm would appear in her bedroom, waking her to tell her that he was wet. Half asleep, he wouldn't be able to make sense of what had happened and would stand whimpering at the side of her bed, his damp cuddly toy held tight to his chest. Knowing she would be wakened some time in the early hours made it harder for her to drift off. It was one thirty now. She'd had two hours sleep already but she needed another five hours if she hoped to face a new day with any sign of energy.

Thinking about sleep would only keep her awake. Yet she couldn't take her mind off the subject. No pleasant distraction came to the rescue. Sleep, Justine, Bevan, bedwetting – there was no escape. She reached across for the Bible but changed her mind. The truth was she found it difficult to concentrate on the text. Even worse, she had to admit she found it slightly dull. She always had. She liked having a Bible but she didn't necessarily want to read it, too. It was enough to know it was there.

In the living room, discarded on the couch, was a *Woman's Day* magazine. She had been given it that morning by Mrs Young, the woman with the sore hip. It was not unusual to leave a client's home with some cast-off or other. Given the nature of her profession, Maggie had to be careful about what she accepted. There was no way, for example, that she would leave a client's house with an original painting or an antique vase stuffed under her arm. But she saw no harm in accepting things that might otherwise be thrown away. Assorted dinner plates that were surplus to requirements, old electrical goods, videotapes, even shoes. She was happy to take these things but, unlike some of her colleagues, she would never go so far as to ask for them. The gifts had to be offered. She was no scrounger.

Calling into the agency a few days before, she had spotted her younger sister, Carol, sitting at her desk, gloating over a laptop computer. Barely glancing up as Maggie entered, she said, 'Look what I scored today! That rich business man I've been visiting

– the one with the shattered arm and broken ribs – gave me this. Of course I wouldn't have accepted it but he's really more of a family friend than a client. His brother works with Lindsay, and besides, he's already bought himself a brand new one with a voice-activated programme so he can keep on working from home. He said this one didn't have enough memory or wasn't fast enough, or something. I don't know. But, good, eh? The kids will love it. Especially Ashley, for his school projects.' Listening to Carol, Maggie had felt a pang of envy. None of her own clients was in the kind of social bracket that enabled them to give away old computers. Few of them even owned computers. In fact, most of her clients were no better off than she was. It struck Maggie then, that whereas most of her clients were sickness or invalid beneficiaries or sometimes blue-collar workers on accident compensation, Carol's clients tended to be professionals and the self-employed, working in the private sector

As manager, Carol had a way of taking these people for herself. There were only one or two at a time, a couple of hours worth each week, but enough to ensure Carol got the laptops while every one else went home with week-old magazines with the crosswords and sudoku already filled in.

Recalling Carol's face as she tapped away on her keyboard, Maggie couldn't help but feel resentful. Her own daughter, Lisa, could do with a computer. She was one of the few kids in her class who continued to write essays with pen and paper and who relied on computers in the library for internet access. At the end of the year, she would be leaving school, going out into the real world and looking for work. It didn't seem so long ago that Lisa was a new entrant, coming home with Early Reader books and dolls made out of toilet rolls and crepe paper.

Career Night. The words suddenly shook Maggie from her dream. Tomorrow evening, between six and eight, was Career Night; she was expected to meet with Lisa's teacher to discuss her daughter's future. With all the nonsense surrounding Bevan she had forgotten about it. Damn. Somehow, she'd have to persuade Bevan to babysit Storm.

Closing her eyes, she ran through her day ahead. There was the staff meeting at nine, followed by her client visits, then home to prepare dinner, and then Career Night. It might work. Bevan's no-show at court combined with his feeble excuse that he had understood they were to meet at home and go in together meant he would know better than to make a fuss about babysitting Storm for one evening. In fact, Bevan was lucky to be let off so lightly. If only she could persuade him to keep away from Todd and his mates. But, in reality, how could she stop him from seeing them? It wasn't as if she had so much time on her hands that she could keep tabs on his every move. If only Ross had taken a bit more interest in the kids. He should have stepped in and offered to help. If only he hadn't left, she sighed. She needed him.

'SO, MAGGIE,' SAID Carol at the staff meeting the following morning, 'you're all set for the retreat this weekend?' She sounded buoyant, as if there was nothing she liked more than organising 'retreats' for her staff. 'You're dropping Storm round at Mum's, right – on Friday?'

Maggie nodded sullenly. Being around her younger sister for any length of time tended to bring out the worst in her. It wasn't the fact that her sister owned the business that annoyed her, but that she took so much pleasure from performing her managerial duties. She enjoyed being the boss. She welcomed every piece of paper that came her way, every envelope that was addressed to her, every call that was put through to the 'supervisor'. She lapped it up.

Maggie glanced at her sister. She was so enthusiastic. She had so much energy. She worked as hard as her staff and yet showed no signs of fatigue. It was as if work was a hobby, something she did for fun. Which, in a way, it was. Married to an engineer working in management at Tiwai Point, Carol didn't need to work. She wanted to. And because she got so much out of it, she wanted the rest of her staff to enjoy it too. That was why she kept organising retreats. She had the idea she was raising staff morale through creating opportunities for increased job satisfaction. She didn't understand that the rest of her team was worn out by the weekend. The last thing any of them wanted was to go back into work and listen to someone who was paid a fortune to tell them what they already knew. They didn't want to stand around during the tea break drinking from a cup of instant coffee while some woman in a designer outfit made polite conversation about Central Otago wines and Bluff oysters.

Because of this retreat, Maggie was going to have to drive Storm all the way to Winton on Friday after school, and then go and retrieve him on Saturday night after work. Her mother, who had agreed to look after him, would have to rearrange her entire day – just because Carol had got it into her head that a session on 'Understanding Maltreatment' was a great idea. It was enough to drive Maggie crazy.

The staff meeting came to an end, and Maggie stood up to leave. Her first client of the day, Mrs Young, would be waiting. The poor woman wouldn't be able to so much as shower and dress until Maggie reached her. Forcing an elderly client to get on with her day while dressed only in a flimsy nightgown and robe – now *that* was maltreatment.

As she reached the door, Maggie was called back by her sister, who asked, 'How did Bevan get on yesterday?' Maggie bristled, then turned to see the eyes of all her work colleagues upon her.

'Did you get him to apologise to the wheelchair guy?' Smiling, her voice breezy – as if the question was no more than a simple 'How's it going?' – Carol continued, 'What did the guy say? Bet he was ropable!' She burst out laughing, stopping only when she caught sight of Maggie's face.

For her own part, Maggie wasn't sure what was worse: hearing her little sister raising private family business in front of her workmates or the fact that she was making light of a very serious matter. Deciding it was the first that really annoyed her, she snapped, 'This isn't the time . . .'

'Oh, come on Maggie,' responded her sister, 'I know what Bevan did . . .'

Maggie wouldn't let her finish, 'Bevan wasn't involved personally,' she began, 'He was sitting in a car, miles away, when the incident took place . . .'

She paused, catching sight of one of her colleagues, who, meeting her glance, quickly turned away.

'Yeah, whatever,' replied Carol, her voice suddenly quiet. 'Phone me tonight, eh – when you're in a better mood.'

'I've got Lisa's Career Night tonight,' protested Maggie. 'I don't have time for chit-chat.'

She heard Carol sigh, and remark to a co-worker, 'It's been hard since Ross left . . . managing the kids on her own.'

It was all Maggie could do not to turn and storm back into the room and give her a piece of her mind. Instead she snatched a new folder from her in-tray and strode out, slamming the door behind her.

She remembered the folder as she prepared to leave her second client of the day, Mrs Devon. It was her final visit. The woman, the principal of a private high school, was recovering from an operation on her shoulder and was now able to take care of herself. Her arm no longer confined to a sling, she was capable of doing most household chores. Only carrying firewood and heavy bags of groceries were out of the question.

Maggie was pleased to be leaving.

On her very first visit, Mrs Devon had pointed to a wall-mounted shelving unit weighed down with a collection of crystal figurines and asked Maggie to run a duster over them. 'I'm frightened to do it myself,' she had explained, indicating her arm, 'A quick flick. I go over them myself every week.'

A glance of the figurines told Maggie that the woman was lying. Minute clumps of dust and grime filled the crevices on every piece. The crystal itself was dull and greasy; it would take hours to clean them. Holding a tiny galleon in her fingers, Maggie had responded, 'It's a big job.'

'Nonsense,' Mrs Devon had replied, 'It takes me about fifteen minutes to give them a wipe down.'

'I'm only here for an hour-and-a-half and if I do all these,' Maggie had persisted, indicating the collection, 'I might not have time to do all the other things that need doing.'

By way of response, the woman gave a tight smile, saying, 'I'd appreciate your co-operation' and then sat back in her chair to watch.

When Maggie lifted the first figurine from the shelf, she was aware of a sharp intake of breath followed by, 'Please take care. That's a very precious piece.' Maggie had wanted to respond, If they're so damn precious perhaps you should clean them yourself, but instead she bit her tongue and made a show of being extra cautious.

While she worked she became aware that the woman's teenage son had entered the room. Taking a seat on the couch, he too watched Maggie, following her every move in silence. And, as he watched, he picked from a bowl of chips placed on a cushion next to where he sat. Within a short time crumbs appeared scattered across the couch, and the boy brushed them to the carpet by his feet.

Paying him no attention, Mrs Devon said, 'I've been collecting crystal objects since I was a girl. I've almost one thousand . . .'

Maggie nodded, but her thoughts were on the boy. It seemed to her that he was dropping crumbs on purpose and, for the first time in her life, she had the impression that she was being treated like a servant.

Coming to the end of the first shelf, she reached for a small clown which was nestled behind a pair of cats. When she lifted it, she noticed with horror that the coloured ball held in its hands was no longer attached to anything. It had broken off and was merely balanced in the figurine's hands. Before she could do anything to stop it, the ball rolled from her fingers, crashing against a lower shelf before bouncing to the floor.

A moment's silence greeted the incident. Then, as Maggie was about to reach down to retrieve the ball, she heard Mrs Devon snap, 'I told you to be careful. Now it's broken.'

She couldn't be certain but Maggie thought she heard the boy snigger. Scowling at him, she said, 'It was already broken. I wasn't quick enough to see . . .'

The woman interrupted; her voice almost sickly sweet as she held out her hand for the piece, saying, 'Accidents happen.' Then, taking the figure in her hand, she examined it carefully, adding, 'It was one of my favourite pieces. Still . . .' she added almost brightly, 'One mustn't make a fuss. Carry on.'

What a prima donna, thought Maggie. Facing her client, she said, 'I think your washing's done. I'll go and hang it out . . . unless,' she added, looking at the boy, 'your son would like to help?' The boy smirked, slowly lifted a chip to his mouth and took a bite which sent shards falling to his knee. Mrs Devon appeared not to notice. Holding the clown in her hand, she replied, 'Put this back before you do that. I need some aspirin.'

Memories of that first session came flooding back to Maggie as she passed the folder containing a 'Client Feedback' form to Mrs Devon.

'What am I meant to do with this?' asked her client, glancing at the form.

She had no desire to prolong her stay, but Maggie found herself explaining that clients were invited to comment on the service and care offered by the agency. They could respond anonymously if they chose – it was up to them. Even as she spoke, she felt her heart sink. To her way of thinking, the feedback form was a worthless piece of paper. Most of her clients were too kind to write anything less than complimentary about their care, but clients like Mrs Devon were too mean to say anything nice. Women like her were fault-finders and there was nothing they enjoyed more than making their displeasure known.

'There's a stamped addressed envelope,' offered Maggie, by way of a parting gesture. 'Pop it in the post when you've completed it.'

Mrs Devon nodded. 'And the cost of replacing my figurine? I've a quote here from Ballantynes in Christchurch. Do you want that – or should I attach it to the questionnaire when I send it in?'

Maggie could feel the skin on the back of her neck begin

to tingle. She knew she should pay attention to the voice in her head which was cautioning her to rise above the situation, but she wasn't sure she could.

'Actually,' continued Mrs Devon, 'I may as well fill in your form now, while you wait.'

Then, taking a pen from a ceramic pen holder on a low table by the phone, she started to look at the questionnaire, reading each question aloud before delivering her answer as she wrote.

'On a scale of one to ten – one being extremely helpful, ten being not at all helpful – how would you rate the service offered by your caregiver?' Mrs Devon hesitated, and then read out loud the question once more while looking at Maggie. Tapping a biro against her teeth, she frowned, murmuring, 'Six? Seven?' Looking once more at Maggie, she smiled, then very deliberately wrote 'seven' in the box.

'I'm sorry,' said Maggie, moving towards the door, 'but I have to go now. I have a client.'

'But you have to take the questionnaire,' cried Mrs Devon, her self-satisfied smile slipping.

It was Maggie's turn to smile, 'No, I don't. I don't have to take anything from you any more.' Then, lifting her keys from the hall table, she almost added, by the way, you have ink around your mouth, but knowing that Mrs Devon was expecting a visit from her hairdresser at any moment, she let it slide.

She was running late again. Her last visit for the day had taken longer than she expected. It was no one's fault in particular but now she was on the back foot, and she had to feed Storm and get him into the shower before heading out once more to Lisa's Career Night.

She loathed school events. Ever since she had turned down an invitation to join the PTA she had felt guilty, and she was always slightly uncomfortable when talking to Lisa's teacher. Now she was facing the prospect of thirty minutes in the teacher's company and she had no idea what was expected of her. She wasn't good around teachers, never had been. And she had done nothing to prepare for the meeting. The day she had left school had been one of the happiest of her life. She could remember the enormous weight that had lifted off her shoulders as she'd walked through the gates for the last time. After years of confinement, she was suddenly free. The whole world had been at her feet. It was only later she realised that it was the other way around.

'Right, Lisa!' she yelled into the hall, 'In the car!' Then, opening the back door, she called into the garden, 'Bevan! Come inside now!' She could make out her son sitting on his bed, a guitar across his knee, oblivious to her command. Muttering, she stomped down to the shed and stood in the doorway, her hands on her hips. Engrossed in what he was doing, Bevan had not seen her. Suddenly her impatience subsided. Something about his concentration, his clumsy attempt to position his fingers correctly on the strings as he strummed an F chord, struck her as familiar. It took a moment, but then she realised what it was. As a schoolgirl, she had also learnt the guitar. There was a time, she recalled, when she had been quite serious about music. She had a decent voice and a head full of ideas; perhaps she could write songs, sing in public – stuff like that. She sighed. So much for dreams.

'Bevan,' she called, crossly, 'Come inside now. Storm has to be in bed by seven, all right? Then I want you to wash the dishes and do your homework. I want to see all that maths finished by the time I get home. And then I want you to wheel out the rubbish, okay?'

While she spoke, she felt strangely sad. Why couldn't she allow Bevan a few more minutes to practise? Why was she always nagging? She felt something – she didn't know what – grow dull inside her, and then added, 'And listen, give your father a call. See if he can do something with you this weekend.'

She could see her son's eyes glaze over as she spoke and her despondency grew. 'I've already made plans for the weekend,' mumbled Bevan.

'What?' snapped Maggie. 'What are you talking about?'

'That competition I told you about. You know, the car?'

Maggie had a faint recollection about some nonsense to do with a car but she couldn't remember what exactly.

'The car,' repeated Bevan. 'The person who can keep their hands on the car the longest, wins it.'

'Oh, for goodness sake, Bevan. You're not old enough for a car! They're not going to give it to you.'

'They are. I checked it out.'

Maggie turned away. There was no way Bevan was going to take part in some stupid competition. Anger surged inside her as she pictured a gang of teenage kids dressed against the cold huddled around an old wreck of a car while, inside, some oily sales manager rubbed his hands in glee as he imagined all the publicity he was getting. 'You are not entering that competition,' she said. 'Final.' She could see Bevan scowl. He was already at an age where he wouldn't be told what to do. But she had no time now to enter into a discussion. She had to get to school. As she walked away, she called back, 'Homework! Don't forget.'

Signs reading 'Career Night' pointed towards the gym. Although Maggie had not been there before, the smell upon entering the gym was immediately familiar. It took her back to her own high school, which had closed down only recently. In her mind's eye, she could picture herself running towards the vault, jumping from the springboard and landing atop the padded horse, legs spread, arms wobbling, searching the air for balance in the moment before toppling onto the crash pad. She had hated Phys. Ed. It had been one more humiliation.

Now she hesitated, allowing Lisa to step forward and take a seat in front of her class teacher and a career counsellor. Maggie followed, pulling her chair back a little so the focus might fall on her daughter.

'Thank you for coming.' The voice belonged to the counsellor, a woman Maggie had not seen before but who was identified by a name tag reading 'Mrs Weir. Career Advisor'.

Despite the smile on the woman's face, Maggie felt the awkwardness of her own teenage years return. Hadn't she once been to a similar evening? She could remember wandering around the hall, trailing behind her mother, taking in the posters from one display to another, as her mother nudged her, remarking, 'There's not much for you here.'

Had Maggie not agreed with her mother she might have been hurt by the remark. But it was true. The posters encouraging girls to be midwives, nurses, teachers – even engineers and managers – were not aimed at her.

'Now . . .' continued the career counsellor, 'this evening really isn't targeted towards girls like Lisa . . .'

Maggie felt offended. It was one thing to be made to feel stupid herself – but no one had the right to talk about her daughter that way. Lisa, as everyone knew, was a bright child. She was always in the top five.

'What do you mean?' she asked, coldly.

'Well,' said Lisa's teacher – a woman who looked no more than twenty-five, though Maggie knew for a fact she was somewhere closer to thirty-five – 'What I think Mrs Weir is trying to say is that Lisa is doing so well at school, it's unlikely she'll be wanting to leave anytime soon—'

'Yes,' broke in Mrs Weir, 'What I meant is that in Lisa's case we should be considering how best to direct her focus . . . so that one day, she might consider entering one of the professions.'

Unimpressed by Mrs Weir's patronising tone, Maggie prompted, 'Meaning?'

'Meaning . . .' continued Mrs Weir, glancing nervously from Maggie to Lisa, 'Lisa has the potential – should she want to make the most of it – to go to university, to medical school or . . .' She lowered her gaze to the stack of papers on the desk in front of her.

A tight knot formed in Maggie's stomach. Glancing at her daughter, she all but blurted, You've never said anything about wanting to go to university!

It was impossible to read Lisa's face. The girl appeared to have withdrawn from the encounter. If anything, she seemed embarrassed by what had been said. Maggie turned to Lisa's teacher and asked, 'Is this what you think, too? I mean you know Lisa better than this woman . . .'

To her surprise, the teacher nodded, saying, 'Lisa is showing great promise in both science and maths, and if she does well in her exams . . .'

Flustered, Maggie turned once more to Lisa, who smiled self-consciously, and fumbled with a brochure in her lap.

The pain Maggie had felt began to subside, becoming a dull ache. Turning from her daughter to her teacher, the only one of the two experts she felt she could engage with, she said, 'But university is expensive, isn't it? I mean, to go to medical school – or whatever – costs thousands . . .'

Mrs Weir cut in, 'There are student loans . . .' Then catching the look on Maggie's face fell silent.

Maggie fixed her with a sharp glance, 'I've never been in debt in my life.'

'There are scholarships, too,' added Lisa's teacher.

Maggie nodded, saying, 'So, you think Lisa needs to stay on at school for another year or so?'

Both women nodded.

Maggie's entire abdomen contracted. Feeling cornered, she turned to her daughter and asked, 'Is that what you want?'

Lisa shrugged, then looking at her mother said, 'I don't know. I mean . . .' she glanced nervously around the hall, indicating the displays. 'There are other things, aren't there? I mean, medical school and that . . . it would be good, but if it didn't work out . . .' Catching sight of her friend standing in front of a poster, she raised her hand to wave, adding, 'Joyce is thinking of taking a Nanny Certificate. That would be cheaper.'

Maggie felt a clamp squeeze her heart.

ONCE AGAIN, Maggie lay in her bed, unable to sleep. Her eyes fixed on the digits on the clock-radio; she stretched and turned it on. Music reached her ears and she lay quietly listening, following the tune, absorbing the lyrics. The song ended but the sound of music continued, not from her radio but from the one in the next bedroom – Lisa's room. Strangely, her daughter had recently become frightened of the dark. Never before had darkness scared her, but in the past few months she had begun to fuss a little at bedtime. She tried to hide her feelings of anxiety but Maggie had noticed that she frequently fell asleep with the light on, or with her door open so that the beam from the hall light might fall into her room. She had taken a radio into her room, too. Maggie hadn't known where the radio had come from but recently she had been tidying the garage and noticed that the transistor from Ross's workbench was missing. Asking Lisa about it, she had been told that classical music helped her focus while studying. 'It blocks out the other sounds,' she explained.

'What sounds?' asked Maggie, not understanding.

Lisa had looked uncomfortable, as if uncertain about how best to respond. Eventually she had said, 'You know, shouting . . .' She hadn't finished but Maggie guessed exactly what she meant. She meant *Maggie's* shouting, the fact that her voice was raised most of the time. With Bevan spending more and more time down in his shed, she had to shout to make herself heard. But even that wasn't the end of it. He was so slow it drove her crazy. He was forever moping around, rummaging about in the kitchen, sneaking food, getting things out but never putting anything away. To make matters worse, he was still whining about the competition. As if he needed a car at his age. It was one more thing for her to worry about. And why hadn't Ross got involved? He was so irritating, too.

There was a sound from down the hall. Maggie strained her ears, imagining that Storm had woken and was climbing out of bed. She held her breath waiting for him to appear in her room, but he didn't. She'd have to get up for him in a minute anyway. She hated her night-time routine. It would be so much better to be able to stay in bed and sleep through an entire night, undisturbed.

Her mind wandered back to Lisa. Despite the fact that Lisa's teacher had continued to talk for several minutes about careers, Maggie had been unable to take anything in. She had been too caught up by the expression on Lisa's face to hear what was being said. Visible in her daughter's eyes — for all to see, Maggie had thought — was defeat. Lisa was a teenager and already she knew what lay ahead. And it wasn't medical school.

When they'd been set free from the interview, they'd wandered around the gym looking at information brochures. One or two had caught their eye. Anything to do with science or technology was of interest. At one point Lisa had noticed a pamphlet about opportunities in care-giving. Opportunities! What a joke. What opportunities, Maggie had wanted to know? The opportunity to flush turds down a blind man's toilet? The gift of polishing crystal figurines? Very funny. There were certificates for everything these days. Bits of paper took the place of common sense and experience. Everything she knew she'd taught herself. Not that it mattered.

She ought to get up and take Storm to the toilet. Her head on her pillow, her eyes on the ceiling, Maggie listened to the radio. She recognised the song, knew the words. Softly she began to hum the tune. The sound of her voice startled her. Hesitating, she fell silent, and then as the song reached the chorus, she joined in. Her voice, barely audible, harmonised with the performer's. For almost a minute she kept pace with the song and then caught herself. 'Stop being silly,' she whispered. Snatching her robe from the bed, she got up and slipped from her room.

$\mathcal{M}$AGGIE'S MOTHER, Elsie, had recently bought a property in a new housing area close to the centre of Winton. Retired, she and her new husband, Murray, had decided to move while they were still fit and healthy. 'Who knows what we'll be like in five years time?' Elsie had reasoned. 'And I don't want you having to deal with two more old cronies when you've already got enough on your plate, what with Bevan and Justine giving you the run-around.' She had smiled at Maggie and added, 'Murray's getting on, you know. He's not as fit as me.' Elsie had a way of talking about her husband that made him appear older than he was. A keen fisherman, there was nothing he liked more than packing his car and disappearing for days at a time to the Mataura or one of the many other rivers in the district. When he wasn't fishing, he could be found in the garage, making flies and doing whatever else it was that fishermen did when not standing thigh-deep in water.

Murray, reflected Maggie, was nothing like her own father. Whereas her father, Frank, had been both religious and remote, Murray was outgoing and confident. Despite being in his seventies, he thought nothing of slipping his hand into Elsie's as they walked through town or browsed the homeware shelves at Briscoes. And there was also the time Maggie had collected him from the airport and been astounded to hear him call, 'Hello, kiddo!' the moment he laid eyes on her. All the other passengers had turned to see who he was addressing. It was almost as if he was teasing her, which was another thing her own father would not have done.

The truth was, it had come as a complete surprise when, only a few years after Frank's death, Elsie had taken Maggie aside and mentioned that she had found a 'special' friend. At that time, no one in the family knew anything about Murray. A tradesman, he had met Elsie through work – that is, he had spent a week or so re-papering her home, during which time they had hit it off, apparently. Maggie had had little to say about the match – it was, after all, none of her business – but Carol had taken it badly.

In the months following her mother's announcement that Murray was moving in, Carol had been on the phone to Maggie night after night complaining. 'Poor Dad,' she had begun, ignoring the fact that their father had been dead for some time. Later she added, 'Look, Maggie, I understand that Mum doesn't want to rush into another marriage. But she can't invite Murray to move in while she gets to know him better.' Hearing Carol, Maggie could imagine her sister shuddering with distaste at the images that were clearly going through her mind. 'Maggie, you know how people in small towns talk.' Maggie had allowed her sister to ramble on but she didn't have time to worry about gossips. She had more important things to think about.

It was only after the marriage was finally announced that Carol began to calm down. Murray, she pointed out, was a Freemason, after all. What's more, he knew one of the top managers at the Tiwai Point aluminium smelter, where Carol's husband, Lindsay worked. His daughter from his first marriage ran a pre-school in Tauranga. His son, who lived in England, had a desk job at British Rail. 'Honestly, Maggie,' said Carol, 'I was so worried that Mum was going to make a fool of herself. And you didn't seem to care. In fact, joking that Murray was related to Minnie Dean . . . I mean, it was hardly helpful, was it?' Maggie had no recollection of saying any such thing but she kept quiet. If her sister wanted to believe that her future stepfather was related to a murderer, then so be it. It seemed an unlikely connection given that Murray was British and had only moved from Balclutha to Winton, the home town of Minnie Dean, in the early nineties.

Driving down Winton's main street with Storm in the back seat, Maggie glanced from the old established trees lining the road to the shops dotted along the way, noticing how much the latter had changed over the years. The town was prosperous, more so than any of the other towns in the area. Across the road from the charity shop was a beauty parlour. And down the street from that was a café. Not an old-fashioned bakery and tea-rooms but a modern café. Never having been inside, she wondered if it had an espresso machine and piles of magazines stacked on the window sill. It was the type of place Carol would like. She could see her now, striding up to the counter and asking for a mocha before taking a seat right by the window, hoping against hope that someone – one of her mother's friends – would walk by and spot her sipping from a cup and saucer.

Everything about Carol was mocha. The colour of her hair and lipstick, the paint on her walls, the cushions on her settee, even her kids' bedspreads – it was all mocha. The only thing that wasn't mocha was the colour scheme at the agency. Carol had taken over the business during her orange period and had not got around to updating the look.

Maggie could remember how the agency had looked before her sister came on board. Back in the nineties the walls in all the rooms had been painted a creamy off-white. The carpet had been the colour of porridge. But within a week of taking over the business, her younger sister had had the walls patchworked with small squares of paint, colours sampled from numerous test pots she had picked up at the decorating shop. 'Isn't it great,' she had said. 'On the back of New World supermarket receipts are coupons for paint testers. I've asked all my friends and clients to cut them out and save them for me.' Then, narrowing her eyes, she had added, 'You don't buy your groceries at New World, do you?' Maggie had shaken her head. 'I didn't think so,' snapped her sister. 'You might like to consider asking some of your clients to help.' Maggie had no intention of asking her clients to supply supermarket receipts for Carol. In any event, none of her clients shopped at New World. Like her, they favoured Pak'nSave or the local dairy.

From time to time, Carol would now glance around and sigh, saying, 'What was I thinking of? Tia Maria!' Although she wasn't certain, Maggie thought that Tia Maria was the name given to the dirty-orange-coloured paint covering the walls. Having reached this conclusion, she sometimes found herself muttering 'Tia Maria!'

whenever she was particularly annoyed or stressed. In her ears, it sounded as good as any other expletive. She had learnt not to utter it within earshot of Carol because, among other things, Carol had no sense of humour.

At last, Elsie's house came into view. Maggie pulled up outside and stopped the car. Nudging Storm ahead of her, she had barely reached the door before Elsie took her to one side and asked, 'How's the business with Justine going?' To Maggie's response of 'All right, I suppose' she merely nodded, adding, 'And that business with Bevan?' Maggie shrugged but said nothing. 'Well,' said Elsie, 'you know I'm here if you need me.' Then, giving Maggie the slightest of hugs, she guided her towards the kitchen to join Murray.

While she prepared coffee, Elsie brightened and said, 'Carol's been on the phone.' It seemed to Maggie that her mother was stifling a laugh and she felt grateful. Her mother had never taken sides or expressed a preference for one daughter over the other, but Maggie often sensed that Elsie understood her two daughters perfectly – that she knew the score. 'You won't believe this, Maggie,' she laughed. 'But she wants to know where we're planning to spend Mother's Day.'

'Mother's Day? But that's not for ages.'

'Yes, that's what I told her. But you'd best call her as she's talking about booking that posh place in town.'

Maggie groaned. That was all she needed.

Smiling, her mother said, 'Look, I told her I'd be happy to have you all here, but she's got it into her head . . .'

Maggie nodded. There was no escape, she knew that. And

besides, why should her mother cook lunch for them all? Hadn't she done enough cooking in her lifetime?

They sat quietly sipping coffee, while Murray helped Storm into his pyjamas. Listening as Murray told Storm about a trout he had caught in the Eglington River, Maggie couldn't help but think of her own father again. Frank had never made up stories about his exploits. To exaggerate for the sake of entertainment would have struck him as frivolous and dishonest. On the rare mornings when he had eaten breakfast with Maggie and Carol, he'd talked to them about the progress they were making at school, their behaviour at home and their role within the church. The manner in which he questioned the girls made Maggie nervous. She felt cornered, certain that a trap had been set and yet unable to understand the reason for it. Never seeking out conversation, her father gave the impression of filing a report.

Yet, once in a while, he had appeared to soften. Maggie had vivid memories of the few occasions he had come into the girls' shared bedroom at night. During these visits, he would often begin by talking about the Blessed Virgin Mary. Maggie recalled the way his voice had trembled with emotion as he told them that through Mary they could obtain every hope and all salvation. He spoke with such conviction, such passion, that he appeared to forget he was talking to his daughters. It was as if he was addressing the Blessed Virgin Mary and not them at all. Even Carol picked up on the change that took place in him. After he left the room, she would grumble that he was 'in love' with Mary. It was a silly thing to say, but Maggie understood what her sister meant. For her own part, she wondered if her father's behaviour was somehow abnormal. He seemed so different from the other grown-ups she had talked to following Mass.

Either way, Frank would appear gentler as a result of these chats – and for this, Maggie was grateful. He would sometimes indulge the girls with tales about the saints or even hymns they recognised from Mass. Carol preferred to hear her father sing but Maggie craved the stories. After one particular tale, that of St Stephen, she had felt moved to draw a picture of the saint being stoned to death. While Carol filled in images of ponies from her *Bumper Book of Colouring*, Maggie carefully outlined an image of the saint as he knelt before his murderers crying, 'Lord, do not lay this sin against them.' She had given the picture to her father, who thanked her for the gift before folding the drawing into quarters and tucking it into his jacket pocket.

Noticing Maggie's concentration as she illustrated more stories about the saints, Carol had taunted, 'You're gruesome!' But Maggie had paid no attention. She couldn't put it into words, but she felt connected to them. She blushed now at her lack of humility.

Elsie, who had been raised in the Church of England, maintained a respectful distance from her first husband's beliefs. It was enough for her that he had been prepared to enter into a mixed marriage. It had caused a great deal of pain at the time but Frank had, in effect, chosen her above his mother. That her eldest daughter, Maggie, had followed the path lain down by Frank caused Elsie some measure of discomfort, but being mindful of her daughter's conviction, she said nothing.

Over the years, Elsie had noted that on more than one occasion, Maggie's faith had complicated her life. It seemed to her that Maggie relied too heavily on the church. Her daughter had the air of an addict about her. It was as if she craved God, and yet whatever satisfaction she got from the encounter appeared so short-lived that Maggie took it as a sign of personal failure on her part. She could never measure up and, as a result, spent half her life feeling guilty.

Reflecting on her daughter's approach to life, Elsie suddenly said, 'Murray saw Ross yesterday.'

Maggie stiffened at the mention of her ex-husband's name.

'He was out working on the lines at Wilsons Crossing. Apparently he was up the pole doing all the work while the rest of his crew stood around chatting.'

It was strange to picture Ross as a linesman when for so many years he had been employed at the timber mill. From the sound of it, he liked his new job.

'Did he talk to Murray? What did he say?' asked Maggie.

Elsie shrugged, 'Nothing much. Mentioned that he was seeing Bevan this weekend. That's about all, I think.'

Maggie grimaced. Bevan had said nothing to her about seeing his father. But since she had put her foot down over the car competition, he had all but stopped talking to her. Irritated, she asked, 'Do you know when they're meeting? I need to tell Ross a few things . . .'

Her mother shook her head, saying, 'I didn't see him, only Murray did.'

Maggie nodded and looked at the mug in her hands. For days she had been trying to get hold of Ross, with no luck. It seemed to her that her only chance was to hope for a storm or major earthquake and then, at least, she could drive out to the spot where the lines were down and catch him at work.

She should be getting off home. She had to be up early in the morning. Her maltreatment seminar kicked off at half past eight, and she wanted to tackle a few loads of washing before then.

Standing to leave, she was stopped by her mother, who offered, 'Why don't you stay here tonight. You look tired.'

Maggie grimaced, 'I am tired.'

Then looking in at Murray and Storm, she said goodbye and left.

*R*ETURNING HOME, Maggie found the place deserted. A note from Lisa lay on the table next to a pile of brochures collected during Career Night. Scrawled in green felt pen, it said: 'At Joyce's. Justine phoned.' There was no note from Bevan. Maggie wondered if he was with his father or simply wandering around town with Todd and his friends. She wouldn't text him; there was no point. He rarely responded to her messages. Instead, she searched the kitchen for a clue to his whereabouts. What that clue might be – in the absence of a note – she had no idea. Nevertheless, she wandered through the house looking for it.

Finding nothing, she went out into the garden and walked across to the shed. The smell of damp and dirty washing struck her as she entered. Scattered across the floor were small mounds of mud-stained shorts and socks. Next to the bed, also on the floor, was a red-and-white-striped box containing the picked over remains of Kentucky Fried Chicken. Beside that lay a milkshake carton, chocolate-flavoured milk forming a puddle on the chip-board floor. As she bent down to right the carton, Maggie's eye was caught by a scrap of green paper announcing: 'Your Chance to Win! This 1992 Toyota Corolla Could Be Yours! All you have to do . . .' The page was ripped and despite searching the floor for another fragment, Maggie could find nothing else relating to the competition.

Wavering, her mind considering all her options, Maggie began to straighten the blankets on her son's divan. She plumped his pillow, placing it once more at the head of the bed, and then gathering the dirty clothes into a tight bundle she left the shed and returned, slowly, towards the house.

She wandered back across the lawn, and stopped from time to time to pick up bits and pieces of toys that had been left on the grass. A bow with no arrow, a truck with no wheel, an astro-naut with no arm – small objects that Storm had forgotten to bring inside.

She wondered whether she should return Justine's call im-mediately or wait until the morning when she might feel better able to cope with whatever it was her oldest daughter wanted. She was worried that if she didn't call, Justine might get it into her head to contact Elsie, or even Carol. Still wondering what to do, she went into the lounge and dumped her son's dirty clothes on the sofa. She then began to search for the phone, rummaging through the piles of junk left scattered over the coffee table and chairs, before finding it on the floor beside the television. Taking a deep breath, she dialled. She held the phone to her ear, while absently tidying the room, putting the objects she had collected from the garden into a toy basket along with a number of other plastic figures and soft toys. Holding one plastic figure, a clown, she thought of Mrs Devon and imagined the fallout that would result from her feedback questionnaire.

The phone continued to ring, unanswered. She imagined Justine standing in her kitchen, Mischa in one arm, Kayla in the other, cigarette in her mouth as she muttered, 'Hang on, I'm coming' towards the empty bedroom where her own phone rested. Maggie waited, seeing in her mind's eye her daughter rushing, grumbling, and tripping down the hall towards the sound of ringing. She allowed her time to reach the bedroom, put the twins on the bed and make a dive for the phone – and then Maggie counted another thirty seconds, just in case, before hanging up. For a moment she felt lonely, and then picking up her son's washing she walked to the laundry and loaded the machine.

$\mathcal{M}$AGGIE SAT ALONE at a Formica table, listening to the conversation between her sister and the woman brought in to facilitate the maltreatment seminar. Hovering around the coffee machine, the facilitator, Judy, could be heard saying, 'I wanted Julian, my partner, to come with me, but he couldn't get away. We're planning to meet up later in the week in Queenstown and we'll have a bit of a break, visit some vineyards and maybe get in some golf.'

Maggie could see Carol nod her head as she murmured, 'Lindsay and I were up that way a few months ago.'

As she listened, she felt an overwhelming desire to walk out. The day, as she had predicted, had been a waste of time. She had learnt little from the expert and next to nothing from the role-playing exercises she had been forced to participate in. At least all they had to do now was sit back and watch a documentary about a nursing home which was located in a dismal town in Yorkshire.

The camera followed the day-to-day interactions between staff and clients. Every so often Judy would indicate a member of the nursing staff and murmur, 'She could have done that better,' or, 'Watch how she deals with this problem.' Despite these interruptions, Maggie found the documentary itself reasonably interesting given the topic.

Certain that the video was about to end, she stood to leave. Her action was greeted with an annoyed glance from Carol but Maggie chose to ignore her sister, and excused herself to Judy, apologising, 'I'm sorry but I have to rush. I've left my grandson with my aged mother and I should go and rescue her.' In response, Judy thanked Maggie for her contribution and then, sifting through some papers, she found a pink form, which she passed out, saying, 'Fill this in and pop it back to Carol, will you?' She smiled, and pointed to the sheet headed: 'Caring – Together'. Seeing Maggie's puzzled expression, she added, 'It's a questionnaire, so I can get some feedback about today's seminar.' Maggie nodded and stuffed the form into her pocket.

She darted down the stairs, and was peeved to hear Carol's voice calling her back. 'Maggie! I need you a second.' Turning on the stairs, Maggie glowered at her sister but made no move, forcing Carol to come down to her. 'Goodness, Maggie, that was pretty rude. And don't think you can fool me with all that "elderly mother" nonsense.' Then, handing Maggie a manila folder, she said, 'I've got two new clients for you. Starting next week.' She stood looking down on Maggie as if waiting for her to open the file and scan the contents. Aware of what was going through Carol's mind, Maggie took the file and held it against her body beneath her folded arms. She stared at her sister, waiting, forcing her to break the silence. 'You said you wanted some clients your own age so I got you these.' Carol smiled weakly and then corrected herself, adding, 'Well, one of them is kind of young, anyway.'

Maggie frowned. She was tired of always being landed with old men. She had nothing against men in general and, in fact, enjoyed the company of her oldest client, Mr Paxton, but she longed to have one or two more clients who didn't have hairs growing out of their ears or shuffle around all morning in saggy white underpants and flapping dressing gowns. For once in her life she would like to get the executive who threw out laptops.

'Look, Maggie,' said Carol, 'I know what you're thinking but this is all I have at the moment. It's this or nothing and, frankly, after all that nonsense with Mrs Devon, I think you owe me . . .'

Maggie gasped, 'What do you mean?'

Carol frowned, 'You know very well what I mean. I've had her on the phone several times . . .'

Maggie stiffened, responding, 'She's a complete monster. And her son – he's even worse. They both deserve a good kick . . .' She stopped. Standing at the top of the stairway, listening, was Judy.

Still fuming as she reached her car, Maggie threw the files onto the back seat and turned the key. As she drove away, she noticed that the fuel gauge was on empty. She was almost certain it was the gauge playing up again, but she decided not to risk the trip to Winton without stopping first to put in twenty dollars of petrol. Topping up would give her a chance to see Lisa, in any case.

Her daughter worked most weekends at the nearby petrol station – her shift beginning at two and ending at 10 p.m. The pay was not terrific, but the owner of the station, Scott, seemed okay. Maggie had met him several times and, although he had little to say for himself, he appeared honest – but shy. From time to time, he would drop Lisa home after her shift and stay for a few minutes and share a coffee with them. He brought the coffee himself. Three cardboard cups containing flat whites, prepared by him at the station.

The first time he'd arrived at Maggie's door, coffee in hand, he'd looked embarrassed, shuffling slightly as he murmured, 'I thought I'd drop Lisa off. She's on my way . . .' He'd not known how to explain the coffee, and it had been up to Lisa to add, 'Scott thought you might enjoy some real coffee. I told him how we only have instant . . .'

Flustered, Maggie hadn't known how to respond. Inviting him in, she had taken the cups from him and stood awkwardly wondering if she shouldn't perhaps empty the contents into some proper mugs. Then, concluding she mustn't make a fuss, she'd invited Scott through to the kitchen, where she quickly hunted through the cupboards for a packet of biscuits.

Uncomfortable in his presence, she said, 'I don't normally drink coffee at night. It keeps me awake.' She immediately regretted sounding ungrateful, and added, 'I'm sorry about the biscuits, I didn't have time to do any baking this week.'

The reference to home-baking made Lisa laugh. She quickly pointed out that it had been ages since Maggie had baked a cake or whipped up a batch of scones. Maggie blushed and was relieved when Scott paid no attention but reached for a chocolate chippie, which he dunked in his cup. They had sat for several minutes in silence, Maggie fiddling with the plastic lid to her cup, repeatedly squeezing it over the rim then easing it off with a faint 'pop'. She wasn't sure what to do with the top, whether she should drink through the small hole in its surface or discard it altogether. Scott had placed his lid on the tablecloth next to his cup, so she decided to do the same, even though the milky coffee that had settled on the plastic now stained the freshly washed and ironed cloth.

'So, Mrs Keane . . .' began Scott. He stopped, and it seemed to Maggie that he had nothing more to say.

'Call me Margaret – or Maggie,' she had responded after several seconds.

Scott had nodded and then looking at Lisa said, 'Your daughter's a hard worker.'

It was Maggie's turn to nod.

They drank their coffee in silence, and when their cups were empty Maggie wondered if she should offer to make more. But, as Lisa had told Scott, they only had instant and so she stayed in her chair, her eyes resting on the cloth and her fingers edging towards the plastic lid in front of her.

She caught sight of Scott now, standing hunched over a newspaper, as she drove onto the forecourt of the petrol station. He didn't notice her. Lisa was busy round the side of the station filling an LPG bottle for a man who stood by watching. The wind had got up again, Maggie realised. Lisa's hair kept blowing across her face, and as she filled the tank she tried to control the wayward strands, tucking them behind her ears over and over again. Searching her pocket, Maggie found an elastic band she had picked up off the carpet at one of her client's homes the day before. She walked across to Lisa, and offered her the elastic and then nodded a greeting towards the man, whom she recognised as a neighbour.

'Bit windy,' he said as he lifted the full bottle into the back of his car.

'I haven't heard the forecast.'

The man scanned the forecourt. 'It's going to be like this tomorrow – with rain.' He smiled and, addressing Lisa, said, 'Put it on my account, love,' before climbing into his car. The way he looked at Lisa and the manner in which he said 'love' was sleazy. He made Maggie feel uncomfortable. When he drove away, she heard music from his stereo, the steady thump, thump, thump of hip hop – a sound she had heard a thousand times before coming from Bevan's shed but which struck her as inappropriate, for a fifty-year-old.

'How's work?' she asked Lisa now they were alone.

'All right. A bit cold, but not too bad.'

Maggie looked at her daughter. She appeared half frozen. 'I've got Storm's mittens in the car,' she offered. Lisa shook her head, responding they were too small and, anyway, they'd only get in the way. She couldn't do her job properly if she wore gloves. Maggie didn't press the point. She didn't like her daughter working so late at this time of year. There had been one or two incidents at the station during the past six months, and Maggie often felt anxious when her daughter was at work. Sensing what was going through Maggie's mind, Lisa said, 'Scott's here.' They both looked in the direction of the shop and watched as Scott looked up from the article he was reading. He caught sight of Maggie and straightened before waving in her direction. Until now Maggie hadn't paid much attention to his appearance but watching him stretch reminded her of how tall he was. He must be all of six-and-a-half foot, she realised. She watched him come out from behind the counter, and a stray thought entered her mind. It would be so awkward to kiss him, she mused. In that instant she pictured herself using the back of her heel to drag a kitchen chair across the floor to a spot by his feet before standing on it – as if trying to retrieve something from the back of a high cupboard. The image lingered in her mind and she turned away from Scott's advancing figure, disturbed by what she had visualised.

Anticipating that he would come outside, Maggie grimaced. She had thought she might be able to spend a few minutes alone with her daughter, just the two of them. All she'd wanted was a quiet conversation. As Scott came closer, he gestured towards Maggie's car, saying, 'Your tyre's a bit flat there.' Beneath the glowing light of the petrol stand, the three of them gazed at the tyre and, although she knew next to nothing about cars, Maggie kicked it, noting as she did that it felt hard as a rock against the toe of her shoe. 'The tread's a bit worn, too,' said Scott.

Maggie couldn't remember when, exactly, she had last bought tyres but she could remember quite clearly how much they had cost. She recalled that the tyre dealer had told her she could pay them off in weekly instalments, but she had chosen to buy them one at a time, paying for each tyre in full before getting the next one fitted. Because of that, she had had to go without a warrant for several months and had been constantly alert on the road for fear of being pulled over by a traffic cop doing a random check. Even now she shuddered at the memory of coming across a Christmas Eve patrol and finding herself in a line of cars where every second or third car was stopped. By some miracle she had been waved straight through, but the recollection of that episode made her heart race.

Lost in thought, she was startled by Scott's voice. 'You'll have to get that tyre sorted before your next warrant. It's badly worn. In fact,' he continued, 'it might not even see you through till your next check.'

He drew Maggie's attention to a small bulge on the tyre, explaining it was a blister, a sign of weakness which could cause it to blow at any moment. Glancing from the tyre to Maggie, he said, 'And you don't want that to happen – especially if you've got your kids with you.'

Maggie nodded dutifully and replied that she would see to it as soon as possible. In any case, she thought her warrant was due sometime during the next few weeks. Only the other day, she had happened to glance at the sticker on her windscreen and had experienced a sense of dread.

She couldn't say why, but she had always hated taking her car for its test. It had always been Ross's job to see to the car, but since he had left she'd been forced to attend to it. Unable to do without her car for a morning, she would join the queue at a 'while you wait' testing station and then stand nervously, trying to read the expression and gestures of the mechanic on duty as he worked his way slowly through his checklist. At least now, she thought, she could pay Scott to do her warrant. Knowing he would carry out the test without making her feel like a failure was a slight consolation. She could trust him, too, not to make a fuss about how long it had been since the vehicle's last service.

While Scott checked the air pressure in her tyres, Maggie followed Lisa into the warmth of the station and stood at the counter watching as her daughter made coffee. She was suddenly struck by how tall Lisa was. In her mind's eye, Lisa was shorter than herself, but seeing her now she realised her daughter was, in fact, at least an inch or two taller than herself. She was a skinny thing – all bones and angles, exactly as Maggie had been at her age. Her attention fixed on Lisa, she noticed how flat-chested her daughter was. Yet she knew that Lisa had started to wear a bra. The size, she recalled, was 10A. Where and when her daughter had bought the bra Maggie didn't know. She guessed she had gone to H & J's with Joyce or one of her other girlfriends. Lisa must have paid for it herself, out of her wages, as Maggie had no recollection of ever being asked for money. Thinking she would compliment her daughter on her appearance, she opened her mouth to speak but at that instant a car pulled up, and Lisa scuttled outside, leaving Maggie alone with two cardboard cups gripped in her hands.

A voice interrupted her train of thought. 'I think you're going to need two new tyres at least. Maybe three.' Maggie jumped, coffee splashing out of the cups. 'I'll sort something out for you, if you like,' continued Scott. 'I can probably get hold of some re-treads . . .' He could see that Maggie was only half listening, that she was far away, her eyes fixed on Lisa's back as her daughter yanked the petrol hose around the back of the waiting car.

Feeling awkward, he sidled back around the counter and peered down at the newspaper still open in front of him. His eyes fixed on the listings for the cinema, he mouthed the session times to himself as he ran his fingers over the page. A thought crossed his mind and he glanced up hopefully, determined to ask Maggie something. He noticed, too late, that she had already left the shop. He caught sight of her climbing into her car and then, walking back around the counter, he collected her cup of coffee and took a sip from it before dropping it in the bin.

PART TWO

$\mathcal{M}$AGGIE HAD THOUGHT it was typical of Carol to hand over two new clients without mentioning they both lived in Riverton. As if she didn't have enough on her plate already. She would have to travel out of town for only a few hours work each week. Even worse, she had now finished with one of them, a Mrs Riley, and was therefore making the journey for the sole purpose of cleaning up after Angela, a twenty-year-old who had sustained a badly broken leg, cracked ribs and a fractured wrist as a result of a mountain-bike-racing accident. According to her diary, Maggie was scheduled for two visits a week over the next two-and-a-half months. At least she got on with Angela. That was something.

There was another reason why she was upset. Ever since Scott had drawn her attention to the poor condition of her tyres she had felt nervous about driving out of town. Though Riverton was hardly a distant destination, her thoughts tended to stray from the journey itself to dwell on images of skidding off the road and into a ditch where, trapped in her seat, she would either incinerate or sink slowly into an irrigation channel and drown.

Years before, when Ross had bought the car, she had tied a small St Christopher's medal to the rear-view mirror. It had kept her safe so far, but she had to admit to having less faith in its power now, since strictly speaking, St Christopher was no longer a true saint. In reality, she had little need for the medal. She'd never travelled far enough to warrant it. She'd never left the South Island. The furthest she'd ever been was to Christchurch and that was a long, long time ago – when she was a child and her father was alive.

Frank had taken her on one of his trips north. She'd never really understood why her father went to Christchurch but she thought it must have something to do with the fact that her parents managed a motel. Although it was located in a rather run-down street at the southern end of town, Maggie gathered that the motel belonged to an international chain and that, from time to time, her father would have to go to Christchurch and attend to business.

She remembered that they had travelled by train. Although the journey took all day, she could recall little of the trip. One incident she thought she remembered was that towards lunchtime her father had guided her through the train to a car serving hot meals. The dining car, she remembered, had struck her as beautiful. She thought it must look like a restaurant – an expensive one. Sadly, all the seats were taken.

She recalled reaching for her father's hand and holding it tightly as the train jolted and lurched – and then it crossed her mind that her father had brought her to the car because, like everyone else, they were going to take a seat and order lunch. It was one of the most exciting moments of her life. But, in fact, he was only *showing* her the dining car. After several minutes they had returned to their own seats, where, slowly and somewhat ceremoniously, her father brought out two packets of sandwiches and passed one to her before opening his own.

Why her father had taken her to the dining car – if, in fact, he had – was never made clear. Perhaps, she mused in later years, he had intended to eat there, but having seen that all the seats were already taken, changed his mind. Or maybe he had wanted her to witness one of the many ways people squandered their money. She didn't know his motives but even now she had the nagging feeling that he was punishing her in some way. That he was saying, Yes, I am taking you with me to Christchurch; but had you been a better daughter, you might also have been rewarded with this.

Realising from an early age that she was not her father's favourite daughter, Maggie had worked hard at trying to be the better one. But even her attempts to appear more conscientious than her sister failed to capture her father's attention. So she had settled on being only 'the eldest daughter', and for a time that had sufficed.

Now, driving to Riverton, she tried to focus on nothing but the road ahead. She ought to be able to get some pleasure, she reasoned, from spending half an hour alone with nothing to do but drive. It should be relaxing – like a coffee break or sitting down with a magazine. She switched on the radio and tuned in to an easy listening channel, hoping to hear a song she might know or like. Instead, a shrill voice raced through an announcement for a car competition. She listened and realised it was being promoted by the same car sales-yard as the one mentioned on the scrap of paper found in Bevan's room some weeks before. She wondered if he had heard about this new competition. It sounded just the same as the last one. He had not mentioned it, but that was hardly surprising given that he had said barely more than ten words in the past week. The disembodied voice on the radio faded to be replaced by another, even louder one.

Maggie adjusted the volume and then glanced through the passenger window. To her left were windswept paddocks hemmed in by densely planted flax bushes. Standing out against the green fields were groups of sheep and one or two newborn lambs. They were early, perhaps too early – though not being a farmer she couldn't say for sure. If the forecasted cold front came through the lambs would be at risk. Even today, with the weather overcast and squally, a few lambs looked ready to keel over. Others had sought shelter, huddled together for warmth, in the lee of the flax. She hoped the cold snap would hold off for another day.

Tomorrow, Saturday, was Storm's birthday. He was turning six, and Maggie had offered to put on a small party for him. He'd been allowed to invite a few friends to play, and later today Maggie intended to rush into town to buy him a present and one or two things for the celebration. Her mother had mentioned that The Warehouse had some children's masks and other bits and pieces, junk really, that six-year-old boys might like. Maggie figured she could probably get a good selection of stuff for around twenty or thirty dollars. When she added to that the cost of food and a present, she calculated the day would come in at around eighty or one hundred dollars. Having to fork out so much was depressing because she'd hoped to buy another new tyre. Now she'd have to wait until after her next pay day. The worrying thing was that her warrant was due, so for a few days, or even a week or two, she'd have to drive the car without a warrant and pray she wouldn't be caught.

For a while she had toyed with the idea of asking her mother to help out, but really it was out of the question. Since retiring, her mother was no better off than herself. And besides, she had already offered to bake Storm's cake – a fancy Pokémon-shaped thing, which she was copying from a cake-decorating book borrowed from the local library. Where her mother found the time or energy for such things was beyond Maggie. It seemed to her that her mother had become more energetic since her marriage to Murray. The same could not be said of her first marriage to Frank.

Throughout her marriage to Maggie's father, Elsie's life had been all work. Every day she would rise early, get the girls off to school and then make a start on cleaning the motel units before sitting down to help Frank with the books or buying food for the following morning's cooked breakfasts.

Maggie had helped her mother. After school and during weekends she would assist with the laundry, ironing sheets and towels. If her mother was behind with the cleaning she would join her in the units, clearing away empty bottles from the floor, cleaning the bathrooms or washing the dishes that had been used and left out. Her favourite task had been to polish the kettle. It made her laugh now but there had been a time when she had loved cleaning both the kettle and the toaster, rubbing them to a brilliant sheen, free from fingerprints. She preferred that task to any other, but as she'd grown older she'd lost her original fascination with all things shiny and begun to regard cleaning as nothing more than a chore.

Storm's party was another chore. Given it was his birthday,

she felt mean admitting she would rather spend the Saturday afternoon alone than in the company of five young boys. To make matters worse, Lisa would be at work and unable to help. And goodness knows where Bevan would be? Out and about with Todd probably. Dwelling on the party, she couldn't help but feel annoyed with Justine for not arranging to come down. Her daughter's unwillingness to participate in her own son's birthday was disgraceful.

Originally, before the business with the car tyres had come up, Maggie had toyed with the idea of flying Justine down or sending Storm up to Auckland for his birthday. He was old enough to travel alone, and she had thought it would be a nice treat for him. She'd worried about the cost, but if Justine had agreed to contribute a little it was within their means. In making plans, she had not anticipated Justine's current state of mind. Despite the nonsense concerning the twins and her threats to have them placed in care subsiding, there was now a much more worrying problem. Aaron, the twins' father, had returned.

Justine was beside herself with joy. No longer phoning at all hours of the day and night with a list of complaints as long as her arm, she was now calling with news of Aaron's sudden reappearance and his change of heart where the twins were concerned. Through careful questioning, Maggie managed to find out two things: that Aaron's latest girlfriend had dumped him, and second, that he was once more out of work. While neither of these facts seemed to have made much impact on Justine, they chilled Maggie. It was clear what was going to happen. The man had no intention of being a father to the twins; he wanted a roof over his head and someone to pay for his food and board, that was all. While Justine gushed about how great he was and how he had bonded with the girls by taking them down to the park each day, Maggie could already predict the future. In fact, everyone – even Bevan – could see what was going to happen. Hearing the news about Aaron's return, he had looked up from his breakfast and sneered, 'Yeah, and how long is that gonna last? Until she gets pregnant again?'

Bevan would have highlighted more of Justine's failings but by some miracle he caught Maggie's eye and realised Storm was listening. Maggie's relief was short-lived, however, because seconds later he added, 'At least Storm doesn't have a loser for a father. In fact,' Bevan laughed, 'he doesn't even have a father, full stop.'

Bevan mentioning Storm's father in front of Storm was unforgivable. The child had been through enough without needing to be reminded that he had never met his dad. Apart from Justine, none of them knew who Storm's father was, and what's more, it seemed likely that *he* had no inkling of ever having fathered a son. Probably a teenager, he had not been informed of Justine's accident. Obstinate to the last, she had insisted on keeping all details to herself.

Seventeen at the time of Storm's birth, Justine had spent the entire pregnancy in a fantasy world of her own making. As she talked about motherhood, she had taken on the glazed expression of a young girl anticipating the arrival of a new doll for Christmas. Her best friend, Amber, was also pregnant – her child was due a few weeks before Justine's – and Maggie suspected Justine had only fallen pregnant so as not to be outdone by her friend.

Lounging on the couch sometime into her seventh month, Justine had done nothing but complain about the changes taking place in her body. For hours on end she would talk to Amber, comparing notes on what they had been through and how different – how much better – things would be once their babies were born. They'd even talked about names. Between them they'd decided to choose complementary names – 'Sunny' for Amber's child and 'Storm' for Justine's. 'It will be so cute,' her daughter had cooed down the phone to her friend. 'I'm sick of waiting.' And so it had gone on, right up to the night when Amber's child had been delivered stillborn and Justine had found herself stuck at home with a baby while all her friends – Amber included – had got on with their lives.

Storm had developed into a sensible, though somewhat cautious, child. Very quiet, often lost in thought, he kept himself occupied most of the time by making up complicated stories about monsters or playing outside on his scooter. It had not dawned on him to ask if his mother would come to his party. It was as if, without needing to be told, he understood she wouldn't be there and had accepted it. That was the type of child he was. He had succumbed to being good.

Maggie's main concern now was that if Aaron remained in the picture, Justine might start talking about taking Storm back. She could foresee the trouble and disruption that would cause. Storm would be packed off to Auckland, introduced to a man he barely recognised, sent to a school where he knew no one, only to find that within a few months he would be bundled onto another plane and returned to Invercargill.

Maggie hadn't felt an urgent need to pray for some time but, as she continued driving towards Riverton, she asked for spiritual guidance. Suddenly, the noise of a brisk, electronic cancan ring tone sounded, breaking her concentration. She assumed it would be Carol pestering her about work, and so she ignored it. She returned to her prayer, beginning where she had left off, but was interrupted once more by the jingly cancan. Knowing she would have to answer, she pulled over to the side of the road. Barely was the word 'Hello' out of her mouth before her sister chimed, 'Good news!'

Carol had found someone to replace Maggie's former client, Mrs Riley. The new client also lived in Riverton; the address was just around the corner from Angela's house. Without waiting for Maggie to respond, Carol continued, explaining the client was a man –a youngish guy. Although she hadn't met him, he had sounded polite on the phone – friendly, in fact. And he was single. To Maggie's ears, it sounded as if Carol was trying to fix her up with a date rather than a job. She allowed her sister to ramble on for a while and then, certain there had to be some drawback, she interrupted, asking straight out, 'What's the catch?'

'No catch!' replied Carol, her voice rising as if offended by the question. 'What do you mean catch? It's a job, Maggie.'

Maggie grunted. She turned to look across the paddocks, her eyes fixing on a sack caught on a barbed wire fence. The sack twisted and flapped in the wind, and a few seconds later she felt the same gust as it buffeted the car, rocking it as if it were no more than a pram being jiggled by an impatient mother.

Mesmerised by the sight of the flapping sack, she failed to catch what her sister was telling her. It was only after several seconds had passed that she realised Carol was repeating herself, calling, 'Maggie, Maggie! Are you listening?' Maggie jerked, nodded and stammered, 'Pardon?' Her eyes still focussed on the sack, she heard Carol explain that the new client was expecting her later that day, that he would take the time vacated by Mrs Riley. It was all organised. All Maggie had to do was drop in after seeing Angela and introduce herself. Nothing special.

More alert now, Maggie protested, 'But I have to go to town and get Storm's birthday present and the party stuff – you know that. I reminded you the other day that I had to go into town . . .'

Her protest met with no response and a deep silence followed, broken only by the eerie whistle of wind through the gap in the passenger window. Allowing the silence to draw out, Maggie eventually asked, 'What is he, anyway? ACC or sickness benefit?'

She hoped her sister would respond with the former. ACC clients were easier to deal with in her opinion. She believed the government treated them better than people on sickness or invalid's benefits, and because of that, they complained less. Beneficiaries, by comparison, could come across as bitter. Some of them were real hard work.

'He's on a benefit.'

Maggie groaned.

She could imagine his house: a stack of dishes in the sink, rubbish bags in the hall and piles of dirty or damp washing strewn over the backs of chairs. The carpet, if there was one, would be littered with chip packets; crumbs would be all over the place and there'd be some animal – a cat or a dog – perched on the sofa, its fur shedding, making the cushions look white and felted. Her thoughts wandered through the house until they came to rest in the bedroom. She pictured the mismatched sheets lying rumpled near the foot of the bed, the pillows most likely without pillowcases, and the threadbare towels or blankets hung up over the window where the curtains should be. And the smell too. Stale smoke from butts stubbed out in paua shells, mugs and beer cans.

She could see it all so clearly that her heart sank. She didn't want to go. She really didn't want to take on another sickie, they were so much work.

'What's wrong with him?' she asked. With luck it would be nothing too debilitating physically. Maybe he was just depressed? She felt uncomfortable admitting it, even to herself, but experience had taught her that depressed clients were straightforward, work-wise. For a start, they tended to be reasonably passive. They hadn't the energy to make a lot of mess around the house and they seldom, if ever, trailed around behind her chatting as she worked. Furthermore, they rarely cared enough about their surroundings to mention any shortcomings about her work. Clean or dirty, it was all the same to them. Well, maybe that was taking it a bit far, cringed Maggie, ashamed of her own ruthlessness. After all, it wasn't their fault they were unhappy. But their lack of get-up-and-go did get on her nerves from time to time, she had to admit that. In any event, it had been a long time since any of her clients had been depressed. Carol kept those for herself.

'Multiple sclerosis,' said Carol, her voice suspiciously airy.

Unconsciously, Maggie raised her eyebrows. She'd worked for MS clients before. They were okay, sometimes. At least she knew what to expect.

When she arrived at Angela's flat, Maggie noticed that three cars as well as an aluminium boat were blocking the driveway. The last time she'd visited she'd been able to park outside the door, but now she had to leave the car on the road and slog up the steep access path to the house carrying the two bags of groceries she'd bought for her client. It annoyed her to be shopping for Angela. She had two perfectly fit flatmates capable of picking up supplies. There was no reason why she should have to do it. Half the time the girl's flatmates were in bed when she arrived in the morning. Both builder's mates, they only worked when the weather was dry and spent the rest of their time lounging around watching Sky TV while fixing their bikes. Twice now she had arrived to discover bicycle parts scattered across the floor of the living room and oily rags draped over the furniture. Had it been Bevan or Lisa making such a mess she would have given them a clip round the ear, but being clients she couldn't do that. She wondered what their mothers had been like. Had they tolerated such behaviour in their homes? She doubted it.

The peculiar thing was that despite flatting with two slobs and being somewhat untidy herself, Angela was always beautifully groomed. Not only was her hair washed and neat, and her face lightly made up, but her nails, too, were filed into smooth almond-shaped curves and painted a soft pink or vibrant red. Her nails were perfect in every way. Maggie had noticed them the first time she had visited but had said nothing until she got to know the girl better. Only in the past few weeks had she discovered that Angela was a beauty therapist. She lived in Riverton but commuted to Invercargill, where, for eight hours every day, she pampered, massaged, waxed and made-up women from all over town.

Over coffee, Maggie learnt about the most popular treatment of all – the Brazilian wax. Listening to Angela's description of the process, Maggie had felt repulsed. Notwithstanding that the treatment sounded painful, it also struck her as disgusting and pointless. She couldn't get her head around it. Why would a woman need to wax down there? Warming to the subject, Angela had let slip that it wasn't only women who undertook the treatment. For a second Maggie couldn't follow what she meant, but then, slowly, it dawned on her. 'But that's revolting!' she stammered. 'I mean, that's . . . that's . . .' She couldn't finish. The only word that came close to describing how she felt was 'sick'.

Angela giggled, but Maggie shook her head. She didn't even want to think about it.

'It's really good money,' went on Angela some time later. 'I can charge fifty to sixty dollars a pop, no sweat.'

Maggie smiled but she couldn't help thinking that she would want a lot more than fifty dollars to do that to a man.

'It's not all waxing, eh,' continued Angela. 'I do a lot of facials and stuff. You ever had a facial?'

Maggie shook her head.

'Tell you what,' said Angela, 'I'll do you one next week if you want? I've got some product and stuff here, and anyway, it will make a nice change from doing nothing all day. It'll have to be a one-handed facial,' she smiled, waving her plastered wrist in front of Maggie's eyes. 'I'll even get some wax and do your eyebrows and moustache, too. Make a meal of it.'

Arriving at the house of her new client, Maggie couldn't help but glance at her reflection in the rear-view mirror. She traced her fingertips over her top lip and squinted. She'd never really been aware of having a moustache, but since Angela had drawn her attention to it, she had begun to notice that pale hairs were growing along her top lip line. They were longer towards the corners of her mouth. Tilting her head slightly, Maggie saw that she also had fine hairs sprouting from her chin. She curled her top lip and the hairs in her nostrils all but protruded from her scrunched up nose. Her cheeks, the side of her face, and the space between her eyebrows were all covered in pale fuzzy hair.

Disconcerted, she reached into the glove box and retrieved a lipstick she'd bought at the time of her father's funeral. A candy pink stain, she applied it carefully, noticing as she did that the colour caught the tips of the short hairs growing at the outer edges of her mouth. She ran her tongue over her lips and bared her teeth, checking for traces of colour. Now that her attention was focussed so squarely on her appearance, she couldn't help but be reminded of how gap-toothed she was. Her teeth were white enough, but the space in the centre, which had haunted her throughout her schooldays, seemed to have grown wider since the last time she looked. She wondered if her gums were receding; if perhaps, in a year or two, she would begin to lose her teeth and need to have them replaced with false ones. The thought horrified her. She had cared for far too many people with false teeth to ever want them herself. She wasn't vain but there was something about holding a set of teeth in your hand while brushing them that turned her stomach. Her thoughts lingered on images of old women stand-ing toothless and slack-mouthed in front of cracked bathroom mirrors. She checked her reflection once more and then got out of the car.

Across the road from the beach, the house she had been sent to was little more than a crib. This both cheered and worried her. Despite the sand which would, no doubt, be on the carpet, vacuuming would be a breeze. It would take, she estimated, about twenty minutes to do a good job. But the downside was that small houses tended to be cluttered. They took longer to dust than normal houses. Every available surface, window sills included, would most likely be decorated with objects – valueless bits and pieces. Given that the house was also located directly across the road from the beach, there would probably be extra junk lying around, stuff picked up from the high-tide line and kept for a rainy day. She could imagine it: glass balls from nets, pieces of wood, plastic packing tape, lengths of rope – all the stuff that was completely worthless but nevertheless essential for someone who did nothing all day but obsess about all the things he might want to make some day. Then, remembering her new client was in a wheelchair, she brightened a little: she might be spared the beach-combed junk.

As Maggie approached the door she was conscious of a sense of anticipation. Before meeting a client for the first time, she often felt nervous, running through the introductions in her mind. Would the client be welcoming? Would he live alone or be surrounded by family? Was he the type to have some weird collection of glass figurines or 'Dungeons and Dragons' paraphernalia, or would he live in some version of an empty shell? No matter how many times she took on a new client, there was always an anxious moment in the instant before the door was opened and everything was revealed.

She stood back a little, and then knocked. Her sister had told her the client was around her own age, so he shouldn't be deaf or too weak to get himself to the door, she thought. Unless his illness was more severe than her sister had let on. Glancing around, Maggie was relieved to see that the bright yellow vehicle in the driveway was fitted out for a paraplegic. She reasoned that if he was able to drive he must be well enough to come to the door. She knocked once more. Her mind no longer making its slow progression through the imaginary interior of the man's house, she began to feel impatient, her eyes flicking over the rough notes she had scrawled onto the back of her shopping list: Taramea Bay, half kilometre past soundshell, Coloursteel garage door, old weatherboard house. Old weatherboard was right. The place was virtually falling down.

She remembered something she had not thought about since doing a school project when she was around eleven or twelve: Riverton was Southland's oldest European settlement. It had been visited by sealers and whalers at the beginning of the eighteenth century. She couldn't really remember anything else about the place but after a moment's thought decided it couldn't have been visited in the eighteenth century. It must have been the eighteen hundreds. But whenever it was, it looked like this guy's house was built around the same time.

She flicked the paper over in her hand and read through her shopping list. There was so much to do before Storm's birthday and yet here she was wasting time, loitering aimlessly on the doorstep. In future she'd let herself in, but today she'd make a note of how long she spent standing outside and deduct it from the time allocated to cleaning. By her reckoning she had already lost a good three minutes.

Maggie had decided her client might be somewhere outside, when, from behind her, came the sound of the door opening. She twisted around and took in the figure gazing up at her and her heart lurched. Losing her balance, she stumbled forward and for an instant she feared she might actually fall on top of him. She struggled to regain her composure, her heart hammering against her chest. Unable to meet his eye, she looked down towards her feet and gabbled, 'I've been sent by my sister Carol. You spoke to her at the agency? I'm . . .' She stopped. She didn't want to give her name. She remembered she had introduced herself the first time they had met but there was the slightest chance that if she kept her name to herself he might not recognise her. Her previous introduction had been very brief, after all. Just a matter of minutes. And if, like her, he was no good at remembering faces, he might not be able to place her. At that moment a flicker of hope went through her. If she didn't remind him, he might not be able to link her to that woman – the mother of one of the 'little shits' who had tipped him from his chair.

Perched on the doorstep, she tried to remember what had taken place the last time they'd met. Apart from apologising on her son's behalf, what had she said? Her heart sank as she recalled she had mentioned she was a caregiver. Glancing at the man, she couldn't help but wonder if he hadn't set out to find her. A strange smile on his face unsettled her. He could be one of those weird types, a nutter. Wouldn't surprise her, not after seeing the state of his house from the outside. Increasingly anxious, Maggie glanced nervously towards the drive. A number of random thoughts entered her mind in rapid succession: she would tell him there had been a mistake, she couldn't fit him in; she'd give Carol a piece of her mind for sending her in the first place; he'd had a haircut – he didn't have that silly plait anymore; it was pure coincidence – it wasn't as if Invercargill was awash with caregivers; it would be rude to just leave; he might have a gun; she should leave now – escape.

His voice broke the silence and she jumped. Extending his hand, he said, 'My name's Tim. Thanks for coming.'

Unable to meet his eye and struggling over what to do, she realised she was shuffling, stepping from the top step to the one below and back again as she tried to figure out what to say. To her surprise, she suddenly found herself mumbling 'Peggy' as she reached out and shook his hand. It seemed to her that he held on to her hand a fraction longer than was necessary, and once more she glanced towards the driveway. She could outrun him, that was for sure. But no sooner had the thought formed in her head than she began to feel foolish. Why had she told him her name was Peggy? True, her father had often called her Peggy or Peg as a child but it certainly wasn't a name she called herself. Smiling uncertainly in his direction, Maggie saw a look of confusion cross his face. He looked at her for a moment before shaking his head, saying, 'Oh . . . I was expecting a "Maggie".'

Maggie looked away, embarrassed. She needed to pull herself together. He hadn't recognised her. At least, she was pretty certain he hadn't recognised her. He would have to be a pretty good actor to get away with his lack of response, otherwise. If he had remembered her, he would have had to say something, even if it was to tell her to go away.

Relaxing slightly, she said, 'Maggie . . . Peggy . . . They're both my names. Whichever you prefer . . .' Tim looked puzzled and she tried to smile, adding, 'Or Margaret. That too.' She blushed and fell silent, stuffing the shopping list she was holding back in to her pocket. Then, her eyes lowered, she stood and waited. After a moment's silence she became aware of his chair turning to make room for her and then he invited her in. She looked up and nodded but her sense of dread suddenly returned. Something in the tone of his voice made her think she had been recognised, after all. She'd apologise and leave. One of the other girls could take him on. Instead, she sidled around his chair and stepped into a dark kitchen, taking one last glance towards the driveway as he closed the door behind them.

$\mathcal{U}$PON ENTERING the kitchen she noticed a stack of dishes piled high on the bench. The sight comforted her. No one, she thought,' would carry out a murder with so many dirty plates around. A killer, she reasoned, would need a clean kitchen in order not to be distracted from the task at hand. And what's more, a murderer would quite likely have some sort of obsessive compulsive cleaning disorder. There would have to be some kind of sign indicating a disturbed mind. Her eyes focussed on the pots, she was barely conscious of Tim's voice. 'Sorry about the dishes,' he was saying. 'I meant to tidy up before you got here. I'm actually a bit of a clean freak . . .'

Maggie started, 'What's that?'

Tim, she noticed, was staring at her – hard.

'Well, I used to be tidy,' he stated, 'but these days I find my arms get tired . . . and the sink is too high.'

Maggie nodded. Enough, she thought to herself. Stop

behaving like an idiot and pay attention to your client. She glanced around the rest of the kitchen, saw the stack of groceries on the dining table – boxes of cereal, pasta, tins of tomatoes and sardines – and understood immediately why they were there. A quick scan of the cupboards, all positioned high up on the wall, confirmed her suspicions. Like many of her former clients in wheelchairs, Tim could no longer reach his cupboards.

Feeling she had a greater measure of the man, she began to relax. This was familiar territory. It would take only a few hours to size up his house and figure out how to make it work. Then, in no time at all, she would turn the place around and get it to meet Tim's needs. There was nothing unusual about his home. Without glancing up she knew, for example, that the kitchen was dingy because the light-bulb in the ceiling had blown and needed replacing. What's more, the Venetian blind on the small window above the sink had come loose at one end and was obscuring half the window. She walked across the room and, standing on her toes, reached across the sink for the cord and yanked it, locking the blind off securely as she did so. 'I'll replace the bulb in a minute,' she said, her voice sounding more confident than before. 'But first, would you mind showing me around – so I can get a feel for the place.'

They crossed the room, experiencing a moment's awkwardness when they reached the door and bumped into each other. It was a small thing, but Maggie felt embarrassed. Tim might think she was being impatient, pushing ahead of him like that, when, in truth, her thoughts had been elsewhere. She'd remembered she'd left her cellphone in the car and had felt vulnerable, cut off from the outside world should things take a turn for the worse. She was about to make some excuse to fetch it when Tim suddenly laughed. 'It's the ramp. Gets me every time.' Maggie looked down and there, by her feet, was a length of chipboard fashioned into a makeshift ramp, which lay across a low step between the lean-to kitchen and the rest of the house. 'It's a bloody nightmare,' continued Tim. 'I keep meaning to get it sorted out but . . .' He shrugged, adding, 'You know what it's like – it's so hard get good tradesmen.' His reference to tradesmen comforted Maggie. Only normal people expressed such sentiments. It wasn't the kind of talk you'd expect from a murderer. Feeling calmer, she followed Tim into an open lounge and looked around.

Like the kitchen, the room was dark. Whereas the kitchen was painted in white gloss paint, the walls in the living area were timber – not the vertical strips of knotted pine she recognised from homes built in the sixties, but some kind of old-fashioned wood. Covering the walls in wide horizontal lengths, it was unvarnished and dark. Its surface was rough as if sawn by hand. Instinctively, she leant across and ran her fingers over its surface. 'Totara,' said Tim. 'It's part of the original house.' Maggie nodded, the words 'dust trap' forming on her lips as she did so. 'The original house was built by a whaler. A family of eight lived here.' Maggie started to say something about Riverton's European settlers but caught herself and fell silent. She didn't know that much about the topic, after all.

'There used to be a big cauldron thing, an oil pot, in the garden but I took it to the dump. Stupid, eh?' Maggie shrugged. It had nothing to do with her. She was more interested in continuing her tour of the house.

A table lamp was placed at either end of a worn leather couch. Facing the settee was what looked like an expensive stereo system and beside it were several towers loaded with compact discs. It took a moment for Maggie to notice there was no television. That was unusual. Stranger was the number of guitars leaning against the wall where the television ought to be. Three of the guitars looked normal, though dissimilar from one another but the fourth was unlike any she had seen before. Made from dark, almost black wood, it looked like it had a polished metal hubcap attached to it. The hubcap thing covered the area where the fingerboard should be. She had no idea what kind of guitar it was but it was definitely flashy – the musical equivalent of a Cadillac.

Her eyes lingering on the guitars, she remembered the tattoo she had seen on Tim's wrist the first time they met. She was about to mention it when she caught herself and instead hastily asked, 'Do you play?'

'Used to. Not so much now,' came the reply.

Maggie nodded. 'I had lessons once. Don't have time now.'

Tim smiled and then glanced towards the ceiling, asking, 'So, you're able to change light-bulbs?'

Maggie frowned. From the tone of Tim's voice she had the feeing he was being smart. She'd had a few awkward clients in her time but there was no way she was going to let anyone talk down to her. So irritated was she by Tim's remark that she decided not to grace it with an answer. That way, at least, she would be able to set some boundaries right from the start. She sensed Tim was waiting but she pretended not to notice.

'I had to let my last woman go in the end,' continued Tim, 'because she wouldn't step off the ground.'

'What do you mean?' asked Maggie, taken aback.

'Something to do with health and safety issues. She wasn't allowed to take her feet off the floor or move and lift objects.' He paused, and then added, 'A framed picture fell between the couch and the wall, and she refused to move the couch in order to retrieve it.' He scratched his arm absently before adding, 'It took me ages to get it, and then, once I had it, she wouldn't stand on a chair to hang it back up.'

Scanning the room, Maggie's gaze came to rest on a framed photograph hanging at chest height near the couch.

'Yeah, that's it,' said Tim, pointing towards the image. 'After I replaced the string on the back I had to hang it myself. That's the only place I could reach.'

Maggie took a few steps closer. The photograph was of a group of young musicians – four men and one woman, all with guitars or violins in their hands. It was clear to Maggie that they were on a stage and, from the smiles on their faces, she guessed they had just finished performing. The man in the centre was holding the hand of the woman next to him, and she was turned slightly towards him, her mouth open as if she was speaking – or laughing. Looking more closely, Maggie suddenly realised that the tall man in the centre was Tim. He looked so different – so young and strong, full of life.

Turning back to Tim she felt sad. In the partial gloom of the small lounge, he seemed small, fragile. Yet clearly he was – or had been – a strong, tall man.

She caught his eye and murmured, 'It's not right.'

This time it was Tim's turn to look annoyed. Responding, 'I don't need your pity,' he spun around and set off towards the hall before Maggie had time to explain that she had been referring to his former caregiver and not his disability.

She watched him struggle to manoeuvre his wheelchair down the narrow passage-way and felt dejected, a feeling that intensified when, without preamble, Tim grumbled, 'I'd prefer it if you didn't try and clean the Dobro.' Despite hearing the word 'Dobro' clearly, she had no idea what he was talking about. But sensing his irritation she decided against probing further. Explanation could wait.

She maintained her distance from Tim, hesitating when she saw him scrape against the wall, his chair gouging the wallpaper. She glanced away each time he cursed, in case he noticed her watching him. The problem was that the house hadn't been designed to accommodate a wheelchair. Anyone could see that the passage was far too narrow. To make it possible for him to enter the rooms off the corridor without having to carry out a number of intricate manoeuvres, someone had knocked out all the doors, making them significantly wider than normal. Exposed beams and roughly assembled doorframes now took the place of what had originally been solid timber, and in place of the doors themselves were curtains – none of them matching and all unhemmed. 'Some friends helped me renovate,' Tim offered, as he gestured towards one room. 'I thought about moving house but the real estate agents kept taking me around pensioner flats and retirement villages. They were always telling me how "wheelchair friendly" those places were; that I'd feel safer living in a community. I couldn't face it in the end – made me feel old.'

The main bedroom was sparsely furnished – with only a bed and a night table. The spare room was empty apart from a set of drawers and two clothes maidens, one of which was barely visible beneath a noticeably damp sheet. In a clothes basket next to the maiden was a second sheet – dry, by the look of it, and roughly folded. Nodding, Maggie stepped back into the hall and retraced her steps to the kitchen, Tim following behind. Once in the kitchen Tim went ahead, leading through another door, which opened into a laundry and bathroom. The room was surprisingly spacious – as large as the kitchen-dining area itself. Against one wall was a washing machine and dryer, while along the opposite wall was a large bathtub fitted with a shower. This, Maggie could see, was no longer used. Inside the bath were two fruit salad plants, a bar of soap nestled in the foliage of the larger plant. Against the wall between the washing machine and bath, was a toilet. This, Maggie noticed, was not where the toilet would have been originally. Almost brand new, it had been re-positioned so as to allow wheelchair access. There was no hand basin in the bathroom. It must have been sacrificed to make room for the new arrangement.

A new wet room took up the entire space of an alcove off the bathroom proper. Pointing to the shower, Tim explained that the room had originally been the toilet. Gesturing towards a door that took up most of one wall of the wet room, he explained that it opened directly onto the garden. 'My friends knocked everything up for me,' he smiled, adding, 'None of the alterations are legal, of course.' He turned around and smiling more broadly added, 'I paid them in beer – in advance. I think that might have been a mistake. What do you think?'

Maggie laughed. It was clear that the job had been carried out by amateurs or, as he implied, drunken mates. She was sure it functioned well enough but it was undoubtedly one of the roughest jobs she had ever seen. Not wishing to offend her client, she replied, 'As long as it works . . .'

Tim smiled and for a second Maggie thought he looked relieved. Shaking his head, he murmured, 'I wouldn't change it for the world.' He laughed out loud, adding, 'The dryer is completely stuffed, by the way, but I should be getting a new one soon.'

Returning to the kitchen, Maggie was strangely comfortable in this makeshift house. It was by far the most ramshackle place she had ever been in but, for all that, it had a good feeling about it. Some of the houses she had worked in were far less homely. Pensioner flats, for example, were usually practical to the point of being institutional. There was something soulless about such dwellings. For all its short-comings, she liked Tim's place. It felt human.

Later, as she drove back to Invercargill, she reflected on her meeting with Tim. Seeing him had given her a shock. She'd been so certain he would recognise her. In fact, she found it hard to believe that he hadn't. It was almost suspicious. Perhaps he had been so wound up on the day of their first meeting that he hadn't registered her face. They'd only spent a few minutes together after all and it wasn't as if she had a face worth remembering. But maybe he had recognised her? Perhaps the whole thing was a set-up and he had hunted her down with a view to paying her back for what Bevan had done. But she'd avoided mentioning Bevan by name and, besides, Bevan hadn't done anything. Furthermore, she had apologised. So that should be the end of it. Unless Tim really was dangerous. Maggie was uneasy. But nothing in his manner had been threatening or even disconcerting. Their meeting again was pure coincidence, that was all. He'd needed a replacement for his last cleaner and had phoned the first agency in the book. That or one of the social services had given him their name. She'd check with Carol – she'd know. There was nothing to worry about.

Maggie relaxed. She was almost at The Warehouse. She'd run in, grab some party stuff and get out as fast as possible. It would only take a couple of minutes, and then she could go home and sit down for a few minutes before sorting out dinner. She was a bit stressed. First Bevan, then Justine, and then the worn tyres and the birthday party – it was no wonder she was feeling anxious. But everything would be all right.

She drove into the car park. Seeing that the handiest spaces were all taken, she hesitated before pulling into a mobility park. She'd only be a minute. What was that word Tim had used? Dobro? She'd look it up. There was bound to be a dictionary somewhere in The Warehouse. She might even find a new word of her own.

$\mathcal{M}$AGGIE WAS surprised to find Bevan sitting in the kitchen when she arrived home with the shopping. There was no reason why he shouldn't be home, but she hadn't expected to see him and was taken aback by his presence. However, as he barely raised his eyes from a pamphlet he was reading, she concluded there was nothing actually wrong. There was no cause for alarm; he was at home, that was all.

He responded to her greeting with a grunt and kept reading, pretending not to hear when she asked what he was doing. Looking at him, his expression fixed in concentration, Maggie felt a momentary pang. It was a shock to see him so quiet, so still. Usually, he surrounded himself with noise but here, in the kitchen, he appeared young, boyish. There was something about his attentiveness that reminded her of when he was a child. She used to read to him in the evenings before taking him to bed. In the olden days she would spend fifteen minutes alone with

Bevan every evening. She'd done the same with all her children. Yet it seemed so long ago since she had last talked with him. Interrogation had taken the place of conversation. She only ever spoke to him when trying to find out where he had been and with whom. Or, at least, that's how it seemed. For an instant she felt an urge to touch him; but then, remembering the ice-cream cake in the car, she went outside and, on returning, discovered he had sneaked away.

The brochure had been left on the table, and she was surprised to see it contained information about the army. She flicked through it, and saw that Bevan – she assumed it was Bevan – had doodled a gun beside a section headed 'Age'. But before she could read more, Bevan returned. Maggie quickly stepped from the table to the bench, where she continued to unpack the groceries. Originally, she had intended to get everything ready for Storm's birthday before collecting him from after-school care. But the day had gone pear-shaped and she was running behind schedule; she'd only have time to put everything away and have a quick cup of tea before heading out again.

She switched on the jug, and searched for a way of raising the subject of the army with Bevan without antagonising him. She settled on saying, 'I didn't know you wanted to be a soldier.' She had wanted her comment to sound casual, off the cuff, but she saw Bevan frown and registered his wariness.

'It was Dad's idea. We made a deal.'

'What deal? What do you mean?' The words were barely out of her mouth when she saw Bevan withdraw into a guarded silence. Eyeing her suspiciously, he shrugged, and it was only after Maggie repeated her question several times, each time her voice quieter and more controlled than the last, that he gave in a little and responded, 'Dad gave me permission to enter the car competition and said he would pay for my driving test provided I checked out some information about careers in the army and stuff.'

His remark threw Maggie. It raised too many questions. Not only about the car competition and the army, but questions relating to Ross and what he had been saying to Bevan behind her back.

Bevan sensed he had the upper hand and continued, 'I'm not a child anymore. So . . . you know . . . it's not like you can tell me what to do.' Maggie flinched at the brash tone of his voice. 'Anyway, I'm going to need a car when I leave school.'

Confused, Maggie opened her mouth to speak, but in the moment it took for her to formulate her response, Bevan walked from the room and disappeared through the back door. Running after him, her head now clear, she shouted, 'You are not leaving school until I say so and you're not getting a car. I don't care what your father says!'

Bevan did not reply but raised his fist and extended his middle finger in a 'fuck-you' gesture. It was enough to stop Maggie dead. Never before had any of her children displayed such disrespect, and in the seconds following, she felt too stunned to move. Her hands hanging loose by her side, she stood facing the shed, gazing towards the small lighted window and watching as Bevan moved across the room and began to lower the Venetian blind. In the instant before disappearing from view, her son's gaze met hers, and in his eyes she saw nothing but contempt.

At a loss, she glanced back towards the kitchen. There was no sign of movement or life, no one moving back and forth from the sink to the stove to the table. No friendly face gazed out of the window towards her. No witness to what had taken place. The house stood empty. Then, remembering she had to bring in the washing, she crossed to the line and slowly, garment by garment, unpegged and folded each item of chilled, limp clothing before placing it carefully into the basket.

*I*T WAS HARDLY surprising that the mothers of Storm's school friends chose not to stay for the party. Maggie only knew them by sight. For the most part, she'd dropped Storm off in the morning before returning late in the afternoon to collect him from after-school care. Often, Lisa brought him home. If anything, she knew more about Storm's classmates' families than she did. By the look of the other mothers, Lisa was also closer in age as well. Not one of Storm's friends' mothers appeared older than thirty. By comparison, Maggie looked every inch the grandmother she was.

The party seemed to be going well. Murray had taken the kids outside, while Elsie and Maggie chatted and kept an eye on the saveloys heating on the stove. The day was, Maggie admitted, almost enjoyable. None of the kids had caused any problems and, best of all, Storm appeared genuinely thrilled with his presents.

The Lego Bionicle Maggie had bought was by far his favourite gift. He had carried its unopened plastic container around with him all day, never putting it down and talking about it constantly, as if it were the most precious treasure in the world. Maggie didn't like to admit it, but deep down she felt relieved – happy, even – that none of Storm's other gifts had given him as much pleasure. The jigsaw from Elsie had been received with polite gratitude. Storm had placed it on the low table next to his other presents before opening a small parcel from Murray – a fishing fly attached to a note promising a day's fishing. It was a nice gesture, and Maggie was grateful to him for showing such generosity even if Storm hadn't fully appreciated it. Nevertheless, she had been delighted that after all the presents were opened, hers remained Storm's favourite.

The afternoon had been going so well that she had almost forgotten that Justine had not bothered to phone. Earlier in the day, when she had suggested to Storm that he might like to call his mother, she had been surprised to hear him mumble, 'It's all right. She's probably not home anyway.' It had taken a minute before Maggie had understood. Aware of the look of disappointment on his face, she had hugged him, whispering, 'I expect she's waiting until the twins are asleep. That way she'll be able to talk to you for longer, without being interrupted.' Storm had managed a smile but Maggie was ashamed. 'I bet your mum has a big surprise for you,' she added. No sooner were the words out of her mouth than she regretted them. Not only had Justine not phoned but there had been nothing in that morning's post. It seemed unlikely that anything would turn up at all.

Maggie marched down the hall towards her bedroom. It wasn't good enough, she thought. From the privacy of her room she'd phone her daughter and give her a piece of her mind. But as she dialled the number, there was a knock at the front door.

A second later she heard voices coming from the hall and, putting down the phone, she got up to look. It was Carol's youngest child, Gemma, followed closely by Lindsay, Carol – and Ross.

Maggie had been expecting Carol's family, but nothing prepared her for the appearance of Ross. For several seconds she was speechless, unable to think clearly, as she watched all three adults remove their coats and place them on a chair inside the front room. Muddled, she nodded stupidly as first Lindsay and then Ross greeted her before disappearing down the hall and into the kitchen. She could hear them calling out to Elsie and Murray. Then, only half listening, she stood quietly as Carol regaled her with the story of how they had bumped into Ross at the petrol station and how she had managed to persuade him to follow them to the party. Indifferent to Maggie's lack of response, Carol continued to talk, explaining that she had searched high and low for a suitable present for Storm. She thought she had got him something he would really like – something special, the type of gift her son would have liked at his age. Still chatting, she had shoved Maggie ahead of her as they made their way down the hall. Finally, calling to Gemma to fetch Storm inside to open his gift, Carol took a deep breath and turned away.

Maggie watched dumbly as Carol snatched the wrapped parcel from Gemma's hands in order to offer it to Storm herself. In the minute it took for Storm to unwrap the package, Carol did not stop talking. Once more she told everyone within earshot how difficult it had been to track down Storm's present and that eventually she had had to order it off the internet, something she had not done before and had felt anxious about in case her credit card details found their way into the wrong person's hands.

As she listened, Maggie glanced in Ross's direction. Apart

from a mumbled greeting, she had not yet spoken to him. Yet there was so much she needed to discuss. Her brain was flooded. In the first place, what made him think he could turn up unannounced? In the second, since when had he begun taking such an interest in Bevan? From what she could tell they had been meeting on a regular basis for quite some time, though neither one of them had had the courtesy to mention the fact to her. She glowered at Ross – not that he appeared to notice. Like everyone else in the room, his attention was focussed on Storm, who had let out a squeal of delight upon finally catching sight of his present.

'A light sabre! It's a Star Wars light sabre! Look, Nan – a light sabre!' Holding a long box up for Maggie to see, he appeared beside himself with joy. A small group of his friends grouped around as he freed the toy from its packaging.

Once more, Carol's voice could be heard above the murmurs of admiration as she said, 'I wasn't sure which you'd like best: the Darth Vader or the Obi-Wan Kenobi model. Ashley said the Darth Vader was better, more *heinous*, because it changes colour . . . He might come by later, after training. He's at the velodrome.'

A smile tightened on Maggie's face as she heard the word 'heinous'. Who did her sister think she was kidding, using words like that? She sighed, and then in a clear voice reminded Storm to say 'thank you' to his great-aunt. Then she thanked Carol herself, adding for good measure that it was a very generous gift. Suddenly there was a change of tone in Storm's excited chattering. She turned to face him and watched as he examined the toy, rotating it in his hands. 'I think it needs batteries,' he said, clearly disappointed. Maggie reached for the box and noticed as she did so that the price sticker was attached: $64.95. The cost startled her. Flipping the box over, she saw that the toy needed two C batteries. For one brief moment she experienced a sense of triumph. 'He's right. It needs batteries.' She was about to add, Never mind, I can get some the next time I'm at the supermarket, when, to her surprise, Ross interrupted and asked, 'What size?' Before Maggie could respond, he continued, 'I've probably got some knocking about somewhere in my van. I'll go and look.' For a split second Maggie's smile slipped, but seeing the look of hope on Storm's face as he ran after Ross, she softened. Why was she being so mean? What was wrong with her? It was Storm's birthday, after all. Didn't he deserve to be spoiled? Flustered, she offered to make tea for her family and then crouched to pick up the Bionicle box, which Storm had dropped in his haste to follow Ross.

It had been almost half an hour since the arrival of her sister and ex-husband, but Maggie felt no less on edge than before. Despite wanting to talk to Ross, she had not been able to get him alone. It seemed that every time she approached him, someone or something would get in her way. Even more infuriating was the fact that he had not attempted to seek her out. He had remained at a distance, watching her from the far side of the room. It was clear to Maggie that Ross had not remembered Storm's birthday. No doubt Carol had had to remind him when they bumped into each other at the station. Earlier, Maggie had glimpsed her ex-husband retrieving a discarded envelope from a pile of birthday wrapping on the floor before stuffing a $20 bill into it and handing it to Storm. He cleared his throat and said, 'Good on you – you're a big boy, now,' before adding, 'Happy Birthday.' Storm was delighted with the gift, but Maggie was not so impressed. It was simple to buy a child's affection. Even easier if, like Carol, you could afford to splash money around.

Miffed, she snatched a tray of sausage rolls from the oven and tipped them roughly onto a plate. She was about to offer them around when she suddenly caught the sound of her name. She pricked up her ears in time to hear a conversation that was taking place between her mother and Murray. 'No, no, no . . . I've told you before,' her mother said, 'that was Maggie. Frank went to stay with her and she nursed him . . .' Maggie edged closer to where her mother was sitting and listened as Elsie continued, 'No, Carol was in Australia. She didn't come home until some time later . . . that's when she bought the business . . . yes, the home-help agency . . . yes, Maggie was already working there . . . It's not that complicated, Murray.' Maggie strained to follow the conversation above the children's noise, but was interrupted by Carol, who suddenly appeared at her side and, helping herself to a sausage roll, announced, 'These aren't too bad. You can barely tell they're shop bought.'

Her sister's comment was nothing out of the ordinary, and certainly nothing that required a response, yet Maggie could feel a surge of resentment swell up inside her. She hissed, 'What is it with you? What is your problem?' Her sister's dumbstruck expression only intensified her anger. Snatching the half-eaten savoury from Carol's hand, she continued, 'You're never satisfied, are you? You always have to be the centre of attention. I mean, trust you to buy the most expensive present you could find . . .' From the corner of her eye she was aware that Lindsay had stood up and was edging towards them. A sense of panic took hold of her. She would need to rush if she was to get through all the things she wanted to say. 'You never stop,' she continued. 'You come back home and get a big house and buy a business, and you always have real coffee at home – and then you read something in one of your magazines about environmentally friendly cleaning products and you expect us to go all eco . . . and . . .' She couldn't remember what she wanted to say next.

She spun around, searching the faces of her family for inspiration, but seeing their stunned expressions, was suddenly lost. Despite the chatter of Storm and his friends, the room seemed eerily quiet. Scrabbling for some form of escape, some way out of the situation she had created, Maggie continued where she had left off. She couldn't stop. Words welled up from a hidden place, and before she knew it she had relaunched her attack on her sister, accusing her of being self-obsessed and judgemental – especially where the rest of the family was concerned – and, she raged, unable to let the subject drop, an inconsiderate manager. Only yesterday, she continued for everyone to hear, Carol had sent her all the way out to Riverton to take on a new client who happened . . .

Carol didn't let her finish. Snapping, 'Don't you dare talk to me like that! I don't know what's come over you but don't you ever talk to me like that.' She glared at Maggie, who, by contrast, deflated. 'And for your information,' Carol spat, 'that guy Tim asked for you.'

The walls in the room suddenly closed in on Maggie. Gasping, she glanced around. Her eyes roamed across the toys scattered on the floor, over the dishes piled by the sink, and then to her ex-husband and finally back to Carol as she tried to fathom what was going on. She opened her mouth to speak, but catching sight of her sister's expression she lost her nerve. Eventually, she asked, 'He asked for me?' She hoped there had been a misunderstanding – that perhaps she had misheard her sister. Dreading the reply, she asked, 'Is that true? He asked for me? Why?'

A faint smile curled across Carol's face as she brushed aside a loose strand that had escaped from an elaborate clip holding her hair in place. She twisted the strand around her finger, examining the ends of the streaked blonde piece as she did so. Fussing with the clip, she slowly raised an eyebrow, a gesture Maggie interpreted as a provocation. After a few more seconds of staged concentration, Carol gave the appearance of having reached an important decision. She fixed Maggie with a sly smile and said, 'I don't know why he asked for you . . .'

'But you must have asked him?' Maggie interrupted. 'I mean, that's part of your job, isn't it? To find out stuff like that?'

Carol shrugged, then in a slow, deliberate voice, replied, 'Well then, it must have slipped my mind . . . How inconsiderate of me.'

Carol's eyes appeared almost devoid of emotion. This, thought Maggie bitterly, was a new skill. As a child, she had always been able to tell when her sister was lying. All she had had to do was stare at Carol and wait for her to blush. It had been so easy. Now, faced with her sister's stare, Maggie was unsure of herself.

She lowered the tray of sausage rolls to the table, noticing as she did the half-eaten savoury she had snatched out of her sister's hand. Overcome by shame, she picked up the sausage roll and taking a paper serviette wrapped it into a small, tight package, which she concealed in her fist. Then, without thinking, she tightened her grip, squashing the pastry into a hard, solid ball.

$\mathcal{T}$HE DISHES needed to be cleared away but Maggie decided they could wait. Curled up on the couch beside her, Storm snuggled against her body, his light sabre resting across them as he listened to a story. While Maggie read, the small boy pressed the power switch of his new toy distractedly. Nothing happened. The batteries, which had been borrowed from Ross's torch, had drained hours ago. But after a quick phone call to Lisa at the station, Storm had succeeded in ordering a replacement pair. Lisa would bring them home after work – too late, Maggie hoped, for Storm to fit them that night.

The house was quiet. Remarkably, no one had said very much about her outburst earlier in the day. Apart from Carol, who had remained tense and unapproachable, the rest of the family had carried on as normal. It was as if somehow everything she had said had fallen on deaf ears or had never been said in the first place. But despite her family's lack of response, Maggie had the strange impression that they shared her sentiments – that the reason why no one confronted her or rushed to take Carol's side was because, deep down, everyone agreed with what Maggie had said.

Moments after she had spoken, Ross had approached and, unusually for him, given her shoulder a gentle squeeze before beginning to talk. In spite of the fact that he was attempting to help take her mind off things, Maggie had not been able to concentrate. His words washed over her head as she tried to make sense of Carol's comment about Tim. There was no way she could force Carol to tell her more. Not after everything that had been thrown at her. Carol had not stormed out of the house, as Maggie had thought she might, but she had kept her distance all afternoon. Any hope Maggie had of revisiting the subject of her new client was well and truly lost. Sitting quietly as Ross made small talk, Maggie felt distracted and ill at ease as she weighed up the risk of continuing to see Tim.

To her surprise, every time she tried to imagine what Tim might want with her or, worse, what he might try to *do* to her, she was confronted by an image of a wheelchair. In truth, she couldn't see how Tim could harm her. Short of shooting her – and as far as she could tell there was no gun in the house – there was little he could do to threaten her safety. And, even though it gave her no satisfaction, she knew he was far more vulnerable than she was. He was hardly in a position to intimidate her. Not really.

She recalled that once or twice she had tested her strength against Ross. That had been early on in their marriage, when Ross was keen on boxing. They'd never fought with any intention of hurting each other, but during those bouts Maggie had always felt confident of her strength. She was scrawny, but strong.

Scanning Ross's face for signs of the former boxer, she was surprised by how haggard he looked. He seemed worn out, the lines on his face more pronounced than she remembered. His skin was sallow and his cheeks gaunt. Her heart gave a lurch. He was thinner than she had ever seen him before and he looked unwell. But he couldn't be ill, she reasoned. He would have told her, wouldn't he? No, nothing was wrong with his health. She was imagining things.

Her eyes rested on her ex-husband and she made an effort to concentrate. She wanted to figure out what was really going through his head. Once she would have known exactly what to look for, but now she wasn't so confident. It wasn't so much that he had learnt new ways of keeping things from her but that she had fallen behind. The small 'tells' she once read so clearly no longer struck her with any force. She had little idea what he thought or did in his spare time anymore – and, of course, it was no longer any of her business. Yet, when he mentioned Bevan's name her heart began to thump. From what he said, it was clear he had gone behind her back in maintaining contact with their son. Without her knowledge, they had been meeting on a regular basis. And, it appeared Ross had been encouraging her son to stay on at school so that he might stand a better chance of being accepted into the army one day.

Unsettled and annoyed by what she was hearing, Maggie listened impatiently as Ross began to recount a story concerning his own upbringing. 'When I was young,' he began, 'I never had, you know, a role model. In fact, the only thing that gave me any sense of family was rugby and then, a bit later the gang . . .' Maggie had heard his history before and she was angry with him for bringing it up now. She knew where his story was leading – it was heading to a place where Ross assumed he was the only teenager to have experienced how tough the world was. As if that entitled him to decide what was best for their son. He wanted to sideline her and put himself at the centre of her son's life. He wanted Bevan for himself.

'Maggie,' Ross said quietly, oblivious to her grim expression, 'I've owned up to the mistakes I've made and I don't want Bevan to follow in my—'

'Really?' Maggie interrupted.

Ross flinched and looked embarrassed. 'You know what I mean.'

Maggie made a huffing noise and shrugged. Of course she knew. Hadn't she been the one left alone with Justine the time he had flipped, and taken off during the early stages of their marriage? Ross had no idea how hard it had been – working full time, lugging Justine and the pram from one cleaning job to the next. Nor had he had to find money for power and food. He didn't have a clue about what she had gone through during his absence. His decision to get his life sorted out didn't fool her. It was one more act of selfishness on his part and, as usual, she had been left with the mess. She had been the responsible one. It wasn't like she'd even been given a choice, she thought, bitter at the memory.

'I know it was hard for you, Maggie,' Ross continued, 'but it helped . . .'

'So you've figured out what's best for Bevan, have you?' snapped Maggie.

Ross sighed. Maggie glimpsed a slight smile cross his lips, and yet his eyes remained downcast. 'I just think,' he continued, 'the army might offer him something. He might respond to a bit of discipline.' Maggie felt her heart soften. He was right. The army was a sensible option. It would do Bevan good, give him a sense of direction and, more importantly, get him away from his current group of friends.

'I've mentioned it to Bevan a few times. We've talked about it off and on, and I think I've got him interested, but I'm not pushing him . . . you know?'

On hearing his words, Maggie flushed with anger. So, they *had* been talking behind her back. Bevan hadn't said anything to her about these chats. And if she hadn't seen that brochure earlier, she wouldn't have had any idea about their plans.

'So it's all sorted. That's nice.' She'd had enough. She didn't even know why Ross had come to Storm's party. She hadn't invited him, and he'd clearly not intended to pop in. And, for that matter, it wasn't as if Storm had wanted him to come around. Maggie stood abruptly. She'd go and talk to Elsie and Murray. She'd all but ignored them until now, leaving them to entertain the kids. No wonder they both looked exhausted. She'd make them a cup of tea and give them a break. That's what she'd do. Yet as she began to fill the jug, she was called away by Carol, who suddenly announced her intention to leave.

'I'm sorry about before. I didn't mean what I said.' Maggie apologised as she accompanied her sister to the door. She picked up Carol's coat, and held it out for her sister but was brushed away.

'I'm perfectly capable of getting my own clothes, thanks.' Carol's anger, which had become less raw during the preceding hour, resurfaced, and for a moment the two women faced each other, Carol's smartly dressed figure all the more striking opposite Maggie's jeans-and-sweatshirt-clad small frame.

Maggie knew she should try make amends. She attempted to smile. 'Thanks for the lovely gift. Storm . . .' The words stuck in her throat. She couldn't bring herself to add that it was what Storm wanted. That of all the presents, Carol's was the most longed-for, perfect gift.

Carol hissed, 'See you Monday,' and turned away.

Preparing to follow her sister down the path, Maggie felt, rather than saw, Ross edge past. 'I'd better get back to Bevan,' he explained. 'I promised to drop off some McDonald's on my way past the car sales-yard.'

'What do you mean?'

'Well, I left him at the competition . . .' Ross began, uncertain of whether or not to continue.

'What competition?' spat Maggie.

'The competition for the car, of course,' chimed in Carol. 'He's been there all day – since nine this morning.'

Seeing the smug look on her sister's face, Maggie bit her lip. Things were beginning to unravel again. 'Of course. I forgot – that's all. I've been focussed on the party . . . It must have slipped my mind.'

She could tell she had fooled no one.

'Bevan's pretty determined to win,' Carol continued. 'What sort of car was it, Ross?' She didn't wait for a reply but added, 'Some old BMW sedan, I think.' Her smile widening, she turned to her husband. 'Isn't it the same model as the one we traded in a few years ago? You know, the old soft top . . . the one we couldn't give away?'

* * *

The house had not fallen quiet until the departure of the last visitor – Nicolai, a six-year-old boy from Storm's class. Much to Maggie's annoyance the boy had not been collected at the prearranged time but had hovered around the house for a good forty minutes, waiting for his mother. When she'd finally arrived, she'd barely had the grace to mumble an apology before launching into a lengthy account of how she had escaped, with a couple of girlfriends, to the movies where, for the past two hours, she had watched a wonderful film about a New York fashion magazine and its tyrannical editor. 'The clothes,' she gushed, 'were amazing and the shoes . . .' She giggled and then, scooping up her son, she breezed from the house, calling, 'See youse'. The mother, thought Maggie, looked all of eighteen, and despite her obvious interest in clothes and shoes was dressed no differently from any other young woman in the street. Even her hair looked like it could do with a comb; it was completely over-processed and stringy. Yet, given the girl's confidence, she was clearly popular – or at least Maggie assumed she was.

Finally sitting down, Storm beside her on the couch, Maggie had automatically reached for the book lying next to them and begun to read aloud. It had taken her a few pages to settle into the story and she had had to fight the urge to jump up and tidy the kitchen. But as her grandson's body snuggled into hers she had felt calmer, more at ease with the idea of ignoring the chaos around her. She was surprised now, as she had been in the past, by Storm's ability to focus on a book. Despite reaching for the switch on his light sabre, his eyes never left the page from which Maggie read. So intense was his expression that Maggie found herself taking longer and longer breaths between passages so that she might simply sneak glances at the boy.

She became aware that there was a good ten-second delay between the time she finished reading a page and the moment Storm looked up, willing her to turn to the next. Something about his hesitation touched her, and although she hated to disturb the intimacy between them, she felt obliged to ask, 'Would you like to phone your mother now?'

To her relief, Storm shook his head. 'Maybe later,' he said. 'Keep reading.'

She returned to the book, reading in a gentle voice. As she read, she felt a slight movement at her side and, breaking off, saw Storm reach into his pyjama shirt pocket and retrieve an opened packet of chewing gum. He placed two pieces into his mouth and began to chew rapidly, as if scared she would demand the gum before he'd had a chance to savour its peppermint taste. He kept his eyes on Maggie, and then offered her the packet, smiling nervously as he did so.

Maggie tried not to laugh. 'Where did that come from?'

The boy sniffed. 'Gemma. She said I could keep it.' Aware that the smile had slipped from Maggie's face, he added, 'She said it cleans your teeth. It's professional gum.'

'What does that mean?' asked Maggie, genuinely interested.

The boy shrugged. 'I don't know. The dentists on television tell children to chew it.' He slipped the packet into his pocket and pointed to the page, 'You're up to here.'

Storm chewed, pausing from time to time to pull a thin strand of gum from his mouth, which he held for a moment before letting go, allowing it to curl and shrivel as it coiled back towards his mouth. Ignoring him, Maggie concentrated on the book and as she read it seemed as if the distance between herself and the boy narrowed, their two bodies merging, until twenty minutes later she felt a heavy weight against her arm and looking down noticed that Storm was fast asleep. His mouth gaping and his eyes flickering gently, he looked at once fragile and beautiful – more precious than anything Maggie had ever seen in her life. It took several seconds before she was able to manoeuvre out from under him and retreat to the kitchen, where the dishes were waiting.

$\mathcal{M}$AGGIE HAD only been resting a minute when Lisa arrived home, Scott close behind. Seeing her daughter's boss hover uneasily in the doorway reminded Maggie briefly of Ross, of the time when she had first started going out with him and he'd had to visit her at her parent's home, the small unit attached to the motel complex.

Those early days made her cringe. There had been something sordid about the way they'd behaved – sneaking off to be alone or, worse, waiting until her parents were in bed and then slumping onto the couch together, Ross's hands urgently fumbling through any opening he could find in her clothes as she tried to keep him at bay. She had held Ross off for as long as possible and it wasn't until they had married that she had felt entirely comfortable with him. No longer worried about disgracing herself before God or her parents, she allowed herself to give in to their lovemaking right up until the time she fell pregnant with Justine and it was no longer decent.

Maggie glanced at Scott and noticed he was watching Lisa as she took off her coat. There was something in the intensity of his gaze that disconcerted her. His eyes were fixed on her daughter, and he appeared to be paying such close attention to the way she undid each button that Maggie half expected him to step forward and help. Suddenly he caught sight of Maggie and looked visibly startled – as if coming out of a dream. He smiled foolishly and raised his eyebrows, taking a step forward as he passed her a cup of coffee. 'It's for you,' he said.

'We thought you might be tired,' Lisa joined in, 'so Scott suggested we get you some pizza on the way home.'

Scott took the food from Lisa and carried the flat box towards the couch. 'Lisa said you like chilli,' he said, gently laying the box down on the cushion beside her as if presenting a token to a monarch. His eyes rested on Maggie for a second longer than she found comfortable, and she stood up quickly, snatching up the box as she went to find plates. To her surprise, Scott followed, taking the dishes from her before setting them on the table. He stood next to her. 'I've got that tyre for you,' he said. 'If you bring your car in I'll fix it up – do your warrant.'

Maggie said nothing. Grabbing pieces of pizza, she arranged them on the plates, handing them around before hunting out tomato sauce and paper serviettes. The serviettes were left over from the party. SpongeBob Squarepants looked up at her as she handed them to her daughter and Scott.

'I'd be happy for you to take the tyre now,' said Scott. 'What I mean is, you can pay me later.' He took a bite from his food and added, 'You shouldn't risk driving without a warrant.' He glanced at Maggie, a look of apology on his face. 'I mean, I wouldn't want you to get pulled over . . .' His voice trailed away and he focussed on the slice in his hand, peeling away a fragment of red chilli which he placed on his plate. Maggie replied only, 'We'll see.'

She wondered if she sounded cross. In fact, she was exhausted. She was also tired of thinking about money. At times she felt as if there was nothing but a steady stream of sums going through her head, an escalating tally which she desperately needed to keep control of and which prevented her from enjoying life. She doubted that Scott would understand and, in any case, she lacked the energy at that moment to try to explain.

They ate in silence. Lisa and Scott glanced up from time to time and smiled, or fanned their mouths before reaching for a glass of water and taking a deep gulp. Then, as the pizza slowly disappeared, Scott suddenly remarked, 'We heard a song on the radio tonight and Lisa told me it was something you used to sing to her, when she was young.'

Maggie looked questioningly at her daughter. 'What song?'

Lisa raised her eyebrow. 'You know . . . we used to listen to it all the time when you took me with you to work. It was always playing on the radio . . . when you were cleaning. Guess!'

Maggie had no recollection of ever having sung while at work. The thought of herself breaking into a cheerful song as she scrubbed out a toilet was too absurd. True, like Justine before her, Lisa had been dragged from one house to another. But singing at work? She had no idea what her daughter was talking about.

Unable to guess, she shrugged. The room seemed to become very quiet then, with only the sound of the three of them chewing to disturb the peace. Then softly at first, but growing louder, Lisa began to half-hum, half-sing, 'Doo do doo do for my shirt, too sexy for my skirt . . .'

Maggie gasped as her daughter's voice gained in volume, watching in horror as Lisa stood up and began to dance around the room, singing, 'I'm so sexy for my cat . . . My sexy little cat . . .'

Maggie wasn't sure where to look. She made a hasty grab for her plate and stood up in an attempt to escape. But her passage was blocked by her daughter, who giggled, 'Come on, Mum. You used to love that song!'

Opening her mouth to protest, Maggie's throat became dry and it was all she could do to hiss, 'Shush, you'll wake Storm.'

Lisa laughed, 'Come on, you and Dad used to sing it together sometimes. Come on, you must remember!'

'I do not!' snapped Maggie. The room fell quiet once more. Several seconds passed before Maggie felt calm enough to speak. 'I don't know the words to that song,' she insisted. Yet, catching sight of her daughter's disappointment, she was flustered. After a moment's hesitation, she offered, 'I can remember I used to sing you a Dolly Parton song.' She frowned at Lisa, adding, 'At bedtime, *not* during work hours.'

'What song?' Lisa asked, her voice hopeful.

Maggie's mind went blank. She couldn't remember the title off the top of her head. It was all so long ago. To her surprise, Scott broke in. '"9 to 5", "Here You Come Again", "I Will Always Love You"?'

His tone, as he listed the song titles, was matter-of-fact and yet Maggie felt vaguely troubled. It was as if the titles were directed towards her, personally. She coloured slightly, and then pulling herself together, nodded, ' "I Will Always Love You". Yes, I used to sing that.' She smiled at the memory. 'I sang a few other songs, too. The girls used to like them, but Bevan always stuck his fingers in his ears the moment I opened my mouth.'

'Do you still sing?' asked Scott.

'Nah,' said Maggie, after a second's pause. 'Not for ages.'

In the early hours of the morning, song lyrics were still circulating through Maggie's brain as she carried Storm down the hall to the toilet. As she urged him to stand in front of the bowl, she felt dispirited. It had crossed her mind once more that his mother had not phoned. For someone so young, the boy had had a tough start to life, and Maggie felt overcome by her own helplessness. Short of offering him love and a home, there was little she could do for him. She couldn't give him his mother. It was then that she remembered that she had toyed with the idea of flying Justine down for the weekend. However, without even raising the matter with Storm, she had decided against it.

She gathered her grandson into her arms, and was about to carry him back to his own room when she hesitated. It was cold down there and it was almost morning. In a few more hours she'd only have to get up again and wake him. Feeling his sleeping body against hers, she knew he'd be better off spending the rest of the night in her bed. At least there he would be warm and, who knows, he might even sleep in.

She lowered him gently to her bed and nudged his body over as she crept in beside him. Then, carefully pulling the covers up to his chin, she lay back against her pillow and gazed at the ceiling. She thought about the events of the previous day and mused over the suggestion Scott had made as he had left that night. Lingering in the hall, he had suddenly cleared his throat and, without warning, invited her to accompany him to a quiz-night fundraiser the following Thursday. Maggie sighed as she recalled the awkward silence which had greeted his invitation. His words had caught her off-guard and she hadn't known what to do. She'd been conscious of Lisa standing in the background listening. She'd also been aware of how shapeless and droopy the sweater she was wearing had become. Given to her by Carol, it had never fitted properly, and hung off her narrow shoulders like some weird mocha-coloured skin. She didn't know why she even wore it.

Now, glancing at Storm, she sighed again. She wasn't cut out for quiz nights. But maybe she should have accepted, anyway.

A SMALL GROUP clustered around a blue car parked at the edge of the sales-yard. As Maggie approached, her eye was caught by a wind-torn banner, which twisted and flapped from a single rope tied to a pole. A second length of rope, hanging from the banner's lower corner, was whipped by every fresh gust of wind. Maggie was caught by the violence of its movement. It was startling.

Seated on a white plastic chair towards the rear of the car was Bevan. By his feet was a tartan thermos, which rolled on the ground, blown back and forth across the short distance separating the hem of his blanket from the car's rear wheel. The palm of one gloved hand placed on the vehicle, Bevan raised the other in a weak wave of acknowledgement as Maggie and Storm approached.

Running ahead, Storm clambered onto Bevan's knee. Oblivious to Bevan's panicked, 'Get off! You'll knock me over!' Storm began questioning him, his words tumbling ahead of his thoughts as he tried to ascertain how close to winning the car his uncle was. Maggie could see three other people, all with gloved palms pressed firmly against the car. They too appeared bleary-eyed and chilled to the bone, but, like Bevan, their faces seemed set with determination. Maggie felt sick. It was all she could do not to drag her son away. Instead, she pulled Storm to one side before placing a small carton of Kentucky Fried Chicken on her son's knee. 'You need to eat something warm,' she said, her eyes glancing over the faces of the other contestants as they watched her carefully. 'There's soup, too, but I left it in the car.'

She stood back and watched as her son fumbled with one hand in an attempt to open the box. 'You look like you've had a stroke or something!' She snatched the box from him and ripped it open, returning it to her son's knee with a curt, 'There you go, grandpa.'

With nothing more to say, she stepped back and watched as Bevan carefully tore at the chicken, ripping chunks of flesh and skin from the bone as small pieces fell away, dropping to the ground by his feet. Hearing a whisper, she glanced down and followed the direction of Storm's hand, which was pointing towards a clear plastic bottle quarter-filled with yellow liquid.

'What's that?' she heard her grandson ask. 'It looks like pee,' he added, giggling.

'It is pee.' Maggie caught Bevan's eye as she spoke. She stared hard at her son but he returned her gaze without blinking.

Pushing Storm forward, she told him to take a piece of Bevan's chicken. Then she looked around once more, shuffling uneasily as she did so. 'Well . . .' she began, before changing her mind and starting afresh, 'Looks like you're having fun.'

'It's not meant to be fun,' Bevan grunted. 'It's a competition.'

Maggie nodded. For the first time she looked closely at the car. 'It's very bright, isn't it? Is it any good?'

Her son sneered. 'What do you think? It's a 1996 Mitsubishi Evo4 . . .'

Maggie shrugged, 'Carol told me they were offering a BMW soft top—'

'What would she know?' interrupted Bevan, 'Her head's so far up her arse, she wouldn't have a clue.'

Shocked, Maggie was about to reprimand him when she heard a voice from the other side of the car. 'Shit, I've had enough of this.' A plump woman got stiffly to her feet, stretched and took off her woollen beanie. Maggie recognised her immediately. It was Justine's old school friend Amber. Years had passed since she'd last seen her, but even so Maggie was surprised by her appearance. She was no older than twenty-three or twenty-four, but Amber's face was weathered and blotchy, dark shadows encircling her eyes. Maggie looked away in case Amber caught her staring.

At that moment a familiar red car pulled up behind hers. Her heart sank. 'Todd,' she noted, before facing her son and asking, 'What's he doing here? I thought I asked you to stay away from him.' The door of the car slowly opened, loud music preceding Todd as he emerged. When he saw Maggie he hung back, leaning against the bonnet as he pulled from his pocket a packet of cigarettes, which he tapped absently against his leg. To her surprise, Bevan didn't appear particularly pleased to see him. 'I didn't tell him to come,' he said, ignoring the older boy, who was now trying to light his cigarette in the shelter of his cupped palm. Maggie sensed that something had changed in her son's relationship with Todd and began to relax. Perhaps, she thought, things weren't as bad as she'd imagined. 'I'll tell him to clear off, if you like,' she offered. A pained look crossed Bevan's face but he said nothing.

Several seconds passed, neither of them speaking, and then a bell rang. 'Toilet break,' said Bevan, standing up. 'I'm allowed five minutes.' Stretching and rubbing his legs, he added, 'Hand me that bottle, Storm.' For the first time since she had arrived, Maggie saw her son smile, a foolish grin crossing his face as he explained how during the night he'd been caught short between official breaks and that with only one free hand he'd had to wrestle the bottle under his blanket, and, without anyone seeing, empty his bladder. Embarrassed, he explained that he had pretty much missed and had got his trousers all but soaked in the process. He indicated a boy not much older than himself who was also competing for the car, and added that he should have done like him and pissed against the wheel. 'If you come back,' he finished, 'can you bring me some clean trousers and undies, otherwise I'm going to wind up smelling like one of your piss-in-the-pants clients.'

He wandered away, and Maggie watched as Todd trailed after him, catching him as he disappeared into a nearby port-a-loo. She'd intended to remind him that he had school in the morning but it didn't matter, she'd return later. She glanced down at Storm. On his face was an expression of admiration. He looked up at her and whispered, 'It's a really cool car, eh? It looks like one of those boy-racer cars.' He sounded so impressed that Maggie had to smile. They walked back to her own worn-out vehicle. 'I don't want you ever taking part in a competition like that, Storm. You're worth more than that.' She could see that he didn't understand. It was bad enough that Bevan had been sucked in. Watching her son stoop that low filled her with dismay, but he was old enough to make his own decisions. In any case, there was no way she could have stopped him.

By the time she arrived at the museum, Maggie felt much calmer. It was not crowded, and leading Storm into the tuatara area, she was pleased she had made the spur-of-the-moment decision to visit. It had been ages since she'd last been to the museum. The tuatara enclosure was more spacious than she remembered. Given that none of the animals appeared to move more than a short distance away from the heat lamps placed outside the burrows, it was almost too large. Watching the tuataras, she was impressed by how regal they appeared. They struck her as rather proud, and she would have spent more time looking at them had not her cellphone rung, interrupting her train of thought.

Barely had she raised the phone to her ear when she recognised Justine's voice, demanding, 'Where are you? You're not at home.' Taken aback, Maggie forgot to reproach her for her lack of communication the previous day, but answered lamely, 'The museum.' No sooner were the words out of her mouth, than the line went dead. Ignoring Storm's inquisitive look, she shrugged and suggested they go to the café. The truth was she wanted a sit down. She liked tuataras, but the lure of a good strong cup of coffee was more powerful. Besides, they could always return for another look.

It seemed that they had only just ordered when from the corner of her eye she spotted Justine striding towards them. Maggie was so surprised she couldn't move. It was only as her daughter staggered up to their table, a suitcase in one hand and a parcel in the other, that she was able to manage a faint, 'What are you doing here?'

Her daughter ignored her. Turning her attention to Storm, who looked as if he had seen a ghost, she trumpeted, 'Happy birthday, dude!'

Confusion followed. Maggie's coffee and a heated cheese scone arrived, but finding the space on the table taken by the brightly wrapped parcel, the waitress became flustered and, to Maggie's consternation, turned back the way she had come. At the same time, Storm clambered onto Maggie's knee, shyly hiding his face in her jacket, restricting her movement and preventing her from going after the girl. While all this was taking place, Justine took the opportunity to begin grumbling, 'You wouldn't believe how long I had to wait at Christchurch airport for my connection. Four hours! And all I got on the plane was a glass of water . . . Where's that girl going with your drink?' She ran after the teenager and took the tray from her hands. But before Maggie had time to reach for her coffee, Justine took a sip and exploded, 'Jesus, you wouldn't get away with that in Auckland!'

It was another twenty minutes before Maggie received a fresh cup of coffee, during which time Justine barely stopped talking. Breaking crumbs off Storm's cheese scone, she started again to complain about the duration of the journey between Auckland and Invercargill, noting that it would have been quicker to travel to Australia. Then, glancing towards Storm, she began to fuss over the way he was dressed. 'You look like one of those kids dragged around the streets by religious freaks. A Jehovah's Witness boy.' It was lucky she had bought new clothes. Cool clothes, she added, smiling at her son – the type worn in Auckland.

Justine rummaged in her suitcase for a sweatshirt and passed it to Storm. Oblivious to the shaken expression on her son's face, Justine took the boy into her arms and hugged him tight, commenting in a voice loud enough for all to hear, 'There, now you don't look so inbred!' Maintaining a firm grip on Storm with one hand, she began to fuss with his parcel with the other, all the time encouraging him to rip into it. Storm reached cautiously for the gift only to have it snatched away by his mother, who called him a 'slow coach' and began to pull at the wrapping herself.

Maggie was horrified by her daughter's frantic behaviour. She tried to intervene but Justine snapped, 'We don't need her help, do we Storm-boy?' Confused and close to tears, Storm nodded dumbly. But even as his head went up and down he tried to return to Maggie's chair, only to be tugged back by his mother, who exclaimed, 'Look, a Star Wars light sabre. Awesome, eh!' It was too much for Storm. He began to cry. He tried again to return to Maggie, but the more he struggled the tighter his mother held onto him. Her arms linked around the small boy's chest, she glowered at Maggie, hissing, 'Look what you've done. Satisfied?'

Maggie was aware that a group of tourists seated nearby was watching. In a low voice, she warned, 'Stop it Justine! You're upsetting Storm.' In response, Justine rose from her seat and, grabbing her suitcase in one hand and Storm by the other, snapped, 'He's my son – not yours!' Then, facing Storm, she announced, 'Come on. You're coming with me.'

The boy began to scream. He tried to sit down on the floor, but was yanked to his feet by Justine. She began to half-drag, half-carry him across the carpet, towards the exit. His body twisted and turned as he attempted to struggle free. Horrified, Maggie went after them. She begged her daughter to calm down.

Her voice raw, she reassured her daughter that no one in the world could love Storm – or care for him – as much as his mother. She explained that Storm was still tired from his birthday party, that he was surprised to see her, that he was shy . . . Words sprung to her mind and she uttered them without pausing, saying anything and everything to placate her daughter. 'Please, Justine,' she heard herself plead, 'I didn't mean to upset you. Let's just go home.'

Her heart pounding, she felt dizzy. Glancing at Storm, who was now standing quietly beside Justine, she was overcome by the sense that she had betrayed him. She desperately wanted to take him in her arms and tell him everything was all right. She wanted him to understand that she had been forced to lie – that, really, no one loved him more than her. That he meant the world to her, and that she would love him and protect him until her dying day. But, sensing that such an outpouring would only make things worse, she stood silently, helplessly, too scared to move.

Still fearful she might lose the boy, she attempted to speak, croaking, 'Isn't it lovely to see your mother again, Storm?' No sooner were the words out of her mouth than she thought she would be sick. She gagged and quickly searched in her bag for something with which to cover her mouth. All she could find was a tattered SpongeBob paper serviette.

A look of amusement crept across Justine's face. She took in the cartoon figure pressed against her mother's lips and said, 'Why don't you stay and enjoy your party while I take Storm outside to play in the gardens. He looks like he needs some fresh air.' Hugging the boy, she added, 'We'll probably see you . . . later.' She stroked Storm's hair and then led him away, saying, 'Come on, mate. Let's get out of here.'

$\mathcal{I}$T TOOK a long time for Maggie's pulse to return to normal. For the rest of the afternoon she stayed in her house, unable to leave, her ears straining for the sound of a car pulling up outside. Lisa tried to reassure her, but she had been unable to relax, tormenting herself with the thought that Justine might disappear with Storm. That even as she prepared the evening meal, her daughter and grandson might be boarding a plane for Auckland. She might never be allowed to see him again. Nothing could alleviate the pain she felt, and when Bevan phoned at five to say he was one of only two contestants remaining in the competition and that he was waiting for his clean trousers and underpants, Maggie could barely summon the energy to respond.

At six thirty, when a taxi finally pulled up outside, Maggie almost sobbed with relief. She forced herself to ask only if Justine had had a nice afternoon before adding that dinner was ready when she was. She had to be careful not to antagonise her daughter and so stood back, a tight smile on her face, when Justine said Storm had already eaten, in town. At the mention of his name, Storm began to complain of hunger. But Maggie maintained her silence, nodding in agreement when Justine announced she would run a bath for the boy.

Less accommodating was Lisa, who snapped, 'You heard Storm say he was hungry so why don't you wait and give him a bath after dinner? Mum's made a special meal . . .'

Maggie shrugged. 'Another ten minutes won't make any difference.' Then, sidestepping Storm's shy request for her to bathe him, she smiled and suggested, 'Wouldn't you rather your mother gave you your bath? She's come all this way to see you.'

Only then did she realise that she had no idea how long her eldest daughter was staying. More than that, she consciously took note for the first time that the twins weren't with her. 'It must be nice to have a break from the girls,' she said, adding 'I expect you must miss them, though.' She was aware that Lisa was watching, and that she seemed puzzled. Yet, Maggie felt unable to do anything but play it safe. Conscious of Justine's unpredictable mood swings, she had to be careful – at least until her daughter calmed down and made her intentions clear.

Just when Maggie thought she could hold back no longer, Justine began to smile, and pulling a bottle of sparkling wine from her bag said, 'The bath can wait, let's crack open a bottle.' Remarkably, with that suggestion the weight that had descended over the room lifted slightly. On edge, Maggie decided to play along – even going so far as to search out the special occasion wine glasses she kept in the crystal cabinet in the lounge.

She watched as her daughter poured the wine. 'That looks good.'

Justine shot back, 'It should look good – it cost thirty bucks.'

Immediately the weight began to settle once more – but this time only on Maggie. Unsure of how to tackle the subject of her daughter's spending, she found herself saying, 'Having Aaron around must have made things a bit less difficult at home – money-wise.'

Justine didn't miss a beat. 'If you mean having a new credit card has made things a bit less difficult – the answer is yes.'

She desperately wanted to find out what was going on, but Maggie said nothing. Taking a sip from her glass, she felt the bubbles burn her throat as she calculated the amount of money her daughter had spent so far on this visit. A figure of five or six hundred dollars taunted her and, unable to take another sip, she blurted, 'You put this trip on your card?'

'Yeah, of course. How else would I pay for it?'

Justine's casual response made Maggie feel sick. She watched her daughter refill her glass. 'Don't worry about it, Mum – it's cool.'

Later, Maggie could not shake the figure of six hundred dollars from her mind. With every mouthful of dinner, with every sip of wine, she felt increasingly ill, trying to work out the level of debt her daughter was in. Seeing the clothes bought for Storm, the Star Wars light sabre and the packaging from a brand new MP3 player, all strewn across the lounge floor, Maggie wanted to cry.

It was only as she lay awake in bed that night, her mind going through the sums, that she realised that her daughter was probably no worse off than herself. She thought the combined income from the Domestic Purposes Benefit and other allowances must add up to six hundred dollars, or more. With a couple of cleaning jobs on top of that, her daughter might be earning around seven hundred dollars a week.

Maggie's anxiety eased a little, and yet she was disturbed by her daughter's behaviour. Justine didn't appear to understand that it was wrong to live off the DPB while sharing a home with a partner on the dole. Moreover, her daughter seemed unable to comprehend that the various authorities might take a dim view of both her and Aaron's false claims. Justine was being reckless, but although Maggie disapproved of her daughter's behaviour, she was even more afraid of what would happen to her grand-daughters should Justine be found out. More than anything, she didn't want the twins to suffer. Yet in protecting her family, she was conscious that she, too, was being less than honest.

As the hours ticked by, Maggie became more and more wound up thinking about Justine's actions. She couldn't help but feel ashamed of her daughter. Going round and round in her head was the knowledge that everyone else in her family had jobs. Everyone *worked*. Even Carol, who didn't need the money, put in long hours at the agency. Lisa spent most of her weekends pumping petrol and Bevan, too, mowed lawns for ten dollars an hour. No one else would do what Justine was doing. It was a mat-ter of self-respect and it saddened her to think that her daughter cared so little. Awkward though it was, she would have to speak to Justine. There had to be some way out of the situation. There was some other way – it was called hard work.

It was almost five. She'd been half-awake most of the night worrying and unless she fell asleep immediately she'd get no more than two hours rest. She tried to think of something to take her mind off Justine's money troubles. Exhausted, her thoughts wandered to the twins. Earlier, she had discovered that Justine had left them in the care of a friend. Their father, Aaron, had not wanted to take responsibility for the girls, and so Justine had dropped them at her girlfriend Kelly's house – the same woman who had 'delivered' Storm.

Imagining the worst, she pictured the twins lying unattended in a squalid room. Their nappies soiled, the girls were crying, calling out for their mother as they tried to reach the handle of the closed bedroom door. From another room, she heard the grunt of their 'caregiver'. Slumped on a sofa, an ash tray balanced between her and some man, she would be watching a DVD, her eyes not so much as flicking away from the screen despite the girls cries.

Maggie gasped, fully awake as she turned to face the small figure standing in her doorway. Sitting up, the image of the twins in the back of her mind, she asked, 'What is it, Storm? What's wrong?' as the young child shuffled towards her, crying softly. She heard him mumble, 'I'm all wet. I had a bad dream and then I was all wet . . .' The distress in her grandson's voice touched her deeply. Reaching for her gown, she slowly climbed out of bed and went to the boy, hugging him gently as she led him down the hall towards the bathroom. There, stripping him of his wet clothes, she began to wash him with warm water from the shower. Reassuring him, she towelled him dry and sent him back to her room before ripping the sheets from his bed and searching out clean pyjamas. Only after she had placed the sheets in the washing machine and put them on to soak did she return to bed. Snuggling up next to her grandson she closed her eyes, and feeling the warmth of his body next to hers, took a deep breath and whispered, 'We'll be okay,' before closing her eyes at last.

$\mathcal{I}$T WASN'T until she left home the following morning that it suddenly hit Maggie that Bevan hadn't returned the night before. Guessing he was at the car sales-yard, she ran back inside, pulling the first pair of trousers and underpants she could find from the ironing basket and stuffing them into a plastic bag before running back to the car where Justine and Storm were waiting.

Justine had insisted on accompanying her to work that morning. Dismissing Maggie's suggestion that she might be better off going to town or visiting old friends, she had remained determined to stay.

Justine had started the day by making Storm's breakfast and packed lunch before hustling him off to the bathroom to clean his teeth. Despite finding it difficult to work around her daughter, Maggie knew it would be unwise to undermine her decision. Nothing was said, but Maggie thought Justine's offer to help was an apology, a way of atoning for her poor behaviour the previous day.

Certainly, since waking, Justine had made a real effort to be pleasant. She had even managed to stop bitching about Carol and the fact that she had also bought Storm a light sabre for his birthday. Provided Storm played only with her gift, Justine seemed content to let the matter rest. This was a far cry from the previous evening when, for several hours, she had moaned about Carol's manipulative, self-centred motives and her show-off, superior ways. The list of complaints mirrored those raised by Maggie during the debacle at the party. Nevertheless, Maggie felt obliged to defend Carol. She didn't like hearing her sister being torn apart. Justine's nose was out of joint and she was being cruel.

In the short time it took to deliver Storm to school and drop by Bevan, Justine's mood swung around. What began as snide remarks levelled against Invercargill's too-wide streets, developed into an attack on her mother: a list of her shortcomings and a critique of her appearance. Maggie knew her daughter was highly strung but she didn't remember her being as manic as she was now. Justine's behaviour made her not only uncomfortable but nervous, too.

Then, without warning, Justine suddenly changed the subject. She announced her intention to start a business, to move from Auckland to the Far North in order to be closer to Aaron's family, and her desire to buy a house with him because it would make their commitment stronger. Forgetting all about her earlier intention to broach the subject of her daughter's dependency on welfare and credit, Maggie became increasingly agitated as, with each passing minute, she waited with sickening dread for her daughter to mention Storm. Finally, she could control herself no longer. She blurted out her worries, only to hear her daughter laugh, 'Storm? God, I hadn't even thought about that!'

'Him!' Maggie snapped, her voice far louder than she intended. 'Not "that",' she continued. '"Him".'

She glanced across to her daughter and registered the girl's startled expression. It was enough to give her courage. 'He's settled here . . . with us. What's more, he's doing well at school, his friends are here and his family is here . . .' Even as she spoke, she knew she had pushed things too far. If only she had paused to think before talking.

'Not me,' interrupted Justine. 'I'm not here and I'm his mother.'

A stabbing pain went through Maggie's chest. She desperately wanted to take back what she had said and yet at the same time she needed to sort things out with her daughter, once and for all. She had dared to raise the issue of Storm and now she wanted to know where she stood.

A memory of her marriage break-up nudged at her thoughts. She recalled the confrontation, the bitter arguments about who got what, or kept what, and her heart sank. Negotiating with Justine was going to be as bad, if not worse. But, as far as Maggie was concerned, Storm was staying with her. She would make that very clear. The best thing for Storm was to remain where he was. He needed stability and security. No sooner had she decided to stick by her demands, than Maggie was struck down by fear. Up against her daughter's stubborn determination, she felt powerless. She lost her nerve.

* * *

At the home of her morning's client, Angela, Maggie found it almost impossible to carry on a conversation. While Angela and Justine discussed beauty products and treatments – procedures Maggie had never heard of – she worked through the house, moving slowly from one room to the next as she vacuumed and cleaned. Every chore was familiar and yet she felt somehow disconnected from what she was doing. Carrying empty beer bottles out to the rubbish, she caught herself standing, staring – not knowing at what, exactly – until suddenly the spell broke and she realised she was looking at a sheet that was tangled around the neighbour's television aerial.

The sheet was wound tightly around the aerial but one corner remained free and flapped in the wind, creating a noise like hand-clapping. The sound was cheerless, and Maggie was about to return to the house when she stopped and fixed her attention once more on the white cloth. A memory relating to an event from her early childhood gradually formed, becoming clearer as each second passed. How exactly the recollection was related to the sheet she didn't know, but when she was a child her father had taken her to a river where, for an hour or so, they had stood watching salmon struggle upstream. The tattered condition and size of the fish had amazed her; she'd never seen anything like them before. But, more than that, she had been overcome by sadness. It had struck her that the fish were attempting the impossible, but because they didn't know that, they wouldn't give up. Worse, no one was helping. She recalled she had wanted to catch the fish and carry them above the rapids, and yet when she had mentioned this to her father, pleading with him to intervene, he had firmly rebuffed her, telling her that it would be wrong to interfere, that only God had that right. God, he insisted, knew what He was doing.

In the end, the sight of the fish battling against the current had been too much for her. She'd burst into tears. At that point, her father had taken her hand and told her that the fish's struggle was all part of God's great design. But she hadn't understood. Whatever lesson she was meant to learn – and she was sure there was one – was lost on her. Angry with her father, she was conscious, too, of a sense of failure. Despite what he told her, she should have helped.

Later, with increasing anxiety, Maggie drove to Tim's house. She had tried to dissuade her daughter from joining her, but Justine was determined. Now, as they stood at Tim's door, Maggie made one final attempt to discourage her daughter. Tim, she explained, was a new client. He might not want a stranger around. Taking family members to work wasn't professional. At this last remark, Justine scoffed, 'Since when? Half my childhood was spent entertaining your clients while you stripped their beds.' Maggie had no response to that. It was true, after all. She had no choice but to let Justine stay. Nevertheless, she decided not to give out any information about Tim. She feared that Justine would put her foot in it if she learnt about the connection between him and Bevan. It was better to keep quiet.

Hearing a muffled sound on the other side of the door, she called, 'Tim! It's me, Maggie,' and stood back to wait. Earlier, she had resolved to keep her eye on her client and if there was any hint at all that something was amiss, she would leave. Even now, she had to fight a sudden, overwhelming impulse to return to her car right away. Weighing her options, however, she decided that spending time with Tim might be preferable to spending the rest of the day alone with Justine. She took a deep breath, smiled and greeted Tim cheerily before introducing her daughter. To her surprise, he appeared pleased to see them both and even went so far as to offer his hand to Justine, shaking it somewhat formally before inviting them in.

Following close behind as he moved into the kitchen, Maggie was astounded to hear Justine breathe into her ear, 'You didn't tell me he was a hunk.'

'He is not a hunk!'

Then, catching sight of Tim, who was looking at her, puzzled, Maggie explained they were talking about someone else. Immediately, she wished she hadn't said anything. She excused herself with a brusque 'I'll start the vacuuming' and fled down the hall, grateful to escape.

As she settled into her chores, a sense of calm took hold of her. From past experience she knew housework often helped clear her mind. The thoughts that filled her head became ordered and less overwhelming as she worked. The tidier the room, the more in control she felt of her own life and after an hour or two she might actually attain a state resembling peace. Cleaning not only made her feel better but it gave her a sense of accomplishment.

Crouching in the shower, scrubbing the soap scum from the Formica panels, she momentarily forgot about both Justine and Tim as she took pleasure in nothing so much as the task in hand. Recalling a piece in a magazine she had glanced at while in the supermarket, she realised there was a special term describing her state of mind. She was 'living in the moment'. She smiled wryly and then turned her attention back to the panels.

Immersed in her task, it took a while for her to notice that music was coming from the lounge. But as she worked she discerned her movements were following the rhythm of a slow, steady tune played on something which resembled a mournful guitar. Listening more intently, she put down her cloth, and as one chord followed another she began to recognise the tune.

Curious, she sidled towards the living-room door and saw Tim sitting with the strange silver and wooden guitar balanced awkwardly across his lap and the arms of his wheelchair. While he plucked the strings with the fingers of one hand, he ran the neck of a glass bottle over its fret board with the other. Fascinated, Maggie stepped into the room, her presence immediately noted by Justine, who whispered, 'Isn't it cool,' before adding, 'You know this song, don't you? You should join in.'

No sooner were the words out of Justine's mouth than the music abruptly stopped. The room fell quiet, the only noise that of Tim's breath, which was surprisingly heavy. The effort of playing seemed to have tired him, and several seconds passed before he spoke. 'Justine asked me to play something but I'm so out of practice. I used to be a lot better.'

He addressed Maggie, but looked at the guitar and for a second she had the impression he was apologising to it. There was something so mournful about the way he looked that Maggie felt compelled to speak, if only to cheer him up. 'My father liked that song.'

'Yuck, that creepy Christian,' said Justine, pulling a face. 'But you used to sing it when you were putting me to bed, remember?' Maggie shook her head. For the second time in as many days, she had no memory of performing a song. At least, she thought gratefully, this tune wasn't about being too sexy for a shirt.

Warming to the subject of music, Justine continued, 'Tim actually found a bottle washed up on the beach out there and cut its neck down so he could use it on his Dobro.'

Dobro. There was that word again. Maggie had not remembered to look it up in the dictionary but now she wouldn't have to. Catching Tim's eye, she smiled. To her surprise, she heard him ask, 'Sing along?'

Maggie shook her head and gestured towards the Dobro. 'I wouldn't know how to accompany that thing.'

'He's got normal guitars too, you know,' interrupted Justine and before either one of them could say anything, Justine took the Dobro from Tim and replaced it with an acoustic guitar. 'Don't say you can't sing along to this. It's the same as yours.'

Maggie flushed a deep crimson. 'I've got a lot of work to do,' she said, exasperated, waving a cloth limply in her hand as if to emphasise the point. 'There's the dishes—'

'No, there's not,' cut in Justine. 'I've already done them so you'd better start singing, okay?' There was an edge to Justine's voice, which became even more apparent as she added, 'No excuses.'

Maggie found her daughter's manner annoying. Why was it so important that she sing? It made no sense. Even worse, Tim was staring at her, waiting. The more uncomfortable she felt, the more Tim appeared to relax, encouraged, it seemed, by Justine, who insisted, 'Come on, will you? Even I can remember a few words. Something about gathering shadows and waiting death-beds. What's wrong with you? Do you want to spend the day cleaning toilets?'

Maggie felt inclined to answer, Yes, I would prefer to clean the toilet – at least then I could get some peace. In truth, she felt disturbed by the lyrics. They struck her as inappropriate, offensive even, given Tim's state of health. Annoyed, she shook her head and muttered, 'Work. Cleaning.'

To her horror, Tim piped in, 'Come on. It's not often I get the chance to perform alongside a professional . . .' Maggie couldn't believe it. To be victim of her daughter's bullying was one thing, but to have some man in a wheelchair tease her – that was pushing things too far.

Looking from Tim to her daughter, she stated, flatly, 'No, I don't think I can even remember the words. I haven't heard them for so long . . .' As the words left her mouth, she recalled the time her father had sung the song – not to her, but to Carol who had perched herself upon his knee. So clearly could she hear his voice that she turned around, as if he might walk into the room. It was disconcerting. She felt shaky, and the feeling was only made worse when Tim prompted her, murmuring, 'Shadows are gathering . . .'

Later, years later, Maggie would look back on this day and the instant when she had opened her mouth to sing would haunt her. She felt as if time had cracked open. The space she occupied was unrelated to her past or her present. It was a vacuum – a void. And in this fractured second she encountered herself. It was such a fragile beginning and, extraordinary though it was, it was one she might easily have failed to recognise, or worse, shunned. Yet, for some unaccountable reason, she accepted the moment as a gift and this, more than anything, filled her with wonder.

Determined not to sing, she shook her head and took a step back towards the bathroom. Then, without understanding why, she hesitated. 'All right – just one verse.'

PART THREE

$\mathcal{I}$T WAS A BEAUTIFUL clear day. The sky was bluer than Maggie could recall ever having seen it. It appeared flawless and smooth as a river-worn boulder. And, like a stone, it seemed solid – like a blue rock, she thought – and she imagined that if she could extend her hand she would find it cold at first, becoming warmer under her touch. Craning her neck, she could see no clouds – just a vast expanse of impassive blue sky. Just her luck she had to work.

She stepped back from the window and asked Bevan if he had anything planned for after school. He shook his head. Her eyes fell on the scar which extended from the corner of his mouth to his cheek. Some time had passed since his accident at the car competition, but even so she could not think about what had happened without becoming angry.

Fifty-two hours after first placing his hand on the car he had been one of only two competitors remaining when he'd fallen asleep. He had toppled from his chair, catching the rear bumper and twisting awkwardly, before hitting the metal arm of his upended chair. His cheek had been badly gashed and he had knocked out two teeth.

By the time Maggie had reached him, he was sitting in a corridor in the hospital. Unattended, he had been there almost an hour, his face covered in blood and a flap of skin hanging from his cheek. That no one from the car sales-yard had thought to accompany him incensed her. Yet, even as she stroked his hair and comforted him, she could not help but feel relief over the fact that he had not won. As the words 'Never mind, there's always a next time' formed on her lips, an equally strong conviction settled in her mind – one that said, I will never allow you to do anything like this again.

Unfortunately, she had not foreseen the media attention his accident would create. Within twelve hours of the incident, the manager of the car sales-yard responded to criticism from the local news and radio stations by offering a 'good sport' prize to Bevan. The prize, a white Holden Commodore with over 300,000 kilometres on the clock, was presented to him in a short ceremony; one which again attracted a great deal of media attention. Everyone, it appeared, was happy.

The Holden was parked in the driveway, its paintwork gleaming in marked contrast to the dull brown of her own car. Bevan had lost no time in getting his learner licence. The fact that he was not permitted to drive unless accompanied by a licensed driver made no impact on him. What's more, Maggie believed the car was uninsured. Whenever she'd raised the subject with her son, he'd brushed her off with a curt, 'It's under control and it's not your problem.' Trying to gather information was impossible. She had rifled through his drawers on several occasions but had found no evidence of insurance papers. The only good thing to have come out of the whole experience, as far as she was concerned, was that he sometimes volunteered to drive her to the supermarket or into town. These journeys seemed to Maggie to be 'safe'. Less safe, were the trips he made in the company of his friend Todd.

In recent weeks Todd had become a much more frequent visitor to the house. His presence alarmed Maggie. Often accompanied by Todd's dog, the two boys would drive down the road, their destination the park where, Maggie presumed, they exercised the animal. It was after one of these short excursions that Maggie came home to discover Bevan storming through the kitchen, cupboards crashing as he searched for food. Maggie was surprised to hear him fume, 'Stupid dog. It's always running off and it gets on my wick, big time. We spent ages calling it. Everyone was looking – except Todd, of course – on account of his bad leg.'

At the mention of Todd's leg, Maggie bristled. She'd almost forgotten about that incident – about the time Todd *got angry* because he decided his girlfriend wasn't paying him enough attention. The story went that he'd caught her talking to one of his friends and had got so wound up that he had gone home, got drunk and taken a shot at his own leg with his air rifle. The pellet had gone right into the fleshy part of his thigh and had had to be removed by a doctor. That had been Todd's method of getting his girlfriend to take notice. But that had happened almost a year ago. It didn't really explain why Bevan was so upset about the runaway dog.

It was only later, when talking to Lisa, that Maggie was able to uncover the real reason why Bevan was angry. Lisa had reluctantly let it slip that Todd's dog responded to the name 'Raper'. Todd had settled on the name, Lisa explained, because the dog spent all its time prowling the streets looking for bitches. The thing was, the dog was always running away, and although Todd got a kick out of standing in the park calling its name at the top of his lungs, no one else did.

Recalling the conversation as she prepared to leave, Maggie asked Bevan, 'Will you be seeing him today?' Bevan looked at her blankly but the mention of Todd's name was so distasteful to her that Maggie could not bring herself to utter it, saying only, 'That friend of yours – the one with the mongrel?'

Bevan shrugged, 'Todd?' he asked. 'Dunno, eh?'

'Well,' snapped Maggie, 'Don't. I don't want him in my house. He's got a part missing in his head.'

'Whatever.' Bevan looked at his watch. 'Better get going. Got to be on time for the old psycho.' Catching Maggie's eye, he sneered, 'Maths teacher, first period' before disappearing out the door.

Maggie passed him a few minutes later on her way to work. Hunched over the handlebars of his bike, he refused to return her wave. Then – for her benefit, she thought – he cut dangerously in front of a car in order to make a right-hand turn at the lights. His helmet, Maggie noticed, was unfastened. She could see the strap flapping, ribbon-like, as he rode along. She wondered if she should have forced him to visit one of her young paraplegics a year or so ago, when she'd had two accident victims as clients. Perhaps an introduction to a seventeen-year-old in a wheelchair would have made some kind of impression on him? She doubted it.

Despite the reasonable start to her day, she began to feel anxious. She wasn't sure why she was upset, but recently she sometimes felt panicky. Her chest was tight and her stomach churned. It crossed her mind that it might be the onset of early menopause, but it was far more likely that she was worried about Bevan and Justine. It had been a while since she had heard from her daughter and Maggie found Justine's silence disturbing. It was a bad omen that they'd spoken only once since Justine's return to Auckland.

During their last morning together, Maggie had managed to sit down with Justine and have a proper conversation. Her daughter had broken down and cried, apologising to Maggie for being such a bitch and promising to be nicer in the future. Maggie had been taken aback by Justine's outpouring of emotion and was almost relieved when Justine added that she wouldn't have been forced to behave so horribly had Maggie been more supportive and less judgemental. Used to confrontation, Maggie had been discomforted by this awkward display of self-reproach.

When her daughter's flight was called, she was even more disconcerted to find herself the recipient of a strong embrace; Justine's damp face pressed into her cheek as her daughter clung to her, mumbling over and over again, 'Sorry, sorry, thanks for everything . . .' Maggie had stood awkwardly, her arms flattened against her body, as she whispered, 'It's all right, don't worry.' It was only as Justine continued to cry that Maggie remembered that a show of remorse following a long period of rage was typical behaviour for her daughter.

Justine could be hateful, but her outbursts were more often than not attention-seeking devices which masked a deeper, un-identified emotion. In the past Maggie would have stood up to her daughter, secure in the knowledge that Justine would inevitably crumple when her behaviour was challenged. Not being around

Justine for so long had made Maggie forget this simple fact and she'd been rattled by her daughter's spiteful goading.

She didn't know what had prompted her daughter to eventually soften but she guessed it might have something to do with their visit to Tim. Shortly after she'd started to sing, Maggie had glanced across to Justine and seen – or at least thought she had seen – tears glistening in the corners of her daughter's eyes. Justine had hastily wiped them away, but she had not been able to disguise the tremor in her mouth. Observing her daughter's emotion had caused Maggie to falter and lose her place.

The first song had reached its end but Tim had continued to play, beginning a new tune which he'd invited Maggie to sing along to. Reluctant at first, she nevertheless had done as requested, and so it had continued, one well-known song blending into another, for almost twenty minutes. A strange sense of peace had come over her. With each verse, she'd felt increasingly at ease. She had began to regard recent episodes in her life as less complicated, less doom-laden, than she had previously imagined. Her falling out with her sister had become a silly spat, her nervousness around Tim the result of an overactive imagination, and even her fear of Justine had seemed suddenly misplaced.

By the time the final note faded, Maggie had felt elated. The last time she had experienced such a strong reaction was when she was a teenager. She had been at a religious retreat, she recalled. The weekend had been arranged by her church. At one point she had been saying her rosary when she had looked up and caught the eye of a nun, a woman not much older than herself. Maggie couldn't remember what, exactly, happened next but she could recollect feeling swamped by a surge of love and gratitude. It was as if the nun had made a promise, as if she was telling Maggie there was something beyond daily life worth looking forward to. Maggie had almost laughed out loud and, seeing her, the nun had smiled and nodded her head before lowering her eyes.

Maggie's memory of that experience had lingered in her mind as she'd watched Tim rest his guitar against its stand. It had been all she could do not to ask him to continue playing. She'd been greedy for more. The thought of stopping had been somehow unbearable, as if it sign-posted the return to some barren region where she would be forgotten.

Tim appeared to have been similarly affected by the music. Although she couldn't be sure, she had the impression that he, too, had been transported to some other, restful place – a world that was somehow his alone and yet, at the same time, shared by her. It didn't really make sense when she thought about it, but, for all that, he looked as she felt – rested.

But within minutes, she had been self-conscious and embarrassed. She'd begun to see herself through the eyes of some imagined stranger. Here she was: a middle-aged dowdy-looking woman, standing centre stage in a cold drab room while a man in a wheelchair played and a tall, skinny girl watched, crying. Viewed like that, the performance was pitiful. Yet she hadn't felt humiliated while singing. If anything, she had felt in control – invincible.

Returning to Tim's house, the memory of her 'performance' fresh in her mind, Maggie was conscious of her heart beating. Since arriving in Riverton earlier in the day, she had felt increasingly distracted and jittery. It was a weird feeling; something like excitement mixed with fear.

She had been unable to avoid an awkward situation at her first client's house. Much to Maggie's horror, Angela had insisted she ignore the dishes and instead enjoy a complimentary facial and makeover. It was Maggie's last scheduled visit to the girl and it was clear she wanted to give her a treat. Had not everything already been carefully laid out on the coffee table, Maggie might have managed to wheedle out of it. But seeing the bottles of creams and treatment products, the white towel and the recliner all set up for her use, Maggie had felt unable to refuse.

She'd been unsure of what to do. Instructed to remove her sweatshirt and bra and slip into a white robe, Maggie had felt exposed. Despite Angela's insistence that she should simply relax, she hadn't been able to unwind. When Angela's fingers massaged her face, Maggie had to resist the urge to push the girl away. Rather than soothing her, the girl's gentle strokes had irritated her.

It had been such a relief when the facial was finally over that she hadn't been able to think clearly and without understanding why, she'd agreed to have her eye lashes and brows dyed. She'd been instructed to keep her eyes tightly closed for ten minutes while the tint took hold. She'd listened as Angela moved around the room and nodded when she'd heard Angela announce she was going to leave for a few minutes in order to heat the wax and go to the toilet. Alone, Maggie had felt vulnerable. More than once she'd heard footsteps approaching and fearing that it was one of Angela's flatmates, she'd grasped the lapels of her robe tightly, holding her breath in anticipation of the moment when the door would swing open and John or Ty would come crashing in. Finally, after what had seemed an age, Angela had returned and asked quietly how Maggie was doing, to which Maggie had replied, 'Fine.'

Her eyelashes tinted and her eyes stinging, all that had remained was for Maggie to have her brows shaped. Relieved, at least, to be able to see, Maggie had been taken aback to feel hot wax applied to the area under her brows. She had occasionally plucked her own brows, but to have them waxed had been an altogether new experience. She'd been thinking how warm the wax felt when suddenly, without warning, she'd felt a rip followed by a sharp, burning pain. It had been all she could do not to cry. 'I'll be finished in a minute,' Angela had comforted and again Maggie had experienced a sharp pain like that of a sticking plaster pulled from a fresh graze.

'The first time is always the worst,' Angela had smiled. 'The roots get weaker after a while and the hairs kind of pop out, by themselves. Next time will be easy.' Maggie had grimaced, raising her fingers to her eyebrow. She'd been surprised not to see blood on them. Ready to get dressed, she'd sat up but had been pushed gently back against the seat as Angela had murmured, 'Just the moustache and you're all set to go.' Had the word not been 'moustache' Maggie would have called a stop to the procedure. Most of her female clients had moustaches and often wiry hairs covering their chins, too. From time to time Maggie had been asked to pluck stray chin hairs and she knew how tough they could be. The thought of having her own top lip waxed filled her with dread – but so did the thought of having a moustache.

Now parked outside Tim's house, she raised her fingers to the area above her top lip as she checked her reflection in the driver's mirror. Despite the application of a soothing balm, Maggie thought her skin looked red and swollen, as if she was about to get a cold-sore. Had she known this would happen, she would have brought face powder. That way, at least, she could conceal the pale rash which was spreading from one corner of her mouth to the other.

At Tim's door, she let herself in, calling 'hello' as she entered the kitchen. The room was cold; she could see her breath. She decided to leave the dishes until last. In an hour or so the kitchen might warm up a little. It was a sunny day, after all, and some rays might seep into the room.

Taking off her coat, she heard Tim's voice calling 'In here, come through' and following the sound, walked down the hall towards his bedroom. Given the cold, she supposed he might be in bed, but was relieved to find him dressed and in his chair. She had cared for bedridden clients in the past but she was never entirely comfortable in their company. She knew it was important to treat them with respect and care, and yet from time to time she could detect a note of impatience creep into her voice. It was hard to stand around and wait while some old man slowly raised a spoonful of hot soup to his lips. During such times she tended to dwell on all the chores that needed her attention. She would catch herself willing the client to hurry up and she would feel ashamed. It was not only her lack of patience that made her uncomfortable but her suspicion that her clients could see beyond her exterior warmth to the fraud below.

Watching Tim as he edged around the bed, her spirits raised. He was a youngish man and, it seemed, in reasonable health. She wouldn't be losing him any time soon. A small pile of papers that was balanced on his knee tumbled to the floor. As she picked them up, she was surprised to see several sheets of music notation. 'I used to write a lot of music – but these days all I can manage are quavers,' said Tim, watching. He raised his arms and Maggie noticed his hands were trembling. Funny she hadn't noticed before. But, she realised, Tim tended to rest his hands on the rims of his chair wheels most of the time. In doing so he succeeded in drawing attention away from his shaking hands.

Tim laughed, startling Maggie. 'Don't look so serious!' he smiled. 'It's a joke.' Maggie didn't know what he was talking about but nodded anyway. Following him down the hall, she listened as he told her about an article he had recently seen, one that discussed the use of cannabis and its potential in treating spasms, tremors and the like. 'I decided when I first got this disease,' Tim went on, his back turned to Maggie, 'that I would draw the line at my hands.'

Maggie hesitated. At a loss, she responded, 'Sorry? What do you mean?'

Tim spun around, his expression unexpectedly cold. 'I mean,' he growled, 'that it's one thing to lose your legs but another to lose control of your hands.'

'What do—' began Maggie, only to be turned on by Tim.

'It's simple. I am not interested in staying alive if I can't write music or play the fucking guitar!'

The atmosphere was tense but, as Maggie's discomfort subsided, she also began to feel angry.

She burst out, 'You can't be serious. Suicide is not . . .'

'Why not? Do you expect me to be some kind of role model? Can you see me going on TV and telling other MS sufferers that it's possible to live to a jolly old-age? Are you stupid?'

Startled, Maggie stammered, 'No, I guess I mean it would be a crime against God to take your own life. Life isn't yours to take . . .'

Registering Tim's dumbstruck expression, she kicked herself for having spoken. She had no right to say what she had said, yet, at the same time, she knew she couldn't have let his remark go unchallenged. Chances were he was simply upset about something and had no intention of committing suicide. She kept her eyes on Tim and as she watched she saw his expression transform from one of surprise to one of resolve. He meant what he said.

It took more than an hour for her to calm down. Leaving Tim alone in the living room, she had gone about her chores as quickly and quietly as she could. It was freezing in the kitchen, but she said nothing, washing and stacking the dishes before wiping the stove top and cleaning the fridge. It was only as she finished hanging the washing, her hands red with cold, that she decided to take a break. It would be silly to drink her tea alone in the unheated kitchen. She decided to take a cup through to Tim. It was time to make a peace offering.

To her relief, he looked more relaxed than before. Taking the mug from her, he said, 'I don't believe in God and I'm not interested in being converted.'

'Swap the word "God" for "suicide" and you know where I stand.'

Tim nodded, then smiled, 'Okay.'

The tension lifted. They drank in silence and then, putting down his cup, Tim crossed to the stereo. 'I was listening to this song the other night and I wondered if you would know it.' His smile broadened.

Her ears cocked, Maggie listened to the opening bars and shook her head. 'No, I don't think so . . . but I know the voice, I think.'

'It's k.d. lang,' replied Tim. He fell silent, listening to the tune before saying, '"Hallelujah". That's its title – not a reference to our earlier conversation.' He listened for a moment. 'Her voice reminds me of yours.'

'Rubbish,' Maggie protested. Yet, even as she spoke, she couldn't help but feel pleased. No one had ever compared her voice to that of a famous singer's before. Of course, she knew Tim was exaggerating – probably trying to make up for his rudeness in calling her stupid. There was no way she sounded as good as k.d. lang.

She listened, then slowly began to hum along, joining in with the chorus. She looked up and caught Tim's eye, who smiled back, saying, 'You look different today. Have you done something to your hair?'

Maggie raised her fingers to her mouth in a self-conscious gesture. 'No,' she murmured. 'Nothing's changed.'

She could feel Tim's eyes on her and she turned away, cursing herself for ever agreeing to a facial. She heard Tim mumble, 'Funny, you definitely look different.' Then, almost as an afterthought, he added, 'You remind me of someone. It's like I've seen you before . . . somewhere.' Choking on her tea, Maggie excused herself from the room.

As she prepared to finish up for the day, Maggie was called back into the lounge by Tim, who handed her the CD, telling her to listen to it and 'report back'. No one, she realised, had lent her a CD before. What's more, no one had ever sought her opinion on a song. Flattered by his interest, she would have liked to have been able to offer some insight about music, but nothing came to mind. Instead she promised she would take good care of the CD and bring it back next time.

With the CD clasped in her hand she found it difficult to

leave the room. It was as if it somehow tied her to Tim and that by leaving she would appear rude. She was tempted to sit down and spend a few more minutes chatting with him about music. Not that she had a lot to say. She realised he was watching her, puzzled. 'I'll report back then,' she stammered, waving the CD.

Tim nodded. 'Sorry,' he said. 'The teacher in me must be coming out.'

It was Maggie's turn to look lost. 'Teacher?' she asked.

'Yeah,' replied Tim, 'I taught music . . . high school – before all this.'

Maggie looked down guiltily. 'I didn't do music at school, or anything.' She was about to add, I wasn't allowed . . ., but stopped. It was probably clear enough already that she hadn't finished school. There was no need to spell it out. Instead she said, 'You don't look like a teacher.' She paused, wondering what it was that he did look like. Maybe a fisherman, or a tradesman? It was impossible to say. The fact was Tim looked like he could have done all sorts of things, once.

'I'm really sorry about before,' Tim said, his mouth turning down at the corners. 'I get pissed off sometimes.'

Maggie nodded, 'Yeah, me too.' She narrowed her eyes, 'Not often, though. And it's not something I'm proud of . . .'

Tim laughed. 'So, I'll see you soon then,' he continued. 'Look forward to it.'

$\mathcal{G}$ALE-FORCE SOUTHERLIES with hail was forecasted. Heavy rain had been falling all evening, and strong winds had brought lines down around the region. Maggie sat in her car listening to the weather bulletin, her thoughts wandering to images of Ross, dressed in safety gear, perched high up on a ladder, clinging to a telegraph pole. Poor thing, she thought, as she unbuckled her seatbelt. He'll be freezing. When she stepped from her car the wind grabbed the door, jerking it from her hand. The weather was even worse than she thought. She wouldn't want to be out on a night like this.

As she walked to her sister's door, she realised that she had been putting off her visit for some time. Things had more or less returned to normal at work, but Maggie was ashamed of the way she had spoken to Carol. Unfortunately she needed to borrow one of her sister's sleeping bags for a trip Lisa was planning. It was a minor but awkward request. A few days earlier, when she had first raised the matter, Carol had responded, 'Couldn't you buy her a cheap one at The Warehouse? Ours are brand new and cost a fortune. I'm not sure it would be a good idea . . .' Her manner annoyed Maggie. Carol had a whole cupboard full of sleeping bags and it hardly mattered which one Lisa used. Her daughter wouldn't care if it was old.

Maggie was even more exasperated when Carol appeared not to cotton on to the reason for her visit. A look of mock concern on her face, she hustled Maggie in. 'Has something happened? It's not Mum, is it?' Maggie had never been able to keep up with her sister's games and now, hearing her mother mentioned, she panicked, 'No, why?' It was only when she saw her sister's sly smile that she knew she had been tricked. 'Oh nothing . . . it's merely that she was worn out by Storm's sleepover the other night.'

Elsie had said nothing about being tired. 'You know what it's like,' murmured Carol. 'Having to get up in the middle of the night to strip the sheets . . . I thought Storm had stopped wetting?'

Maggie made no response. Her mother had said nothing about a wet bed. Having been warned that Storm might have an accident, Elsie had nodded and said that he was probably still unsettled by his mother's visit. She hadn't made a fuss, and Carol was troublemaking in raising the topic now.

Maggie followed Carol down the hall, towards the kitchen. Catching sight of Ashley as she passed the lounge, she cleared her throat and asked if Lisa could borrow his sleeping bag. Though her voice had clearly startled him, he smiled. 'Sure, no problem – which one?' The exchange was so quick and easy that Maggie almost laughed. She was about to reply when Carol said, 'She wants to take it to Christchurch.'

Ashley gave his mother a withering look. For one crazy

moment, Maggie was tempted to give the boy the 'thumbs up' or say, nice one. But there was no point in antagonising her sister. Instead, she thanked him and apologised for interrupting his television programme. 'No worries!' he responded. 'Is there anything else she needs? A camera?' He caught his mother's glare, and asked, 'What?' He shook his head, rolling his eyes and turned back to the screen. 'I'll get the bag in a minute.'

Before Maggie had the chance to ask for anything else she was ushered out of the room and into the kitchen, where she was instructed to sit while Carol set about fussing with a small espresso machine. Her sister had been busy since her last visit. The dining chairs were new. No longer pale wood, they were a rich brown leather with dark legs. They looked expensive. The table was also new. It crossed her mind to ask what had happened to the old furniture, but she was afraid her sister might think she wanted them so said nothing. Instead, she asked after Gemma. Carol described every aspect of her daughter's day – her success in the school production, her promotion to captain of the swimming team – and Maggie listened, her mouth fixed in a smile.

Carol turned the focus of her conversation towards Ashley, describing his recent successes on the bike track and his hopes of representing Southland in the finals. She rambled on and on, and although Maggie listened quietly, she wanted to shout, Hang on a minute! Don't you want to hear about my family? I have children, too, you know! But Carol, she realised, never asked after her kids. In fact, they didn't even register. Maggie knew better than to be surprised by Carol's behaviour but she resented it. Her sister's lack of interest offended her. With nothing to lose, she interrupted, 'I'm thinking of sending Lisa to medical school.'

No sooner were the words out of her mouth than she wished

she had kept quiet. Nothing irked Carol more than being forced to acknowledge that Lisa was brighter than both Ashley and Gemma. Maggie could see her sister's mouth tighten and twist. Seconds later, she snorted, 'But that's ridiculous. She's not even sat her exams yet.' She stared hard at Maggie and continued. 'Besides, how much does university cost? You've not asked Elsie for money, have you? You know she can't afford to help you.' She frowned, and then her brain reached a conclusion Maggie could not have predicted. 'You're not asking me for money, are you?'

Maggie laughed. 'You don't get it, do you? I'm not even talking about you. Of course I'm not asking for money.'

At that, Carol's mouth curled into a smile, 'It's not like you to have such unrealistic expectations.'

Maggie sighed, worn down by the futility of trying to have a conversation with her sister. Continuing was pointless; she'd only wind up angry again. It was easier to back down. 'I don't know,' she murmured, 'I kind of hoped you might be able to give me some advice. I mean, you have such a head for money . . . you know.'

Replaying the conversation as she drove away, Maggie couldn't help but shake her head. It was pathetic. To have reached forty and still be sucking up to an insecure little sister – it was sad. But it made life easier, she reasoned. And it didn't matter, really. It was just talk.

On the spur of the moment she decided to call in at the service station and tell Lisa she had the sleeping bag. The poor kid had taken on extra shifts, and although Maggie wasn't happy with her working until 10 p.m. on two school nights, she didn't have the heart to stop her. Having planned her trip to Christchurch weeks before, Lisa needed extra cash. She and her friend were going to take the bus and stay with her friend's aunt, a teacher at a private girls' school.

Maggie intended to chip in, too. A hundred bucks or so. Knowing she wanted to give her daughter some money was part of the reason why she hesitated before entering the service station. She guessed Scott still had a tyre put aside for her and she was embarrassed that, once again, she would have to put him off. Money-wise, things were getting worse. She predicted it would be two months, at least, before she could find the cash for his tyre. She'd only recently managed to recover from paying for Storm's birthday and her share of Justine's air ticket. And now Bevan needed to see a dentist and her warrant of fitness was overdue. The way things stood, there was no way she could splash out on a new tyre.

It was at times like this that Maggie questioned her resistance to using her credit card. After all, and for reasons she couldn't understand, her credit limit had been raised to $7000 – an incredible amount given that she never used her card. She would love to buy a tyre, a new sleeping bag and pay for Lisa's trip to Christchurch without having to worry about how much it came to. It would be so simple to put everything on her card. Six hundred bucks would do it. Everyone else used credit cards, and it wasn't as if she was irresponsible with money. She needed a little help to stay on her feet, that was all.

She had considered Scott's generous offer regarding the tyre. He'd told her she was welcome to take it and pay for it later. It was such a kind gesture and it made sense to take him up on his suggestion, and yet she couldn't. It wasn't a matter of pride so much as fear. To have access to credit would ease so many problems, would free her from so much stress that she worried she might become dependent on it. And then, she could imagine borrowing even more money – for comfort, more than anything, against an increasingly uncontrollable life.

Frank, her father, had used alcohol as a comfort. Strictly speaking he was not an alcoholic, but few evenings would pass without him opening a couple of peters, from which he poured his beer. Carol's husband Lindsay was similar to Frank in that respect. He was rarely seen without a glass or bottle in his hand. Like Frank, he seldom appeared drunk – but he never appeared entirely sober either.

Believing herself to be more like her father than her mother, Maggie feared she might have inherited his addictive nature. Provided she didn't tempt fate, everything could remain in her control. That was the main thing – not to tempt fate.

At the petrol station she was surprised to see Scott standing at the pumps. There was no sign of Lisa. For a second Maggie considered leaving, but Scott waved in greeting and she wound down her window. 'Lisa's gone,' he said, coming up to the door of her car. 'It was so quiet I sent her home.' He paused as if unsure about continuing, and then added, 'Bevan collected her.'

Maggie nodded. The thought of Lisa being in a car with Bevan at night time was hardly what she would have wished, but she felt she couldn't make a fuss. 'Thanks,' she said, beginning to wind up her window.

'Wait a minute,' said Scott. 'Why don't you come in for a coffee. I haven't seen you for a while and it would be nice to . . .' He looked at the ground, shuffling awkwardly. Then, after a moment's thought, he said, 'I wish you'd let me give you that new tyre.'

Maggie sighed. She was tired. She wanted to go home.

'My wife once . . .' Scott began, but his voice quivered and he fell silent, shaking his head, and added, 'Nothing.'

Maggie had the impression he was going to cry and, feeling disconcerted, said, 'I shouldn't really drink coffee at night. It keeps me awake.'

'I can make hot chocolate,' countered Scott. 'I mean the machine can. I just press the buttons.'

Maggie nodded, reluctantly. She wanted to leave, but there was something so eager about Scott's invitation that she couldn't refuse. Sighing, she unbuckled her seatbelt and opened the door. She was about to step out when she realised she had parked in the middle of a large puddle. Annoyed, she considered swinging her feet back inside and driving away. But glimpsing Scott's extended hand, she was obliged to carry through her decision to stay for a drink. It would only take a few minutes and then she could be on her way. Nothing appealed to her so much, at that moment, as the prospect of crawling into bed.

On previous occasions Lisa had always been present, acting as a kind of buffer between them. Being alone with Scott was an altogether different proposition. She felt trapped. She hadn't wanted to chat but confronted with his hangdog expression she was sorry for him. Now, she felt manipulated and, what was worse, her shoes and socks were soaked through and her feet freezing.

She decided to follow up on Scott's reference to his wife. In general, most people found it relatively easy to talk about their family. Family and weather, the two constants. She smiled ruefully.

'Your wife . . .'. She hesitated, suddenly uncertain. Something about Scott's expression made her think that she had made a mistake – that she'd chosen the wrong subject, after all. Yet, in spite of that, she was curious. She hadn't pictured Scott as a married man. To her, he seemed to be one of those men who would be forever single. He had a note of quiet desperation about him. Perhaps desperation was too strong, but he definitely struck her as lonely, somehow lost.

'Your wife . . .' Maggie repeated, wishing she'd chosen to talk about the weather, 'Does she work?'

'No, she's dead . . . now.' Maggie heard him laugh faintly and then he corrected himself, saying, 'I mean she's dead – without the "now".' He sighed and added, 'It's been almost ten years. She was killed in a car accident . . . our daughter, too.' His head bowed, Scott explained, 'We were on holiday at Glenorchy, but on the second day the car skidded on some ice and went down a bank into Lake Wakatipu. They drowned.' Then, in a voice so faint she could barely hear, he finished, 'I was driving.'

Maggie was stunned. She had had conversations with clients who had revealed tragic events from their past, but nothing in her experience had ever come close to this. How was it possible, she wondered, to say what Scott had said without disintegrating? Not only was he standing upright, but he was operating a machine that dispensed hot chocolate into a paper cup! The fact that such ordinary words and actions could contain such terrible news shocked her. But even worse was the sight of Scott's stricken face, contorting into a self-conscious smile, as he held out a cup for her to take.

Maggie took the drink and stared at it, her thoughts whirling. She was aware that Scott was busy making himself a cup, but there was no way she could pretend nothing had happened. She couldn't act normal. Scott's comment had transported her into another world. One where the horror of what had occurred to his child intensified as she imagined a similar thing happening to any of her own children. There was no way she could live through that, she thought. Even if she somehow managed to keep breathing, she wouldn't be alive. Not if her child were taken from her.

'I'm sorry.' Scott's voice broke through the silence. 'I shouldn't have said anything but . . . I had to.' He explained that in the past he had seldom raised the subject of his family with acquaintances. It was too painful. But then he realised he was beginning to avoid social events and invitations because he didn't know how to deal with the topic. If things went unspoken, socialising with new friends became awkward. He'd begin to feel anxious, constantly steering conversations away from anything to do with his past. Life became too hard. It was easier, he apologised, to be up-front from the beginning. He was sorry if his behaviour struck her as callous. That wasn't his intention.

'If you don't mind,' he said, 'I don't want to talk about it, any more.'

Maggie nodded. 'Does Lisa know?'

Scott shook his head, frowning. 'The other day I was watching Lisa,' he said, 'and I worked out that my daughter must have been in her new entrant's class at school. I think they would have played together.' He held Maggie's eye, his expression soundlessly asking, 'Do you remember her? Can you picture my daughter? Don't let me be the only one left in the world to recall her face.'

Maggie shook her head. 'What was her name?' she asked.

'Morgan.'

Maggie had no recollection of a girl named Morgan. Lisa had only ever talked about one or two girls in her class and, as a working mother, Maggie had had little to do with the school. Back then she had been too busy to be involved.

'I remember her,' she lied. 'She was lovely. Very bright and friendly, very kind.'

$\mathcal{M}$AGGIE HUMMED softly to the music on the car radio as she drove towards Tim's house. When she walked in he was at the table, sheets of paper strewn around his wheelchair. Some pieces, she noticed, had been tossed in the general direction of a waste-paper basket that lay near his chair – but most had missed. Maggie had been looking forward to talking to him. She had listened to his CDs and hoped to start the day by going over the songs and performances. Yet seeing the look of concentration on Tim's face, she was reluctant to intrude. He frowned as he worked and, in spite of herself, Maggie laughed. It was like stepping into a movie – the type of costume drama Lisa brought home on DVD. She imagined a story that depicted the relationship between a musical genius, like Beethoven, and a servant. She was part of the scene where the genius gets stuck for an idea, looks up and notices the servant girl. The genius would ask for her opinion and then get grumpy when she answered truthfully. That created tension. But, deep down, the genius would know she was right and he would have to admit it sooner or later. Glancing towards Tim, she realised she was being silly and so set off down the hall to change the sheets on the bed.

As she worked, she daydreamed. It was pleasant to picture herself as an artist's muse. From the little she knew, muses didn't have to do much. They hovered around the artist and exchanged knowing glances from time to time. If that became a little dull, they dressed up in an extravagant outfits and accompanied the artist to dinner.

There was a second type of muse, too, she remembered. Usually the wife, she also hovered around all day, attending to business and annoying tasks. She rarely had the opportunity to go out to dinner – she was far too busy working. Instead, she brought her husband snacks and drinks late in the evening. And, as the genius relaxed, she would rest one hand on his shoulder and examine his day's work. Their relationship would be quiet; they would communicate with few words. Every now and again he would show her a finished poem or song, and there, in black and white, would be proof of his love and gratitude. She would know, then, that he valued her.

A thudding noise interrupted her train of thought. It was the washing machine. The sheets must have balled up during the spin cycle. She would have to go and fix the problem.

She hated overcast days. The sheets would never dry, and if she hung them outside on the line, they would have to stay there until her next visit. There was no way Tim, or any of her other clients for that matter, could bring in the washing. Fortunately, Tim had a wet weather line strung up in the garage. It was only just high enough. When weighed down with laundry, the sheets had a tendency to trail on the ground and their hems picked up dust from the floor.

Despite its new-looking door, the garage was pretty horrible. The only good thing about it, as far as Maggie could tell, was that it was dry and weatherproof. Lengths of wood and tools were piled clumsily along the end wall. These, she guessed, were the bits left over from Tim's house renovations. Paint cans were stacked along one wall, and along the other were craypots and scallop dredges. There was even a collection of old diving tanks, their bright yellow cylinders one of the few splashes of colour in the otherwise gloomy space. Most disturbing of all, was the dried remains of a cat. She had glimpsed it the week before when she'd been asked to fetch a piece of underlay from the garage.

An entire corpse, the cat was wafer-thin and flat. This struck Maggie as odd, because, given its location in the shed, it couldn't have been run over. Most unsettling was the cat's head. Its eyes were open and its mouth was frozen into a grotesque grin. What's more, its lips were drawn back and its teeth bared, as if it were on the verge of attacking something. Maggie didn't want to share the garage with a dead cat but she couldn't bring herself to remove it either. Instead, she had covered it with an old sack.

When she'd mentioned the cat to Tim he had looked blank. He never ventured into the garage. What he meant, he explained, was that he didn't park inside. He could operate the door by remote control and drive in, but there wasn't enough space for him to get out of his car once he was stopped. 'It was fine before I had the chair,' he explained, 'because I could squeeze out of the driver's side. But now,' he murmured, 'I'd be stuck for good.' He smiled and added in a theatrical tone, 'Like the cat.' His manner startled Maggie, sending shivers down her spine. Quickly she changed the subject. The garage was unpleasant enough without having to joke about such things.

Tim had no intention of treating her like a muse. He barely spoke to her all morning, managing little more than an impatient 'No' when she offered to make him lunch. In his presence, Maggie became irritable herself. She was reminded of the first time she had met him, when he had struck her as arrogant and self-absorbed. It was a shame, she thought, because she really had been looking forward to discussing the CDs. She had hoped he would talk to her. No one else shared her interest in music, and she had imagined they might sit together for fifteen minutes or so and play music and have a discussion. That was all she wanted — a chat.

After Tim's, her day got worse. As usual, she was confronted by the sight of waste matter floating in Mr Paxton's toilet bowl. Not only that, but there was an awful smell in his entrance hall, which upon close inspection was clearly related to something he had trodden in. She guessed he had stood in dog shit while collecting the morning paper. He kept no pets himself, but both his neighbours owned dogs that roamed free, often relieving themselves on his verge and lawn. In the past she had spoken to both households about the problem, but nothing had changed. If anything, she had only managed to offend them and make things worse.

She was pleased when she caught sight of Mr Paxton setting up his chessboard. Her mood was so flat she thought it would make a pleasant change to sit down for thirty minutes and have a game with him. During her previous visit he had begun to tell her about his experience of the Murchison earthquake, and she hoped he would pick up the story again and carry on. She wanted to find out more about how his family had coped during the weeks following the quake. He'd already told her that all the houses in his street had lost their chimneys and that his family, like those of his neighbours, had been forced to cook outside on makeshift stoves. But Maggie wanted to hear what happened next. New Zealand history was unknown territory where she was concerned, and to have the opportunity of spending time with someone so old he had actually lived through a major historical event was quite something.

She had experienced history first-hand only once in her life. She had been a school girl when the department store H & J Smith had installed an escalator. From memory, there was only an 'up' escalator but it had been the first in Invercargill, and her class had made a special trip into town to see it. Lines of children had filed onto the escalator and travelled up to the first floor before being ushered through the furnishing department to the stairs which had taken them back down. They had been allowed to make their journey twice, each time lining up patiently to await their turn to travel up the escalator and each time walking through racks of soft furnishings on their way to the stairs which had taken them back to where they had started.

The day had been so exciting that she'd tried to persuade her father to take her back the following week. To increase her chances of success she'd tried to include Carol in her scheme, but, being more interested in horses than escalators, her younger sister had not responded with enthusiasm. Maggie's disappointment had been great. Alone in her room she had drawn countless pictures of herself and her father riding the escalator. Headed 'A Great Day Out', the pictures had remained pinned to her wall for weeks. She'd kept them there in the hope that her father would see them and give in. He'd known the pictures were there, of course. He'd seen them during prayers, going so far as to commend Maggie on her realistic portrayal of the escalator, the accuracy of its detail. Flushed with pride, Maggie had carried her father's compliment around with her for days. Knowing he appreciated her drawing was almost as good as taking him to see the spectacle itself.

One day she'd arrived home from a friend's house to discover her father had gone into town, taking Carol with him. As Carol's voice rang out, 'We rode the escalator, we rode the escalator!' Maggie had felt sick with hurt, conscious of the gross injustice. Never before had she felt so unfairly treated, so betrayed.

Plucking up her courage, she had approached her father. 'Why did you take Carol and not me?' She'd carried the faint hope that he would say her turn was next. She'd thought he would have to take her – it was only fair. Maybe she would get to ride the escalator and then have something to eat at the Copper Kettle, the dark tea rooms located inside the store. She had gazed at her father with such intensity that he ought to have been able to read her mind, to guess her thoughts. Smiling at her, he had laid his hand gently on her head and murmured, 'I took Carol because *she didn't ask.*'

That short sentence had taken her breath away. Sobbing, she had promised never to ask again if only he would take her. In fact, she would never ask for anything, ever! She'd kept her word. Though at times she was tempted to ask for *something*, she had kept her mouth shut.

Only once in her life did she travel up the escalator with her father. The trip took place shortly after Frank had been persuaded to move into her house. He had suffered from Parkinson's disease for years, but when his condition finally deteriorated, Maggie offered to take him in. At the time her parents, although not divorced, were no longer living together, and Carol was in Australia. Already working full-time for the firm Carol would eventually acquire, Maggie had to juggle her clients around caring for Frank. She had thought he would be with her for months rather than years.

On this particular day she had needed to go into town, and noticing there was a sale at H & J's, had led Frank into the building, negotiating the various counters before reaching the foot of the escalator. Unconscious of it at the time, she had realised later that there was something premeditated about her actions. There had been no need to take her father up the escalator. He could have found a chair on the ground floor and waited while she nipped upstairs. But, she had wanted him to ride with her. Standing behind him, her hand supporting his back, she had been a third of the way up when, to her horror, she had began to sob. Confused, she'd choked back her tears as she'd tried desperately to regain control of her emotions. At the same time, she'd been aware of her father's own weak, trembling body through the palm of her hand. Somehow, by the time they reached the first floor she had managed to all but stop crying. She'd helped her father off the escalator and, without saying a word, ushered him across the floor. Her father had noticed nothing and Maggie was struck by a painful sensation. From that moment on she had felt cut off from her past and disengaged from him. As far as she was concerned, he was good as dead.

It was almost dinner time and she had the shopping to do. Driving towards Pak'nSave, she realised she couldn't face going in. The idea of negotiating the aisles, feeling overshadowed by the high shelves while trying to remember what to buy, required too much effort. She was too tired. She'd call in tomorrow instead. But tomorrow would be no different from today. She might as well get it over and done with.

For a while after the introduction of the new coins in 2006, Maggie had continued to pay for her groceries with cash. It helped her keep track of her budget. But, as Lisa had explained, cash was no longer the best option. 'It's because of the way things are rounded up,' Lisa said. 'Say something costs ninety-eight cents, for example. You're going to be charged one dollar. So, if I was you, I'd pay by eftpos . . . unless the bill is ninety-two cents, of course. Then it's better to pay by cash.'

Waiting as the cashier scanned her groceries, Maggie wished again that she didn't have to consider all that stuff. The man in front of her had whipped out his wallet and withdrawn a fifty-dollar note without even stopping to think. It didn't cross his mind that he was forking out three cents more than he had been charged. He flapped down the note, and then took his wine and pre-packaged pumpkin–capsicum soup and began to walk away with out so much as pausing to check his change. He wasn't interested in making sure he hadn't been overcharged. He wanted to get out as quickly as possible. She could understand that. He wasn't alone there.

*J*USTINE'S PARTNER, Aaron, had disappeared once more. Woken at eleven thirty by her tearful daughter, Maggie had been forced to listen to the whole sad tale from start to finish. It wasn't particularly complicated. Aaron had taken her car and driven away. He'd told Justine he wanted to go north to check out the work situation. Now he had been gone for several days, and Justine hadn't been able to reach him by phone. None of his friends knew where he was. Aaron had said he was going to his sister Melanie's place but having rung Melanie, Justine discovered they hadn't seen each other for over six months. Aaron's sister certainly wasn't expecting him and, if anything, appeared annoyed by the mere mention of his name. He still owed her fifty bucks from his last visit. He was scum. Unnerved, Justine slammed down the phone. Her heart pounding, she had sat snivelling for several minutes before ringing Maggie and repeating the whole sorry story for her benefit.

Propped up in bed, Maggie gazed silently at her clock-radio. The minutes ticked over as Justine became more and more agitated. 'He could be anywhere! He might be lying in a ditch,' she sniffed. 'Or worse . . .'

It was all Maggie could do not to scream with frustration. How was it possible that she had raised a daughter so prone to self-deception, so lacking in pride? What was it going to take for Justine to see things clearly? If she hadn't felt so aggravated Maggie might have been sorry for her daughter. But how could she feel sorry for someone who was determined to ruin her own life? There had to be some reason for Justine's blindness. Something genetic. Deep down, there must be something inside Justine that had made her seek out such a creep. It was as if she wanted to be treated badly. It didn't make sense, thought Maggie. That guy had made her daughter's life a misery, and still Justine came back for more. And now look at what had happened. Aaron had stolen her car and left Justine alone with the twins. It was too much. Maggie was inclined to ring the police and have Aaron locked away. That's what she should do.

But, of course, Justine couldn't be made to understand. She insisted something must have happened to Aaron. She knew in her heart that he wouldn't leave her alone with the girls. He'd been so happy, so settled. They'd spent hours talking about their future. Their business was about to take off and they were planning to move north, buy a property and settle down. It was all worked out.

At the mention of the word 'business' Maggie felt her heart freeze. 'What business?' she asked, barely able to utter the question for fear of hearing the response. Her question was greeted with silence. 'What business?' she repeated.

'Biros. I was going to tell you but I knew you'd do your nut.' Maggie listened numbly as Justine began to explain that she had started a business printing company names and logos onto biros. 'At the moment I'm reading about basic business management, and when I've got it sussed Aaron and I plan to establish a client list. My girlfriend Kelly does the same thing. She reckons there's so much demand she can't keep up. She says I can't fail.'

Maggie winced at the mention of Kelly's name. Hadn't Justine learnt by now that it was a mistake to get involved in any of her friends' madcap schemes? Years ago, she had got pregnant because her school friend Amber had convinced her it would be fun to have a baby. Now she was falling into a similar trap. And it didn't take a brain-box to predict what was going to happen. Justine continued in a sly voice, 'It was you who wanted me to find work, remember? I'm only doing what you told me to do.'

Maggie could not bring herself to speak. Glancing around her room, she searched for something to hold her attention – a photograph or an ornament – something solid she could rest her eyes on while she tried to come to terms with her daughter's news. But her bedroom was featureless. Never having had the money to do it up, it had remained pretty much unchanged from the time she had first laid eyes on it almost twenty years before. Ross had begun to cover the wallpaper with off-white paint but had never got around to doing the ceiling or re-varnishing the cupboard doors. A sheepskin rug, a wedding present from her mother, still lay over the bald spot on the carpet where water from a potted plant had leaked. Even the light fitting, a pale-pink tulip shade, had been in the room since the time she had moved in.

Finally her eyes came to rest on a family portrait Carol had had taken during a Mother's Day dinner. She examined her own face. 'It's late, Justine.' She hoped her voice sounded sympathetic. 'Get some sleep. Everything will seem clearer in the morning. I'll phone you.' She could hear her daughter begin to snivel once more, but she couldn't bring herself to offer anything more. Nothing she could say would make a difference.

Now wide awake, she continued to stare at the photo as she tried to decide what to do next. Nicely framed, the photograph was one of only a handful in her possession. It had been taken by a professional – a man who had made the rounds of all the restaurants during Mother's Day – and he had made her look almost radiant. That the glow was due to two glasses of wine and soft lighting was not lost on her.

At times like this she missed Ross. He had always managed to remain patient with Justine. Not one to be flustered or messed around with, he had always known what to say and, more importantly, how to word it. He could have told Justine to come home and, more likely than not, Justine would have agreed. She had always listened to Ross. Whereas from the age of thirteen she had given the impression of not being able to stand Maggie, she had grown increasingly closer to her father. At times their relationship had been almost impenetrable. They were more like accomplices than father and daughter, and Maggie had felt excluded. Yet, in the past year or two Ross had withdrawn from the relationship. It was as if he'd washed his hands of Justine. Perhaps, thought Maggie, he resented the fact that he was no longer the most important man in her life.

She drew her knees against her body, thinking about the way Ross had behaved when he had lost his job. He had been so bitter, she remembered. Not over the fact that he was unemployed but because she'd had to work so hard that she was no longer able to spend enough time with him. He had felt ignored, and they had grown apart. But perhaps he figured that withdrawing from the relationship was the best way to gain her attention.

More awake than ever, Maggie rolled over and pulled the covers tight around her neck. She clung to the blanket but could feel a draught edging its way around her collar and down to the small of her back, and no matter how low she squirmed under the blankets, she couldn't make the chill go away. Shuddering, she yanked a pillow down and wedged it against her body, hugging it tight against her belly. Why was it always so cold, she wondered? No matter what time of year it was, regardless of the season, her room was dank and miserable. She could never get warm. There was always some gap that let the draught in. It never let up.

WHEN MAGGIE pulled up at Tim's house, she caught sight of him sitting by the front window. He reminded her of a dog waiting for the return of its owner. She was about to wave when she realised he had not seen her. His gaze was fixed on the beach and the sea beyond. He was oblivious to the fact that she was unloading his groceries from her car. As she struggled with her bags, she recalled that her ex-husband had always become engrossed in some minor chore — like pretending to fix a sticking drawer — whenever she had arrived home with their food shopping. It wasn't until the groceries were all packed away and the kettle put on to boil that he'd look up from what he was doing. He'd smile, then, and offer to carry the rest of the bags from the car. When Maggie responded, 'You're too late', he would look at her accusingly and mutter, 'You should have told me you wanted help.' At this point they would either squabble or Maggie would turn her back on him and make tea. She would ensure that his mug was left on the kitchen bench. She would not pass him his tea; she had a point to make. It was only when it became clear that he couldn't be bothered fetching his hot drink, that he was going to let it stew, and that he also had a point to make, that she lost her temper. It was this final snub which most irritated her. Seething, she would dwell on it for the rest of the day. Of all the minor irritations that punctuated their marriage, it was this fundamental lack of respect that most rattled.

To Maggie's surprise, Tim reached the back door before her. He held the door open with the wheel of his chair as he reached forward to take a bag from her hands. 'I saw your car,' he said. 'I was waiting for you. You're late.'

'I'm not late. I was at the supermarket buying your groceries.' Even if he was pleased to see her, she wasn't going to let him get away with a remark like that. What was it with men, she wondered? It was as if they thought food cupboards filled themselves. One day there would be no tea or coffee, and the next morning, abracadabra, there it was. If only she could gain admittance to a man's world, her life would be so much easier.

She had barely taken a step into the kitchen and gathered her breath before Tim was beckoning her into the lounge, insisting she listen to something he wanted to play. He butted her with his chair, jostling her towards the door. With Tim following too close behind, they became jammed, neither able to move. 'Wait a second!' snapped Maggie.

It was only as Tim reached for his guitar that she fully understood the importance of the occasion. Talking as he tuned the instrument, he explained that he had spent several days working on a song, and that he wanted her to listen and tell him what she thought. His head was cocked to one side as he continued to tune his guitar, and Maggie couldn't help but notice that his progress was hindered by severe tremors affecting his hands. At one point it appeared he would lose grip of the guitar altogether, and he was forced to stop. Maggie heard him swear beneath his breath and when she caught his eye he grimaced. He shook his head with impatience and tried to strum the instrument, stopping a moment later when it became clear he could not control his hands.

The minutes ticked by; Tim glowering at his hands while Maggie stood still and waited. There were so many chores requiring her attention that it was all she could do not to suggest they give music a miss and come back to it later when she had more time. From the look on Tim's face, she could see that that would be the worst thing she could do. She had no choice but to go on waiting.

Eventually, after what seemed like hours, Tim had the instrument tuned to his satisfaction. He glanced at Maggie to make sure she was listening, and then began to play the introduction. Several bars later, and for no apparent reason, he stopped. Squirming awkwardly in his chair, he whispered, 'I've got it now', before taking up the tune from where he left off.

By this time, Maggie's attention was waning. Beyond Tim, she could see a stack of dishes piled up on the kitchen table. She calculated how long it would take to tidy up. Her eyes fixed on the mess in the next room, she heard Tim begin to sing. His voice was clear but he was still having trouble with his guitar. His fingers could not keep up, and the song was fractured by long pauses and discordant notes. For all of that, Maggie felt drawn to it. From the lyrics, she guessed the song was written for a female voice. Not only were the notes too high for Tim, but the words were so unguarded, so fragile-sounding that they had to come from a woman. No man would say that stuff. As Tim's halting voice continued, she was carried along by the tune, and joined in for the chorus. Never having heard a song written and sung by someone she knew, she was proud of Tim. It seemed a shame that no one else was around to appreciate his talent. Without doubt, it was the best song she had ever heard.

The song ended, and although Maggie wanted to say something about it, she lacked the confidence to begin. She simply nodded and smiled. 'You have a nice voice,' she eventually said, adding, 'The song was good, too. Bit sad.'

She was offended to hear Tim laugh. True, she hadn't known what to say and her comment wasn't brilliant, but all the same he didn't need to laugh. Anyone would think he had been waiting for her to say something dumb. Perhaps that was all he expected from her. In order to be taken seriously, she continued, 'It must be hard to put yourself in a woman's place – to write from a female point of view. You managed okay, though. It was believable.'

Her comment was greeted with silence. Seconds passed, and then speaking quietly, Tim responded, 'The song isn't about a woman – it's about me.'

'Yeah, right.'

She expected Tim to smile or at least come clean about the joke but seeing his grave expression, she said, 'Well, I guess it could be about anyone really. Even you.'

Tim shrugged and put down his instrument.

Throughout the morning, Maggie's thoughts returned to the song. She couldn't remember its exact words, but she felt touched by it, nevertheless. It was beautiful and painful, all at the same time. But it lacked hope, she realised: it was such a lonely tune.

At eleven thirty she filled the kettle and set out two mugs.

Humming as she waited for the jug to boil, she happened to glance across to the garage and in that instant felt a chill run down her spine. An image of the dead cat entered her thoughts and lingered there as she continued to sing softly to herself. The faint steam-whistle and the noise of boiling water echoed the tune and then distorted, becoming like the sound of air being expelled, a death rattle. The jug clicked off, and the noise made Maggie gasp with surprise. She glanced at the kitchen bench and then out of the window, but everything was as it should be. Nothing had changed.

Unaware that Tim had entered the kitchen, she heard a shuffle and jumped, spilling tea down the front of her trousers. She thought she heard him say, 'I'd like you to record that song, for me,' but she ignored the remark and continued to pat her trousers with a tea towel. 'I want to enter the song into the Gold Guitars,' Tim said, loudly. 'The song-writing category. I'd like you to sing it for me.'

Maggie was only half listening. 'You can sing it yourself, surely? You've got a good enough voice.'

Tim shook his head. 'I think you'd make a better job of it,' he said, watching her scrub violently at her trousers. 'You'd be more thorough.'

'Thorough?' asked Maggie, looking up.

'Yeah, thorough.'

It was hardly a compliment, mused Maggie later that evening as she stood behind the couch, looking down at the back of Storm's head as he watched a DVD. On the plate next to him was a pie. Not one of 'Millar's Killers' — the pies she remembered from her childhood — but a Pak'nSave mince and cheese. She had taken it from the freezer and heated it in the microwave, noticing as she cut it into quarters that the centre had barely warmed through. Storm had not noticed. With his eyes fixed firmly on a fight taking place between Spiderman and Venom, his fingers sought out a quarter of the pie and raised it to his lips without even looking. He didn't take his eyes from the screen, but nevertheless managed to avoid touching both the carrot sticks and the three small pieces of broccoli that sat on the plate next to the pie. Smiling to herself, Maggie said, 'Green Goblin eats his vegetables, you know. That's why he's so strong and green.' Her remark went unacknowledged, but a few seconds later she watched as Storm's fingers crept back to the plate, this time taking a small head of broccoli which he raised slowly to his lips, holding it at the edge of his mouth, before lowering it, untasted, back to his plate. 'Storm!' snapped Maggie. The boy jumped, and instantly his hand retrieved the broccoli and delivered it to his mouth, whereupon it vanished as if swallowed whole. Following his flurry of activity the boy fell once more into a dream, and it became too much for Maggie to watch.

Tonight, like most nights, she had laid the table for one and then forced herself to go through the ritual of sitting down to eat. She made herself chew slowly and pause between mouthfuls. The kitchen had felt particularly deserted and quiet this evening. With Lisa away and Bevan out, somewhere, she had found that rather than enjoying the peace of being alone she missed the bickering that punctuated most meals. Even Storm had been unusually subdued, turning away from his film only once in order to ask if his father was dead and if he was an orphan. Where he had got that idea, Maggie wasn't sure. It was possible Justine had told him his father was dead but it seemed unlikely. The drama and tragedy of a dead father might have appealed to Justine but Maggie thought she would be more inclined to paint Storm's father as a loser. That way there would be less chance of the boy creating a hero out of him. And knowing how insecure her daughter was, Maggie could guess that she wouldn't want her son to look up to his father more than her.

It was only as she was clearing away her plate that Maggie recalled Spiderman had been an orphan cared for by elderly relatives. That was a relief. She had anticipated there would be a time when she would have to sit down with Storm and tell him everything she knew about his father but she wasn't looking forward to it. It bothered her that she had so little to tell. That, in reality, she knew nothing – only that there had been someone – a man. It seemed an unpleasant fact for a child of Storm's age to grasp.

Maggie's concern over raising the topic of Storm's father appeared not to be shared by Justine. She was so intent on keeping everyone, Storm included, in the dark that she refused to accept that there was anything to discuss. On the few occasions when Maggie had raised the subject, Justine had been dismissive, if not completely illogical. Once, Maggie recalled, Justine had stopped the conversation dead before it had even started by saying, 'Tom Cruise was raised by his mother and sisters, and look where he is today. Only one of the richest men in Hollywood.' To Maggie's protest that that didn't prove a thing, Justine had retorted, 'If you're so worried about him having a "father" why don't you try to get Dad to move back in.' Then, realising that she had hit a raw nerve, she continued, 'Of course, if you hadn't been such a grumpy man-hater, he might not have gone in the first place.'

Her daughter's comments were out of order but Maggie had dropped the subject. Provided the boy felt loved and had a stable home, what did it matter if he had a father or not? In one of the magazines Carol had lent her, Maggie had read an article about the 'changing face' of New Zealand families. In view of what she had learnt, Maggie had to admit her life wasn't so bad.

With Storm settled back in front of the television and all thoughts of being an orphan gone from his mind, Maggie walked out to the garden and crossed the lawn to Bevan's shed, where she intended to collect his dirty clothes. But, before she reached it, a new thought entered her head, and returning to the kitchen, she searched in her bag for the song lyrics Tim had given her.

Out in the shed, she cleared a space on Bevan's bed and lifted his guitar gently to her knee. She ran her hands over its soundboard and ribs, feeling the smooth cool wood beneath her fingers. Then, she eased the plectrum from where Bevan had left it between the strings and neck, and strummed, noticing how out of tune the guitar was, before returning it to its place against the bedside cabinet. Sitting on the edge of the bed, she looked about the room. Clothes, both clean and dirty, were piled on the floor. On top of the piles were shoes, cartons and CDs – everything she might have expected in such a pigsty. Only the guitar seemed out of place. It was a beautiful instrument, given to her many years before by her private music tutor.

She remembered her first lesson well. She had biked to her teacher's house and been invited in by a woman who appeared grey and tired. Shown into a small sunroom, she had sat alone, staring at the various instruments while waiting for Mr Turner, her tutor. Moments before he entered she had heard the toilet flush, and because of that she had felt awkward. Noticing that his fingers were on his belt, that he was in the process of threading the leather strap through the keeper on his pants, she had been even more shocked. Yet, nothing was to prepare her for what had followed. Smiling cheerfully, he had handed her a school exercise book, the first page of which was filled with the words and chords for 'Rock my soul in the bosom of Abraham'. It was only when he noticed her blush that he had paused to ask what was wrong. She hadn't been able say. Barely twelve, she'd felt too embarrassed to explain that the word 'bosom' was the problem. She'd managed to stammer only that she had never played before, that this was her first lesson and she had no idea what a chord was. What's more, she had no guitar.

Only her last comment had made any impact on Mr Turner. Genuinely surprised that she had turned up to lessons guitar-less, he had asked how she intended to practise without one. It had been almost too much for Maggie. She would have left then and there but she knew that her lessons – all eight of them – had been paid for in advance. They had been a special gift from her mother and so she had to stay and see them through.

A year passed before Mr Turner gave her the guitar she still had today. Following that first dismal lesson, when she had strummed hesitantly at the tune but remained too shy to sing, Mr Turner had lent her an old three-quarter-sized instrument. She'd had to buy new strings but that guitar had kept her company through many months. By the end of term she was obsessed with the instrument, spending what little free time she had shut away in her room practising barre chords and variations on strumming. Progress was slow but she had felt encouraged by Mr Turner, and on the anniversary of her very first lesson he had handed her a new guitar, saying she had worked hard and deserved a better instrument.

That had been the last time she had seen Mr Turner. While practising for the following week's lesson, she had been called out of her room and told by her mother that her lesson had been cancelled. No reason was given. The next week the same thing happened. And the next. Then one day a cheque arrived in the mail. Addressed to her mother, a brief note written in pencil informed them that Mr Turner would no longer be available to take lessons. A refund was enclosed but there was nothing by way of explanation. Of the whole baffling episode, only a short postscript reading 'Keep the guitar' seemed clear and straightforward.

Even now Maggie had no idea why her lessons had come to such an abrupt halt. Neither her mother nor father contacted Mr Turner. They had accepted what had happened – and that was that. Maggie sent Mr Turner a note thanking him for the instrument, but she did not attempt to see him. After a few more months, she gave up playing altogether.

Looking at the guitar now, she realised that it was one of the few things of any value she possessed. Years ago she had seen a similar one in a shop in town and had been amazed by its price tag. New, the instrument had cost more than five hundred dollars – an amount that seemed all the more remarkable given that it was several hundred dollars more than the only other things of value she owned: her engagement and wedding rings. That evening she had gone home and polished the instrument with furniture wax, vowing to take better care of it in the future. She hadn't, of course. The fact that it had been left in Bevan's damp and untidy shed proved that.

Suddenly annoyed by the filth in Bevan's room, she stood up, and grabbing armfuls of clothes, CDs and litter, flung everything through the door and onto the lawn outside. Breathing deeply, she took a seat once more on the edge of the bed. Lifting the guitar back to her knee, she glanced around, feeling at ease in the small, uncluttered space she had created. It would be nice, she thought, to move in here herself. She could leave the house to the kids and spend her evenings out here, alone in peace and quiet. She could put a lock on the door to prevent anyone from coming in and disturbing her. She'd wallpaper the room, make it more homely – more like a small crib than a shed. Above the door she could nail a sign reading 'The Retreat', or something similar.

She carefully arranged her fingers across the strings and strummed an F. The chord plunked, but she pressed down harder and tried again, before moving her fingers down a fifth. Once more the plunk sounded. Ignoring it, Maggie continued, working her way slowly through the chord changes while silently singing the words of Tim's song in her head. She recalled the way Tim's foot had tapped the beat as he sung. She had noticed that movement in particular because it was strange to see someone in a wheelchair moving his foot. Seeing Tim in a wheelchair each day had become so familiar that she had forgotten his legs were not paralysed.

Her own foot tapped the rhythm, and she began to sing out loud, the chords trailing behind as her fingers failed to keep pace with her voice. She sang the song twice more, then stood up and went outside. Gathering together her son's shoes and discs she flung them back into the shed, watching as they fell on his bed and floor. Collecting his dirty clothes she walked back to the house and placed them in the laundry bin before returning to the garden, where she picked up the last pieces of litter and stuffed them into the rubbish. Finally, dragging the wheelie bin down the drive, she hesitated a moment, looking down the road as if expecting someone. In the distance she could see the neon sign flickering above the fish and chip shop, but, apart from a dog several houses away, the street was devoid of life. Deserted.

A DULL TWANG sounded from the guitar. For the past five minutes or so Tim had been struggling to control the instrument. But now his fingers appeared to have lost all their strength. His hands fell to his lap, and though he fixed his gaze on them, willing them to work, there was no change. He was clearly frustrated, and the atmosphere in the room grew tense as he waited.

Watching from the corner of the room where she stood folding washing, Maggie found she could maintain her silence no longer. 'That must be incredibly annoying,' she said. She immediately regretted her remark. She'd intended it to appear spontaneous and sympathetic, no more than a passing observation. Somehow, she had misjudged the tone of her voice and her comment had come out all wrong. It came across as something she might have said to one of her children – Bevan, in particular. A remark which, to her ears – and from the look on Tim's face, his too – sounded impatient, critical.

Tim glared at her. So hostile was his expression that Maggie retreated, stepping back from the pile of washing and apologising as she did so. Had Tim not been in a wheelchair she would have felt threatened.

For several seconds she stood, waiting for something to happen. The silence in the room was eased only by the sound of rain on the roof. The downpour was so heavy the gutters overflowed and a torrent could be heard splashing against the concrete path outside the window. As the rain strengthened, the room became increasingly gloomy; so much so that when looking at Tim, Maggie was reminded of a picture of an animal crouching and cornered in the back of a cave. The only difference between Tim and, say, a bear, thought Maggie, was that Tim had a guitar on his knee. The thought of a guitar-playing bear made Maggie smile. She knew it had as much to do with nerves as anything else but she couldn't control what she was thinking, and as the image of a country-and-western-playing bear took hold in her brain, she grinned. She attempted to regain her composure, but even as she turned away from Tim and bit the inside of her cheek she began to giggle.

There was nothing funny about the situation she had found herself in. If anything, she was making things worse. She knew that and yet she was powerless to stop. It was only when she glanced back at Tim and realised that his rage had been replaced by hurt that she at last managed to control her laughter. Ashamed, she wiped at her eyes and tried to think of some way to explain what had happened. Nothing, she thought, would make much sense to Tim. She cleared her throat and apologised. She offered no explanation, choosing instead to steer the conversation towards some neutral territory – music.

'Last night,' she began, 'I tried to play your song . . .' She tried to imagine how she might convey the sense of peace and well-being she had experienced while sitting on Bevan's bed. She explained she hadn't played for years and that she found the tune far too complicated. Despite that, she had enjoyed playing and, more than that, she had forgotten about everything else – even Storm who was sitting alone in the house watching television. The thing she would have liked to get across to Tim was that when she had left the shed and gone outside and seen all the stuff she had tossed out on the lawn, she had been surprised. She had no recollection of having thrown anything out. Seeing everything scattered over the ground had forced her to re-enter the world – a less beautiful world than the one she had inhabited only minutes before. It was really strange, she wanted to explain. The music, the song – Tim's song – had allowed her to go somewhere far away, and she didn't understand.

Maggie shook her head. She hadn't explained it. There was something more. The song was about death, about vanishing off the face of the earth. It was an idea that made her uneasy. 'Sorry. I know I'm not very good at putting my thoughts into words. I don't spend much time thinking about deep stuff like that. There's always too much to do . . .'

Tim looked at her. 'What do you have time to think about?' he asked, his voice emotionless.

Maggie shrugged. She didn't know. Her kids, she supposed. Work, shopping, housework, family, Carol. How to get through each day without going crazy.

Tim gave the impression he found her response unsatisfactory. He put the question to her once more. Maggie cringed. She didn't like to talk about herself. Describing her life made her feel like she was boring. Nothing she had done was exceptional, or interesting. She hadn't achieved much. She was like everyone else in her family, in her street – she took care of her kids and she worked. But, she thought, at least I am a good worker.

She began to apologise, but Tim stopped her. 'No,' he said, 'Tell me. What about Justine? For instance.'

His interest was so genuine that Maggie was reminded of her priest. During reconciliation she had found herself in a similar situation. Then, as now, she would sit opposite a man and talk and he would listen. It was that simple. Looking at Tim, she felt she could trust him. Whatever she said to him would go no further than the room, she was sure of it. Frowning, she shook her head, sighing, 'Justine . . .' She shrugged and took hold of a tea towel, which she began to fold into quarters.

'She struck me as having a lot of energy,' said Tim. 'The way she moved about—'

'Yeah,' interrupted Maggie, 'She can never sit still. Stand up, sit down, stand up again – that's Justine.'

Tim lowered his eyes. The room fell quiet.

'I used to hate mowing the lawns,' he suddenly said.

'Yeah, me too,' responded Maggie, 'I can usually get Bevan to do . . .' She stopped, looked away and then, biting her lip, glanced back at Tim.

'Bevan? Is that your son? I haven't heard that name before.'

Maggie picked up another tea towel.

'How old is he? What does he do?'

Maggie kept her eyes on the washing, taking the remaining items one by one and folding them tightly. 'Bevan's a teenager,' she said, not looking at Tim. 'He's at school.'

'What does he look like?' asked Tim.

Maggie shrugged, her brain working overtime as she tried to figure out how best to answer. 'Like his father, I suppose.'

'Boys can be hard work at that age,' murmured Tim, 'At least they were at the school where I taught.'

Maggie shuffled.

'They usually turn out all right,' continued Tim. He smiled at Maggie, and then asked, 'Do you think he could cut my grass? I'd pay him. Maybe he could clean the gutters, too?'

Maggie froze.

'Even though I hated doing the lawns,' Tim sighed, 'I'd give anything to be able to do them now.'

'Yeah,' said Maggie, 'I wish you could, too.'

Tim was no longer facing her but had turned to the window. Seen in profile against the grey sky, he appeared gaunter than the last time she had seen him. In her mind, he was stockier than he was in reality. Weeks before, she had imagined him as a tradesman or a fisherman, but now, seeing him like this, he appeared too frail to have ever been capable of any physical occupation. She saw him brush his cheek and then, lowering his head, he rubbed his eyes as if he were a child ready for bed. He glanced back towards her. 'I'm tired.'

Maggie nodded. 'Shall I take you to your room?'

His lips curling into a wry smile, he asked, 'What would you do in my position?'

The question took Maggie by surprise, confused her. Whatever his train of thought, she hadn't followed.

'I'm in my mid-forties,' continued Tim. 'In a month's time, two months' time . . . do I book myself into a rest home? Do I spend the next thirty years of my life "in care", being wheeled out each morning to sit in a communal lounge with people twice my age, or do I . . . ? What would you do in my position?'

'I don't know,' replied Maggie, 'I haven't really thought about it—'

'Well,' interrupted Tim, his voice bitter, 'I think about it all the time.'

As Maggie drove away, she felt uneasy. When she'd left, Tim was asleep in his room. She'd wanted to go in and check on him. If only she had more time she could have stayed. She could have cooked him a proper meal and sat with him a while, listened to music – even tried to sing his song once more. She'd never been in his position but she knew what it was like to feel abandoned. In her mind's eye, she could picture him lying flat on his bed, his eyes open and fixed on the ceiling. She could see the room become gloomier, the greys deepen and she could hear the wind whistle through the gap in the window frame. It was an eerie sound, one that startled you the first time you heard it. After a while the noise subsided, becoming like a kettle reaching the boil before cutting out and then suddenly reheating once more. The sound would continue as long as the wind blew and if one were to focus on it, it would be possible to feel trapped by it. With the strong gusts, Tim's house shook. Facing south, it took the full impact of the wind. Stretched out on his bed, Tim would experience every shudder, every creak and, alone, he had nothing to do except listen and wait for it to go away. He hadn't given in to his illness, but it seemed he believed in nothing. And, as far as Maggie was concerned, that was as good as having nothing to live for.

In the main street of Riverton, Maggie pulled over. She did a U-turn, and drove back to Tim's house. She'd been gone less than a quarter of an hour. Her windscreen began to mist over, and she could barely make out the faint shadowy structure of Tim's front room. Winding down the driver's window to allow a gap for fresh air, she remembered she had to call in on Mr Paxton before collecting Storm from school. She had planned to take him something for afternoon tea, but now that she was held up here she wouldn't have time to shop – not unless she called in on him after collecting Storm. Storm wouldn't mind. It wouldn't be the first time he'd been dragged along to one of her clients and, in fact, he might enjoy himself. Mr Paxton's house would be cosy on a day like this and perhaps, if he was in the mood, he'd teach Storm the basics of chess. Now that there was a chess club at school, it would be nice if Storm learnt the game. He was, Maggie thought, the kind of kid who would do well at a game like that. It was far more his style than, say, basketball or table tennis.

A man walked by. Despite being dragged along by a dog, he had to lean into the wind in order to make progress. One big gust, thought Maggie, and he'd lose his balance and get blown back a step. There was no way Tim would go outside in these conditions. In this wind it was unlikely he'd be strong enough to open the door to his car, let alone close it after himself. It was far more likely that after his nap he'd get up, make himself a sandwich, and listen to some music. After twenty minutes or so he might even regain enough energy to give his guitar another go. That would keep him occupied for most of the evening. Then, next time he saw her, he would ask her to perform the song and, she hoped, he might record her and send the tape in to that competition he was talking about.

Maggie struggled out of the driver's seat and eased the door shut behind her. She walked up to the garage, checking that the man with the dog was out of view. She reached down and took hold of a railway sleeper that edged the path near the back door. It was heavier than she had imagined. Dragging it towards the garage, she could feel her back strain from the weight. She tried to manoeuvre it between the front of Tim's parked car and the door of the garage. She imagined she looked like a gangster dragging a heavy sack containing a corpse towards a shallow grave. What she was doing suddenly struck her as so odd that, despite the pain which was spreading from her lower back to her shoulders, she began to smile. The sleeper thudded to the ground in front of the car wheels, and she straightened, admiring her work. No one would drive over that in a hurry. She felt happier now than she had all day.

$\mathcal{M}$AGGIE WOKE with a start. Someone was standing near the end of her bed. Taller than Storm, the person hesitated, glanced around the room and then tip-toed towards the chair where Maggie's bag was perched. Maggie watched as the man – for she could see it was a man – reached for her belongings. Her heart beating wildly, she saw him remove her cellphone. To her amazement, he appeared to check the time, before returning the phone to her bag and pulling out her purse. Maggie lay quietly, her eyes following his every move as he fumbled inside her purse. Only then did it occur to her that his behaviour was odd. Why didn't he just take the whole purse? And wasn't there something familiar about the way he stood and slouched? Less afraid, she edged her hand from under the covers and switched on the bedside lamp. In the seconds it took to adjust to the light she detected a flurry of movement, and there, staring back at her, his eyes wide with surprise, was Bevan.

Before Maggie could ask her son to explain what he was do-ing, he began to mumble something about not wanting to wake her. The absence of apology in his voice grated. Minutes ago she had been fearful but now, face to face with the source of her fear, she felt irritated by her son's nerve. It was as if his decision to come into her room during the early hours of the morning was not only acceptable, but of no significance. Bevan repeated he'd not wanted to waken her, that he needed the money for school and that he had forgotten to mention it earlier because his mind had been elsewhere – on his homework assignment. Had he fallen silent before mentioning the word 'homework', Maggie might have found it in her heart to give him the benefit of the doubt. Knowing he had spent less than fifteen minutes with his books open cemented her anger. Her voice steady, she asked what, *exactly*, the money was for? Standing awkwardly, Maggie's purse in his hand, Bevan shifted from one foot to another, muttering something about 'stuff'. Fully awake and disinclined to let the matter drop, Maggie probed deeper, asking how much money he needed. She continued that it was strange that none of his teachers had let him know how much was required for 'school stuff'. He shrugged and when he raised his eyes from her purse there was a hint of defiance in his gaze.

'You've only got five bucks, anyway,' he sneered.

Maggie ordered him to put the purse down. Watching him turn to walk from the room, she was overwhelmed by a desire to leap from her bed and drag him back. 'I haven't said you could go, yet,' she said.

Stillness came over the room. Maggie was aware of her heart, a thudding in her ears. As each second passed her mind raced, repeating, what will you do if he ignores you and leaves the room?

She had no answer. When Bevan turned to look at her a wave of relief flooded through her. 'What do you want now?' he asked. 'It's late. I need to sleep.'

Maggie gestured towards her bed, and asked her son to sit down. He shuffled awkwardly, refused her invitation and stood waiting. Surprised when she said nothing, he offered an apology, adding, 'I would have asked, honest. But I forgot.'

It didn't take much imagination to understand why Bevan needed the money. In the past fortnight he had lost two regular lawn-mowing jobs. One family had moved to Christchurch, and the other could no longer afford to pay the fifteen dollars he charged. Desperate for cash, he had approached his Aunt Carol for gardening work, but she had turned him down, saying one employee in the family was as much as she could handle. His father had been just as bad. It didn't help that he didn't have a lawn – his front garden being nothing more than an asphalt parking area rented out to the panel-beating company next door. Even Elsie and Murray had been unable to help. Bevan had driven out to see them but they hadn't cottoned on to the reason for his visit. They had invited him to come in, offered him scones and tea, and chatted about school, the weather and even his new car. Not once, Bevan complained, did they ask how he was off for money. 'You'd have thought, being grandparents, they would have given me something. I know they love gardening and do their own lawns but even so it wouldn't have killed them to give me a few bucks – seeing as I was nice enough to visit.' The return trip to Winton had pretty much used up every last drop of petrol. He had barely made it back to town.

Brightening slightly, he mentioned that Scott might have something down at the service station. He was thinking of increasing business hours, in which case Bevan might be able to pick up some work, if he was lucky.

'You could sell your car,' suggested Maggie.

Bevan shook his head. 'I need it.'

Again the room fell quiet, the only sound coming from the radio in Storm's room. Like Lisa, he now preferred to sleep with a radio playing. Sometimes, awake in the night, Maggie would find herself listening to the jumble of sounds coming from their rooms, the soft classical music from Lisa's transistor competing with the talk-back station Storm preferred. With her own radio tuned to the country station, Maggie was surprised her ears didn't shut down in protest. Moreover, since Bevan had been given the car, there had been an additional noise to contend with – the booming base from his car stereo as he returned home from his late-night jaunts around town.

Hesitating before raising the subject, Maggie asked if Bevan remembered the man in the wheelchair. She was certain her son would not recognise him by anything other than 'the man in the wheelchair'. Instantly on guard, Bevan shrugged. 'Might do.'

Tempted to let the matter drop, Maggie waited. But hearing Bevan ask why she wanted to know, she mentioned the offer of lawn-mowing and gutter-cleaning work. She asked if Bevan might be interested.

'How much?' asked Bevan.

Maggie frowned. Given her son's involvement in 'the incident', she thought he might be a little less demanding. In fact, if anything, he should consider volunteering his services. Bevan only laughed, responding that the 'wheelchair man', as he continued to call him, didn't know him from a bar of soap. As far as the victim was concerned, he could have been a passer-by, someone who helped him back into his chair *after* the incident.

'He never even noticed me,' said Bevan. 'He was too busy fussing around with his legs and checking his bag to pay any attention to me. And anyway,' he added, slyly, 'I wasn't anywhere near him. I was in the car, remember?'

The slight change in detail – the hint that Bevan was nearby when Tim checked his bag – caught Maggie's attention. For the first time she felt suspicious about the role he had played in Tim's attack. Up to that moment she had believed that Bevan had remained alone in Todd's car but now she wasn't so sure. More uneasy than ever, she told Bevan to go to bed. But as he walked from her room she called him back and choosing her words as carefully as possible, asked, 'Did you have anything to do with the attack on Tim?'

'Tim?' her son responded, hearing the name for the first time. 'Nope,' he said, frowning, 'I had nothing to do with it.'

'Are you telling me the truth?' asked Maggie.

'Of course I am,' said Bevan, taking a step into the room. 'I'm not interested in beating up handicapped people, eh.' And then he was gone.

'OKAY,' SAID TIM, glancing up, 'I'm almost ready. All you have to do is stand here and sing. Direct your voice down.' He nodded, indicating the small microphone that was propped on top of a large pile of books.

Less than two days had passed since Maggie had last seen Tim and yet he seemed so much happier that it was difficult to believe he was the same man who had caused her concern during her last visit. Walking up the drive that morning, she noticed that the sleeper she had dragged in front of Tim's car was still in place. Now, thinking about what she had done, she felt foolish. Clearly he had been going through a bad patch but now he was on the way up again. Before she'd even had time to unpack his groceries, he'd hustled her into the lounge and shown her the 'recording studio', as he had jokingly referred to it. 'Things have changed a bit since your last visit,' he said, as if she had been away for some time. 'I'm not going to use the guitar but the Dobro, it's easier to handle.

It won't make much difference to you, but for me it's better.'

Pleased to see that he had got some of his spark back, Maggie smiled happily, forgetting for the moment her doubts concerning her own performance. It was one thing for him – someone who, by his own admission, frequently played at folk and country music festivals – to climb back on stage but it was quite another for her to do the same. However, such was Tim's enthusiasm that she felt she had no say in the matter. She would follow his lead and do what he said.

Watching as he struggled to get set up, Maggie had to control her desire to step in and help. She could see how much effort it was costing him to carry out the most simple of tasks. Small, fiddly adjustments which she would have completed in seconds were causing him a great deal of trouble. Raising the height of the microphone, which was balanced on top of a pile of books stacked on the table, took several minutes. Tim wheeled across the room to his bookcase, grabbed a few books, balanced them on his knee, and then, keeping them in place with his chin, rolled himself back to the table where, cautiously, he lifted them up onto the existing pile until he could reach no higher. Finally, gesturing towards the books, he asked Maggie to help. As she took each book, she glanced at its title, reading it aloud and pausing to listen as Tim explained where – or how – he had come by each volume. An anthology of New Zealand poetry caught her eye and, curious to learn where it had come from, she held it up for Tim to see. 'It was a gift,' he began, 'from the principal at my last school. She gave it to me when I left. I was a little surprised by her choice. It's not the type of book I'd imagine her buying.'

He held out his hand and took the book from Maggie, continuing, 'To tell the truth I suspect it was an unwanted Christmas present. She probably thought she could get away with passing it on to me. As you know, that's the kind of woman she is.'

Maggie started, 'What? What do you mean?' Confused, she snatched the book from Tim and opened it. There, in small, neat writing was the inscription, 'With thanks for your valuable service. Regards, Joanne Devon.'

Though she reread the message, Maggie couldn't place the woman's name.

'She spoke well of you,' said Tim, his lips curling into a faint smile. He paused, measuring the impact of his words on Maggie. He registered the look of puzzlement on her face, and his smile broadened. It was clear he was having fun, teasing her with these small snippets of information.

Maggie shook her head. She didn't know anyone called Joanne. Perhaps, once – at school – there had been a Joanne, but it wasn't a name that had entered her world in recent times. And then it hit her. Devon. Mrs Devon. A vision of crystal figurines swam into view, the countless rows of knick-knacks; and that boy, too, her son – the overweight kid who had slumped on the sofa snacking from a bowl of chips as she vacuumed around him.

'Mrs Devon!' cried Maggie. 'That doesn't make any sense. All she did was complain . . .'

Tim laughed out loud. 'Yeah, she's like that. Terrible people skills. It's a wonder she was ever appointed principal.'

He shrugged and took the book from Maggie's limp hand, adding, 'I bumped into her a while ago and mentioned I was looking for a new cleaner. She immediately took it upon herself to write down your name. Said you were competent.'

'Competent!' exclaimed Maggie. 'She hated me!'

Tim laughed. 'Well, join the club. She didn't like me much,

either. I guess she thought we deserved each other . . . '

Then, as the significance of Tim's words gained momentum, Maggie began to smile. She had not forgotten that he had originally asked for her, but she had always been too nervous to broach the subject with him. And, because Tim had never raised the issue, she had decided to keep quiet. The prospect of being confronted with an awkward situation didn't appeal to her. It was safer to say nothing. Because of her decision, she had always remained slightly on edge.

She recollected all the times she had caught Tim looking at her, frowning as he wondered aloud why her face looked familiar. Every time he had brought up the subject, she had frozen, anticipating the moment he would finally put two and two together and place her. She had been so sure he would eventually remember their meeting. She had even thought she should pre-empt his discovery and invent some other location, or some other opportunity where their brief encounter might have taken place. With luck she could trick him into thinking they had met elsewhere – at a concert, perhaps. She was hopeless at thinking on her feet and yet, try as she might, she hadn't been able to work out what she would say when he did, finally, spring her.

But maybe she shouldn't have been so worried.

Straightening the poetry volume on top of the pile of books, she started to hum and, catching Tim's eye, she beamed. She felt giddy from relief and excitement. She was going to sing for Tim and if she was any good, he'd enter the song in a competition. It was so cool. Nothing like that ever happened to women like her. From the look on Tim's face he had no idea why she was suddenly so happy. Puzzled, he smiled back, but quickly turned his attention to arranging the microphone.

'You know the tune, eh?' he asked, without looking up. 'Take it slowly, as I won't be able to keep up otherwise.' He gave a wry laugh and then wriggled back in his chair, lugging the Dobro onto his knee. 'Slowly,' he repeated and then, nodding his head, indicated the recorder and laughed. 'Let's rock this joint.'

The tape recorder running, Maggie felt her nerves return. She opened her mouth as Tim's introduction came to an end but she was aware of a tightness in her throat and before she knew what was happening, she missed her cue. Abruptly the music stopped. 'Not that slow,' murmured Tim. Maggie apologised, rewound the tape and indicated her readiness. Nothing happened. Glancing over to Tim, she saw that he had slumped in his chair and was staring at his left hand which had begun to shake, uncontrollably. In a low voice, he explained he'd lost his place. He wasn't sure where they'd got to. He gave an apologetic smile and then nodding his head, said, 'Oh, that's right.'

Seconds passed. Maggie didn't want to pressure Tim but she was worried that if they didn't get started, the opportunity to continue might slip away. They had come so far, she thought. She mentioned the name of the song competition and asked if he had ever entered it before. Distracted, Tim mumbled something about always being the runner-up. Then he raised himself in his chair.

Conscious that this might be her only chance, Maggie focussed on the beat, counting silently until Tim gave the signal to sing. As the first notes rang out, her confidence increased – it was no more difficult than the other night, alone in Bevan's room. With each bar, she was aware that Tim was losing time, and as the first verse eased into the second she found it difficult to follow his erratic playing. More than once she opened her mouth to sing but, hearing no accompaniment, checked herself and took up the tune a fraction later than intended. By the time they reached the third verse, the performance had become a shambles, and although she didn't want to be the one to call a halt, she could no longer keep track of either the music or the words. Her voice faded. A moment later Tim also stopped. Neither of them spoke.

The silence deepened, isolating them from each other. Maggie sat down and reached for a book which had been placed next to the stack supporting the microphone. She flicked through a few pages and then, noticing it was upside down, closed it, letting the palm of her hand rest on its faded blue linen cover. Avoiding Tim, she examined the marks on the table top: the circular stain from a red wine glass, faint scratch marks and then a deeper gouge which ended in a notch at the table's edge. The triangular dent was large enough for her fingernail and she picked at it absently, running her nail back and forth, increasing the depth of the scratch with each pass.

She needed to say something. She wanted to say something – anything that might suggest that what had happened wasn't so bad, that there was always another day – but the power of speech had deserted her. She was aware that Tim hadn't moved, that the Dobro was balanced across his knee and that, if nothing else, she ought to stand up and free him of its weight. But she didn't have the strength to move. Looking across the room towards the small window, she caught sight of a seagull which was being blown sideways by the force of the wind and, despite herself, she sighed.

A sound, a soft 'thunk', caught her attention and turning towards the sound she saw the Dobro had fallen to the floor. In the short time it took for her to stand up, Tim pushed down hard on the rims of his wheels and drove his chair hard against the instrument. Without looking up, he reversed several inches and then, grimacing with the effort, propelled himself forward, catching the edge of the Dobro under his wheel and shunting it an inch or so. Once more he reversed, this time putting more distance between him and the instrument before running at it. Transfixed, Maggie watched, dismayed, as his wheels once more struck the Dobro. Then, played out in gruelling slow motion, the wheel rose up off the ground and Tim began to topple. As he fell, his body twisted, sending him down on top of the Dobro, the neck of which splintered under his weight.

'What are you doing?' cried Maggie, aware even as she spoke that her question came too late, because whatever it was had already happened.

A cry – animal-like in its rawness – filled the room. Sobs, merging with the sound of the wind outside, grew in strength, buffeting Tim's shoulders as he drew his legs up to his chest and wrapped his arms around them, scrunching his body into a ball.

Nothing like this had ever happened to Maggie. She had dealt with distraught clients in the past, but never anything like this. It was as if some violent, invisible force had punched and kicked Tim to the ground. But then, as she listened, she thought, no – his cries are childlike, abandoned. Defining the sound made her feel more in control, more adult. She felt calm. Lowering to the ground, she lay down beside him and gathered him into her arms. Gently, she stroked his hair and whispered soothingly into the back of his neck, 'I've got you. It's all right.'

She had hoped he would calm down, but nothing she said seemed able to reach him. A feeling of panic began to overtake her. She fought to regain control. And then, finding that she had no more words of her own with which to comfort him, she began to softly hum.

$\mathcal{M}$R PAXTON was hunched over the newspaper, a magnifying glass held to his eye as he scanned the page before him. Hearing Maggie approach, he beamed and said, 'I'm checking to see if any of my friends are in here.' He stabbed at the obituary page. 'Four "peacefully" and one "suddenly".' He raised his eyes. 'You know, Maggie, when I fall off the twig, I want you to write "finally" in my column. At my age, it seems more appropriate than "peacefully", don't you think?'

Only half listening, Maggie smiled. She was pleased Mr Paxton appeared so well. During her last visit she had been worried about him. She had not raised the subject but she had noticed – while cleaning the toilet – that something was clearly amiss with his bowel motions. She did not, as a rule, *examine* the contents of his barely operational toilet but she could not help but notice that, on her last visit, his stool was streaked with blood. It was quite possible the old man was suffering from nothing more serious than haemorrhoids but, nevertheless, she had felt uneasy and had wondered if she should mention her discovery. Knowing that Mr Paxton was a private man, she had decided against it.

Although the visit was not scheduled, she had decided to look in on him. At home, earlier, she had been restless and uneasy. Her mind was overloaded, but when she tried, little by little, to separate all the fragments she felt no calmer than before. Unable to settle, she had begun to wipe out the kitchen drawers. As she worked, she heard a shuffling noise and looking up noticed Bevan enter the room. Rubbing the sleep from his eyes, he said, 'Hello' before nudging past her to reach the utensil drawer. He took the knife, and glanced up but, catching her eye, quickly looked away, staring at the ground as he crossed back to the bench, where he waited for his bread to toast.

It was then that the events from the previous day resurfaced from the shadows at the back of Maggie's brain. She turned to speak to Bevan, but at that moment Lisa entered the room and, unaware of the subdued atmosphere, sang a cheery 'Morning', before grabbing the milk from the fridge and resting her back against the bench. Her eyes flicked from Maggie to Bevan and her smile increased as she said, 'You gave Bevan a bit of a fright yesterday.' Maggie stopped cleaning and looked up in time to see Bevan's forehead furrow into a deep frown. 'He told me that when he turned up at that guy's house and saw the two of you lying on the floor, he'd thought you were . . . you know . . .'

'Shut up!' snapped Bevan. 'Shut up, that's not what I said. I said I got a shock.'

Lisa laughed, made a 'wooooooooo' noise and laughed again. 'That's what you told me!' she yelled after her brother as he marched from the room. 'Honest,' she said, smiling at Maggie, 'that's what he said.' Maggie didn't know whether she should go after the boy or not. She could see that he was still upset, but given what had happened, it was hardly surprising.

It was true she had been lying on the floor with her arm around Tim when Bevan appeared in the doorway. She remembered hearing a scraping noise and she had looked up to see his startled face, his eyes huge, as he stared down at her. Maggie had been equally surprised. Given that it was a weekday and mid-morning, she had expected him to be at school. It was only later that she had been able to make sense of his sudden appearance. He had bunked school but then, feeling bored and at a loose end, had decided to take up Tim's lawn-mowing offer and bowled up with the expectation of earning a few dollars before the weekend.

Rooted to the spot, he had taken a few moments to respond to Maggie's gentle plea for help. At first he had seemed confused, and she had had to repeat her request several times before he gave any indication of comprehension. 'Bevan,' she had said, 'Come and give me a hand. We need to lift Tim back to his chair.' At the mention of Tim's name her son had flinched, and for an instant Maggie had thought he was going to turn his back and retreat the way he had come. It was only as she said 'Please' that he'd taken his first hesitant, jerky steps towards them. He'd stopped a few feet short of where they lay and looked nervously about as if expecting the floor to open up and swallow him.

Realising that Bevan hadn't grasped the situation, Maggie had spoken softly once more, reassuring him, saying, 'It's all right. Tim lost his balance and fell – that's all.' She'd added, 'He's not hurt. He's all right.' The sound of her voice must have sparked something in Tim because at that moment he'd let out a faint cry, the kind of low groan made by a man caught at the bottom of a collapsed scrum. The sound had made Bevan jump. He had taken a step back and once more his eyes had opened wide as he'd regarded Tim's tightly curled body and the battered instrument next to him. Her manner calm, Maggie had tried again to catch her son's attention, but so intent was he on Tim, he hadn't noticed. He'd began to shuffle, shifting his weight from one leg to the other and then, aware of the noise he was making, had whispered, 'Why doesn't he get up?'

Maggie had been shocked by her son's response – by the fact he was so clearly shaken – but she had forced herself to think calmly. In her mind, she could hear the words, one step at a time, take it easy . . . nothing to worry about; but at the same time, part of her longed to run away. She had felt like a ten-year-old who, witnessing a younger brother fall from a tree, feels obliged to take on the role of the adult. She'd known this was the part she was meant to play, but even so her heart had been racing and a knot in her stomach tightening with each passing second.

'Come over here,' she'd murmured, her voice steady as she stood up. 'Now listen,' she'd smiled encouragingly at her son, 'I want you to put your hands around his shoulders and then, on the count of three, I want you to lift.' She'd been aware that Bevan nodded, but as she reached 'three', he had remained motionless. She'd waited a second, then prompted him, saying, 'Now, Bevan.'

In the following seconds she had noticed two things. The first was that Tim said and did nothing. She'd talked to him and explained they were going to get him back into his chair. She'd asked him to try to take some of his own weight – but he hadn't responded. It was as if, she'd thought, the part of his brain that should be able to comprehend had disengaged and become lost. No, she'd corrected herself, it was more than that. It was as if he was on the verge of dying and, anticipating the end, his soul had abandoned him. It was nowhere to be seen. Only a body, hollow but chained to the ground, remained.

The second thing was that Bevan no longer looked so much scared as stricken. His face had been grey like ash and his presence, like that of Tim, had been more illusion than real. Barely able to follow Maggie's instructions, he'd nevertheless managed to position himself behind Tim, hooking his arms under the larger man's shoulders as he had been told to do. 'On the count of three . . .' Maggie had repeated and, with a grunt, they'd both yanked Tim's prostrate body. Despite their effort, they had only managed to pull him into a sitting position. He was far heavier than Maggie had imagined. She remembered how she had mistaken him for a fisherman or a builder, and feeling the width of his shoulders, she had understood why she had thought that.

They'd tried once more but with no success, and Maggie had stepped back, puffing, and doubled over, her hands resting on her thighs as she'd tried to think of what to do next. She needed Tim to help – that was all. She'd caught her breath, and heard Bevan's voice, whispering close to her ear. Talking through the side of his mouth as if not wanting to draw attention to himself, he'd murmured, 'Todd's outside in the car.' Astounded, Maggie had drawn in a sharp intake of breath and slowly straightened up. Cautiously, Bevan had continued, 'He could come and help. It would make things a lot easier . . . an extra pair of hands.' His voice had faltered, and for a moment his face appeared to go cloudy and he'd bit his lip as he'd tried to regain control of his emotions.

Sickened at the mention of Todd's name, Maggie hadn't been

able to reply. But, seeing Bevan's lip begin to tremble, she'd softened. She'd shaken her head, offering no explanation. 'No.' Exhaling, she had looked up and added, 'Never.' She'd half expected to hear Bevan press the point but, to her relief, he had said nothing.

She had crouched beside Tim. She'd tried again to coax him into a standing position. On television she had seen images of ambulance drivers crouched in a similar way beside crash victims. She'd wondered if they were any more successful than she was. There was something so chilling about Tim's gaze that she had shuddered. She'd turned back to Bevan, but he'd been in no state to offer any more suggestions. Despite his silence, he had been pleading with her to do something, to make things better . . . to make it go away.

Scared that Todd might appear at any moment, she'd begun to speak calmly, telling Bevan what to do. Nodding dumbly, the boy had approached and took Tim under the arms. On Maggie's instruction he had lifted. As he'd taken Tim's weight, Bevan had grunted and then in a low voice murmured, 'I'm sorry.' He had said it again, 'I'm sorry,' and then, like floodwaters washing away a barrier of packed sand, words tumbled from him, 'I'm sorry, I didn't think. It wasn't even my idea. I've got a phone. I didn't want yours. I didn't know they would go that far . . .' Maggie snapped at him to stop. Tim was back in his chair. That was all that mattered.

Once Tim was settled in bed, they had wandered back to the lounge, where both mother and son stood awkwardly looking down at the small splinters of wood that littered the floor. Bevan, Maggie had noticed, no longer looked shocked or scared. In fact, in the minutes since returning to the lounge, his expression had hardened and his manner had become vaguely hostile. Skirting the events of the last fifteen minutes, he'd said, 'Todd came with me because I didn't want to risk being caught driving alone. I needed a licensed driver next to me.' His explanation had sounded like an accusation, but Maggie had said nothing.

They'd stood a minute longer, and then Maggie had broken the silence. 'You should go.'

It was only then that she'd caught a return of fear in her son's eyes. His voice hoarse, he had seemed to falter, before asking, 'Will you be okay?' Maggie had nodded but, unconvinced, Bevan had continued, 'You should stay with him – Tim – a bit longer. Make sure he doesn't have a relapse – or another fit.'

Maggie had tried to smile but she didn't have the energy. Exhausted, she'd gestured towards the road and replied, 'You go. I'll follow soon.'

She had watched as her son shuffled uncertainly from one foot to the other, then, as if making up his mind, he'd glanced up and, holding her gaze, said, 'He couldn't do much, eh? He was pretty helpless . . .' His voice had been harsh and carried a note of disdain. As he spoke, Maggie had seen him straighten, pulling his shoulders back until his chest lifted. He'd reminded her of a schoolboy scrabbling to his feet after losing a playground fight. He'd turned to go. He had walked steadily from the room, but as he reached the ramp leading to the path he'd lost his balance and tripped. It had been barely enough to throw him, and he'd regained control almost immediately. But Maggie had seen it and she saw, too, that by the time he passed the window his head was bowed and his hands thrust deep into his pockets.

$\mathcal{M}$AGGIE FOUND a parking place close to where she was to meet Lisa in town. They had planned to have coffee together – Maggie's treat – and then do a bit of shopping. Early, she sat quietly, staring at the backs of her hands as they rested on the steering wheel. After a morning spent cleaning, her skin was blotchy and red. When she turned her hands over to inspect her palms, she noticed a lacework of lines criss-crossing her skin. Where her skin was particularly dry, the lines were white – as if someone had rubbed chalk over her fingers and palms. Absently, she wondered if hands were like trees. Was it possible to tell someone's age by counting the marks?

Through the rear-view mirror, she noticed a parking warden making her way along the pavement towards her car. The warden moved slowly, dipping in and out of view as she checked each car's windscreen for registration and warrants. The warden was several cars away, and Maggie had time to move, but she stayed where she was, her eyes flicking from her hands to the mirror and back to her hands again. With her attention focussed once more on her hands, her mind began to wander. She thought about Angela, the young beauty therapist with the perfect nails and soft, even-toned skin. She imagined what it would be like to have a manicure. The thought of someone fussing around with her hands made her uneasy. It was too intimate. Where would you look, she wondered?

Maggie glanced up and caught sight of the warden. She realised, then, that she had been so lost in thought that she had forgotten all about her. She ought to move the car. She dropped her gaze and, although she intended to start the engine, she hesitated. Her thoughts strayed, recalling Mrs Devon's puffy white hands and the way the fat on her fingers had rolled up around her gold rings. It looked like her rings were never removed. Mrs Devon's fingers were doing their best to grow around the tight bands – much like the bark of a tree over a too-tightly wound length of wire. Why was she thinking about hands and trees?

A tap on her windscreen startled her. Glancing up she saw the parking warden looking down at her. The woman's nose was almost touching the glass. Maggie could see into her nostrils, the fine crop of hairs – which looked like spider silk – protruding. The warden smiled, and Maggie smiled back. A few seconds passed and the warden's smile, Maggie noticed, seemed to hang on the woman's face. Then her lips straightened and her smile faded, and it was the wrinkles around her eyes that caught Maggie's atten-tion. The warden raised her eyebrow, and straightening up took a step towards the driver's door and tapped on the window. Maggie smiled again. She'd buy some hand cream, she thought. She'd take Lisa to H & J's and she'd buy some hand cream for herself and her mother. It could be her Mother's Day gift. Nothing flashy. Her mother would be embarrassed if she thought Maggie had spent too much money.

In any case, spending money and going over the top was Carol's thing – not hers. Carol had booked a restaurant and organised the family to put in for a gift. And, as usual, she had complained about Maggie's modest contribution.

Maggie could hear her sister's voice, the note of disapproval as she berated her, saying it was not enough, that this year she wanted to make a big fuss of Elsie, buy her a 'weekend escape' to a hotel in Te Anau or Queenstown. Aware of her sister's unsmiling face, however, Carol had given up. It was clear that Maggie would not be moved. There would be no weekend package, not this year.

Maggie started. The parking warden hadn't moved. The woman's face had tightened into an angry frown. She had her pad out and was writing something. As Maggie watched, the woman turned her head like a swimmer taking a breath, and then turned once more to the notebook in her hands. She must be writing quickly, thought Maggie, because she expects me to get out of the car and start an argument. She probably wants to avoid confrontation. Maggie sighed. She knew she should get out and talk to the warden but she didn't want to. What she wanted was to be left in peace so that she could think. Why was it that every time she tried to spend a few minutes alone, someone would come along and disturb her? She needed some time to herself, that was all.

An item on the news the night before had caught her attention. Not the story itself – which had been about the number of thefts of copper from power lines – but the images accompanying the story. There, in all his glory, standing atop a long ladder was

Ross. Although he was doing something to the wires, his actions appeared staged. It was as if he had been asked to play the part of a linesman – as if someone behind the camera had directed him to go up a ladder and give the impression of replacing the copper, or whatever it was he was meant to do. The scene, with the reporter in the foreground and Ross on his ladder behind him, had made Maggie laugh. It was bizarre. At one point she'd almost expected Ross to raise his fingers into a peace sign and hold his hand up in the air, the way kids made rabbit ears above a presenter's head during netball games or Christmas parades. Stealing copper was no laughing matter. The thieves were risking their lives, said the presenter. It was only a matter of time before someone got hurt. Seriously hurt – or killed.

The warden's nose was up against the windscreen. Maggie could see her enlarged pores. Although she had slipped the ticket under the windscreen wiper with a thwack, the warden avoided making eye contact with Maggie. She must think I'm a lost cause, thought Maggie. Sitting here like a dummy, doing nothing.

Suddenly, her thoughts sharpened. No longer wandering from one topic to the next, her mind latched onto one image: that of the street, her immediate surroundings. It happened here, she thought. This is where it happened. Right here. It was all so clear. One minute Tim had been negotiating the footpath and the next he had been surrounded by a group of teenage boys – her own son's mates – maybe even Bevan, himself? It must have taken only seconds for the boys to grab the chair, tip Tim over, snatch his phone. Then what? Did they see the startled look on his face and laugh? Maggie could picture the scene so clearly. She could imagine Todd's response to Tim's humiliation. He would have *enjoyed* it. Todd would have felt like the king of the world:

standing over Tim, mocking him, calling him a 'fucking cunt' as the other boys stood back, watching, loving every minute of it. Was that what Tim was to them? A stupid, helpless 'cunt'?

The anger Maggie felt rose in her throat, choking her. She glanced around. *Here*, she thought again. On this street, in this town, where I live. It happened here. Unable to contain her rage, she opened her mouth wide and yelled, 'You monsters!' Flinging open her car door, she exploded, 'You disgusting little creeps! How dare you! How dare you treat a man like that!'

From the corner of her eye, she caught sight of the ticket slipped beneath the wiper. Incensed, she grabbed it, crumpled it into a tight ball and hurled it to the ground. Trembling, she spun around, ready to take on the group of boys she could see so vividly in her imagination. The pavement was deserted. Her heart pounding, she turned back and glimpsed the warden running away, her feet tripping in her haste to escape

Maggie sobbed. She thought she was going to be sick. She swallowed, then breathed deeply, exhaled slowly and swallowed again. Tears pooled in the corner of her eyes and she swiped at them with the back of her red, mottled hand.

Maggie stood motionless.

A long 'Sssssh' escaped from her lips as she tried to calm down. Seconds passed and still she did not move. Once more she looked at her hands, noticing a thin white scar which ran from her knuckle to the base of her thumb. She couldn't remember what had caused it; some childhood accident, something that had taken place long ago. She traced the line with her fingertip and then, crouching down, she retrieved the ticket from the gutter and stuffed it into her pocket.

$\mathcal{E}$VEN BEFORE STEPPING out of her car, Maggie sensed that Tim wasn't home. His house appeared empty, hollow. There were no signs of movement within. Worried about him, she had rushed coffee with her daughter in order to be here, and now she felt foolish. Yet, even here, she could not shake the image of him lying on the ground from her mind. It was an image that had haunted her throughout the day; so much so that she had had to abandon Lisa and drive out to Riverton. She needed to check up on him, convince herself that everything was all right.

As she walked up the driveway, she noticed the empty space where his car was normally parked and she glanced back towards the road, as if expecting to see him drive in at any moment. She should have warned him that she was coming. It was crazy to turn up unannounced, especially when she had so much to do before driving all the way over to Winton to collect Storm from her mother's. More annoying, she'd forgotten to pack the bottling jars Elsie had asked for. She must have left them on the kitchen bench. But it would take too long to go back for them now. She suddenly remembered she had seen jars on the shelves in Tim's garage. Perhaps she could take those. She would ask him when he came in. Her visit needn't be a completely wasted journey.

There was a spare house key hidden under a smooth grey boulder by the glass-panelled side door to his garage. He wouldn't mind if she let herself in and made a cup of tea while she waited. Who knows, if he was feeling well enough to drive, he might be willing to give their song another go. But even if he wasn't strong enough, he might agree to teach her how to play the accompaniment on one of his guitars. She smiled. Why hadn't she thought of that before, she wondered? It might take a few lessons but she was sure she'd get the hang of the tune, sooner or later. Hadn't she already given it a go at home? If she could master the basics alone, then there was a good chance she'd progress quite quickly. With practice.

The house was cold. It was so like Tim not to bother with the heater. More than once she'd felt cold in his house – even though he complained of the heat. It was to do with his illness, she thought. Conditions like multiple sclerosis did funny things to a person, making them feel hot when everyone else was cold, or tired when everyone else was starting to get going for the day.

There were no dishes stacked on the table. Apart from a mug, there was nothing. Usually when she turned up at his house, there was a pile of unwashed plates, bowls, frying pans – you name it – all waiting to be washed. But then she'd never been to his house during the weekend. Most likely one of his music buddies had called around and done a quick tidy up before taking him out for the day. They were probably sitting in a pub listening to some group. She could see him, propped up in his chair, a glass of orange juice in one hand, an unlit cigarette in the other as he waited for a break in the music before going outside for a smoke. She'd often caught him sitting at the open front door, gazing out across the road towards the sea. Not long ago he had called out to her and gesturing towards what looked like a swarm of black mosquitoes far off in the distance had told her they were titi. Only after he had added 'muttonbirds' had she realised what he was talking about.

As a child he had once been taken to Taukihepa, Big South Cape Island, by a distant relative who had harvest rights. It was his job, he said, to wax the birds. Maggie hadn't followed, so he'd described the process to her. After plucking, the birds were dropped into a vat of molten wax floating on hot water. Once the wax cooled on the birds it cracked, and it was his job to peel it off. That was the way to get rid of the down and small pin feathers that remained after plucking – by waxing.

He had sat gazing out to sea a while longer. It was clear from his expression that he didn't want to say much more. He hadn't been in the mood to tell her about his childhood, where he had lived or what else he had done, and Maggie hadn't asked. All the same, it had struck her that she knew very little about him. Though she cleaned for him, washed his dirty laundry and cooked the occasional meal, she knew almost nothing about his previous life.

If she opened the front door now, Maggie knew she would see a pile of discarded butts littered around the veranda and scattered among the shrivelled rose bushes in the garden border. She didn't liked the way Tim smelled. He had taken up smoking after becoming ill, he told her. It helped calm his nerves. Like most people, he knew smoking was unhealthy, but he didn't feel it mattered that much in his case. He was probably right, but she'd told him to stop.

Wandering into his bedroom, she went to the window and glanced down the road, hoping to spot his car. It was always musty in here. The room didn't get aired as much as the kitchen or the living room and the smell lingered. It seemed strongest near the curtains and the bedspread. The bed was unmade. She hadn't expected it any other way. The weight of his sheets and blankets was too much for him. He always left the bed in a mess but he never forgot to thank her for making it. He thanked her all the time. He was aware of everything she did for him, and several times a day he would say 'thank you'. Sometimes he said it too often. She'd told him not to worry – that most of her clients didn't bother thanking her until she left at the end of the day – and some, people like Mrs Devon, didn't bother even then. It wasn't as if her own kids even thanked her either. Only Mr Paxton, she had told him, made the effort to show his appreciation – but then, he was an old man with old-fashioned manners. She had used the word 'old-fashioned' and it had made Tim smile. She had felt embarrassed then, for implying Tim was also old-fashioned, and, without thinking, had covered her mouth with her hand and looked away. It was strange how her teeth made her doubly self-conscious whenever she felt embarrassed about something else. At least she no longer had a moustache to worry about – Angela had taken care of that.

Maggie smoothed her hand over the straightened bed, making sure the sheets were not tucked in too tightly. She gathered up the pillows and plumped them before replacing them at the head of the bed. There, she thought, it looks much better now. She hadn't meant to crumple the bed but suddenly she felt the need to lie down. She didn't think Tim would mind. Resting her head against the pillow, she stared up at the ceiling, listening to the waves breaking on the shore, anticipating the return of his car, or that of his friend – the sound as it slowed and stopped. He must be back soon, she thought.

She glanced at the clock-radio and realised that it was much later than she had imagined. Elsie would be beginning to wonder what had happened to her. She hoped Storm had behaved. There had been a few occasions recently when he had acted out of character, shoving her or, from what his teacher had told her, one of his school friends. 'It's not like Storm at all,' his teacher had explained, a look of concern on her face. 'Normally he's such a gentle boy, but recently . . .' And then she'd told Maggie that she'd had to send Storm from the room in order to take 'time out'. 'It's not like Storm,' she'd repeated and her voice, Maggie had noticed, had sounded almost apologetic.

The sound of a car drew closer, and Maggie sat up. Glancing towards the window, she waited for it to slow, to turn into the drive, and she swung her feet off the bed, taking a step towards the window before stopping. The car didn't slow. It wasn't Tim.

Returning to the living room, she switched on the light. Instantly the room looked more homely, but it was far too bright. She preferred the half gloom; it seemed more in keeping with waiting. Absently she picked up several cushions, shaking them gently before placing them neatly on the sofa. She noticed that the remote for the stereo was on the floor and picking it up she turned on the CD player. Nothing happened. There was no disc in the machine. She tried the radio but the voice which burst into the room was too noisy, so she flicked over to the tape deck. She didn't expect to hear anything – Tim rarely listened to tapes – but then, coming softly from the machine was a tune she knew. It took a second to recognise her own voice. She listened, her head cocked, as her halting voice carried the tune. She heard her voice hesitate, the accompaniment catch up and the strange connection between the two. Tim must have been listening to the song before he went out, she thought. He must have been playing it to himself, probably thinking about what changes he wanted to make before re-recording it next time. Her breath slowed as the song broke off, to be replaced by silence. She continued to listen. She heard a sound like someone flicking through the pages of a book and then, more faint, a sigh followed by a dull thud. She held her breath, waiting, and there, recorded on the tape, was the sound of Tim's wheelchair being driven into the fallen instrument. Another thud, louder than before and a crack as the body of the Dobro splintered. There was a crash and then, chilling her to the bone, a roar – a cry of pain and anguish – and then the sound of a scuffle and her own voice . . . and then the sound of humming, followed by silence. Nothing.

She walked to the tape machine, pressed eject and took the tape in her hands, reading the spidery writing on a thin strip of adhesive tape: 'For Maggie'. In that instant she glimpsed the future. She saw it as if looking sideways, as if taking it in without really trying. She saw it in the same way that she had noticed that the railway sleeper in front of the garage door had been knocked skew-whiff as if someone had taken a run and driven right over it. She glimpsed it as if it was something remote, shadowy, like the flash of the yellow bonnet of Tim's car or the empty driver's seat which she had seen earlier when she stooped to retrieve the house key from beneath the boulder by the side door to the garage. She recognised it as if it were no more than a flock of birds, a ragged line, flying far out to sea.

She felt the tape in her hand – the tape onto which Tim had written 'For Maggie' – and she knew that that was as much as she could ever expect now. There would be nothing more.

PART FOUR

'IT'S ALL RIGHT to feel sad.' Maggie glanced up at the sound of her daughter's voice. Although she had seen Lisa enter the kitchen and was aware of her helping Storm prepare for school, she hadn't consciously retained an image of her daughter's presence. So when Lisa spoke it had come as a surprise. Noticing her mother's shocked expression, Lisa continued, 'I could stay home. I wouldn't be missing much. I could spend the day with you, keep you company – if you like?'

'I'll stay home with you!' chipped in Storm. 'I don't mind.'

Maggie smiled and shook her head. 'No,' she said, 'I won't be here, anyway. I'm going out.'

Seizing the opportunity, Storm replied, 'We could come with you!'

Again Maggie shook her head. She felt an overwhelming desire to keep them with her – to make sure they were all right, that they were safe – but she knew she wouldn't. She didn't want to disrupt their day – besides which, they didn't need her protection.

'Are you planning to go to the funeral?' Lisa asked.

Maggie shrugged. She hadn't thought about it. Rather, she had thought about it but had discovered that trying to reach a decision was too difficult. She probably wouldn't. After all, she only worked for the man.

'It starts at three,' continued Lisa. 'I read the notice in yesterday's *Times* while I was at work last night. I could come with you . . .'

'No,' said Maggie, standing up. 'You get off to school.' Yet, even as she watched their two figures disappear down the drive, she had a strong urge to run after them and take them in her arms and tell them to 'take care'.

She rubbed her eyes and realised she was tired. She had barely slept. Bevan shuffled into the room but, seeing her, sidled out without talking. A moment later, he reappeared. 'You all right?' She nodded. She saw him frown and he opened his mouth to speak but then shrugged and went down the hall towards the bathroom. She heard the shower, and then Bevan was back, standing in the doorway, his expression immobile as he looked at her. Not knowing what he wanted, Maggie concentrated on the sound of hot water swirling down the drain. It drove her crazy the way Bevan turned on the shower before getting undressed or using the toilet. The words 'You're wasting hot water!' quivered on her lips, but she held her tongue. She waited, praying he would say something or return to the bathroom but, clearly, her anxiety about the hot water was not shared by her son. She heard him sigh and then slowly he gathered his thoughts and said, 'Do you think he knew – that day – that he was going to, you know . . .'

Maggie saw Bevan swallow hard and in that moment she felt

the floor dip beneath her feet. Carefully, she said, 'It had nothing to do with you – you understand that, don't you?'

Bevan said nothing.

'He had already made his mind up – long ago. Nothing we could have done would have made any difference . . .' Her voice cracked. She wasn't convinced by what she said either.

With Bevan's departure, the rooms in the house appeared to grow in size. She rattled about as she tidied away the breakfast dishes and got ready for . . . she didn't know what. Only last week she had been rushing to the supermarket to buy Tim's groceries before driving out to Riverton. Without a client, she didn't know what to do. The house was too quiet. She should call Justine. She'd been putting off speaking with her daughter but, reaching for the phone, she realised she couldn't cope with one of Justine's dramas. In truth, she didn't feel like talking to anyone. She'd rather be left alone. She wanted time to think.

As the morning progressed Maggie became more and more jittery. She had had only two cups of tea, and yet she felt as if she had been drinking mug after mug of strong black coffee. Not having eaten, her stomach was queasy; but more than anything she was restless. Sitting at home was driving her crazy. She had to get out and do something.

It took fifteen minutes to reach the car sales-yard. She hadn't visited this side of town since Bevan's competition but now she found herself outside the same dealership, her eyes scanning over the vehicles lined up in front of the showroom. All the cars, she noticed, had their bonnets raised. They looked disembowelled, brightly coloured, gleaming bodywork ripped open to reveal dark engine-innards.

Heaving her car door open, she felt the full force of the wind against her. From above her head, came the sound of metal clanging against metal. She looked up and noticed that a small karabiner fastened to the corner of a banner had worked free and was banging against the flagpole. How, she wondered, could anyone concentrate with that noise going on? But glancing around, the sales-yard appeared deserted. Perhaps no one did work there. Apart from her, the place was lifeless. Her phone rang but she made no attempt to answer it. Whoever it was could wait.

She opened the door of the third vehicle in the line, a yellow car, and climbed in behind the wheel. Her eyes rested on the raised bonnet which blocked out her view.

The car had both a CD player and a tape deck. That was good. There was a tap on the window, and turning, she caught sight of a man smiling at her. She frowned and then watched as he pulled open the door and popped in his head, asking, 'How are you doing?'

She shrugged. 'All right.'

He nodded and she noticed that his breath smelt of cigarette smoke. The smell reminded her of Tim.

'Are you in the market for a new car? This one just came in at the weekend – it's very tidy.'

'My friend had a yellow car.'

The man flinched, and his smile slipped. After a moment, he continued, 'It's a very safe colour. Do you have children?'

'Yes, three.'

'This is a good car – a very safe colour,' he repeated, reaching into his jacket pocket for a large handkerchief and blowing his nose. 'Would you like a test drive?'

Maggie shook her head. She was quite happy where she was. 'Are the tyres new?' she asked.

The man nodded but Maggie noticed he avoided her gaze. 'It's fitted with mags.'

'Like the wheels on Bevan's car?' asked Maggie coldly.

Disconcerted, the salesman tapped his fingers on the dashboard. He then took out his handkerchief and, with one corner, rubbed at a smear left by his fingers. He didn't have a clue what she was talking about.

'My son got his car from you,' explained Maggie, adding, 'A schoolboy . . . barely old enough to drive?' She caught the salesman's eye, but he looked away.

She smiled. 'I'd like to try the tape deck, please. Can you pass me the key?'

She waited as he walked back to his office. She glanced at her reflection in the mirror. She looked terrible. There were dark circles beneath her eyes and her hair was all over the place. After this she'd go to the hairdresser. She'd noticed a '$10 Cuts' salon on her way here.

The man returned. Dangling from his fingers was an embossed key ring, which he held out to her. 'Toyota,' she observed. She placed the key in the ignition, but stopped turning when the stereo light came on.

'They're very reliable,' said the salesman. 'Plus we offer a one-year warranty, which you can upgrade to three years. There's a CD player and a port for your MP3 player – your children will appreciate that.'

She ignored him. She had already taken the tape from her pocket and inserted it into the machine, mumbling, 'I hope it doesn't eat it.'

Maggie bowed her head in concentration and listened to the tape. She hadn't noticed it before, but she could hear every intake of breath. It was incredible how noisy her breathing was. Now that she was aware of it, she found it hard to focus on the song. Tim's accompaniment faltered for the first time. He came in a fraction too late and then sped up, as if he thought that by rushing ahead he could afford to trail off towards the end. She heard her voice hesitate. She had noticed that Tim's playing was erratic. At that point, she'd hoped she was only imagining the problem. She'd continued to sing – as if nothing was wrong. She'd tried to kid herself into believing that everything would be all right. That it was only a small hitch, that Tim would regain control.

The salesman cleared his throat but Maggie raised her hand and silenced him. The song wasn't finished. Again, he tried to speak but Maggie ignored him. Reaching forward, she turned up the volume and then said, 'Music always sounds better loud, eh? Or, at least that's what my son says.' She laughed when the man nodded in agreement. She rewound the tape and pressed 'play' once more.

Her cellphone rang but she didn't care. She was interested only in the tape. A sound caught her attention. She pressed 'stop', rewound it and started again. It was too fast, she realised. *She* was rushing. No wonder Tim hadn't been able to keep up. She'd been the one to muck it up, not him. He should have told her to stop, to try again. She could have done it better.

Her cellphone rang again. Pressing the eject, Maggie climbed from the driver's seat and took the call. The salesman hovered nearby, a nervous smile on his face. What a shark, thought Maggie. He had taken advantage of Bevan and mucked her around. It was time he had a taste of his own medicine.

Her cellphone pressed to her ear, she turned her back on the man and returned to her own car. Hearing Justine's voice, Maggie felt a thud. It was as if she had reconnected with the ground, as if the world beneath her feet was solid once more.

'Where have you been?' Before Maggie could answer, she heard her daughter cry, 'Aaron's got a new girlfriend.'

Although she could hear the despair in her daughter's voice, she was relieved. Glancing down the street, which stretched out before her, she wanted to say, Thank God. Instead she asked, 'When did you find out?'

The guilt which had been lurking in the back of her mind since her last conversation with Justine suddenly resurfaced. She hadn't been very supportive. In fact, she had been avoiding her daughter. Dealing with Justine's volatile emotions was too stressful. Now, however, she would help out. She'd pay for Justine and the twins to fly home. Then she could take care of them. She would help Justine get back on her feet.

'He's gone to Rotorua,' continued Justine, her voice hoarse. 'He's with a woman he used to know. She's in her thirties . . . two kids.' Maggie heard her daughter's voice break. 'They're not even his kids . . . '

Sobs echoed down the phone and Maggie's heart lurched. It wasn't fair. Her daughter had been through a lot and deserved better. She was so young and fragile. In going straight from childhood to motherhood, she'd been forced to grow up too soon. Once she came back to Invercargill, Maggie thought, she would see to it that her daughter had more time for herself. In fact, she'd give Angela, the beautician, a call and book Justine in for a facial. She needed pampering, looking after. If Justine gained a bit more confidence and self-respect, everything else would fall into place.

'Listen, Justine,' said Maggie, carefully. 'I know it's difficult but maybe it's for the best. Aaron's never been . . .' She hesitated, thought better of discussing Aaron and changed tack. 'I'll pay for you and the girls to come down. I'll book the plane tickets, don't worry.' Maggie sighed. In the past her relationship with Justine had been fraught with conflict. It was time to make amends.

From the other end of the line she heard a sniffle. It sounded as if Justine was calming down, listening. Take things slowly, Maggie cautioned herself. Don't push too hard, too fast. Remember: Justine's proud.

'Justine,' she began quietly. 'Your family is here . . .' She laughed self-consciously and then stammered, 'I do care about you, you know. I love you.'

The words came in a rush. They didn't sound right. In fact, they sounded insincere, false even. With a start, Maggie suddenly realised she hadn't said those particular words since Justine was a girl, a child of Storm's age. Voicing the word 'love' made her uncomfortable. Actors and talk-show audiences could say it, but they weren't like real people. They liked being the centre of attention. She hesitated, breathed deeply and repeated, 'I do love you.'

She could hear Justine breathing and then a long sigh escaped from her daughter's lips. 'Yeah, me too,' she replied, cautiously.

A lump formed in Maggie's throat. She longed to take Justine in her arms and simply hold her. Mother her.

'I'm moving to Rotorua,' said Justine, her voice flat. 'I'm going to get Aaron back.'

Maggie gasped, a tight ball clenched in her chest.

'I love Aaron and I'm not going to lose him again – not like before,' Justine stated. 'He's the father of my twins . . . He's my family.' Her voice grew hoarse and Maggie heard her daughter gulp before continuing, 'I don't want to live in Invercargill.

I don't want to spend my days in some dead-end job.'

Maggie opened her mouth but nothing came out. Instead, she recalled the day Justine had stood next to Tim, a look of ferocious determination on her face as she'd bullied her to sing. What had she said? What was it? Something along the lines of 'Do you want to spend the rest of your life cleaning toilets?' Maggie recoiled at the memory.

'I hate Invercargill,' continued Justine, oblivious to the effect her words were having on Maggie. 'Nothing good ever happens – it's depressing. Look at you. You're forty going on ninety . . .'

The evenness of her daughter's voice – its soft, unemotional tone – stunned Maggie. Had her daughter yelled or sounded angry, she might have been able to cope. At least that behaviour would have been familiar, expected. But, as it was, the words cut into her with the surgical precision of a scalpel. She expected to look down and see a pool of blood ooze across the seat of the car, and drip onto the carpet mat.

Suddenly angry, Maggie wanted to yell, you'll regret it! If you think your life's going to be any better than mine . . . Just wait. It doesn't work like that! She thought of all the years she had spent working, raising kids, caring for her sick father, only to find herself alone, the employee of her younger sister. There's nothing out there, she wanted to cry. Tim knew that! But no sooner had the words formed, than she swallowed them down.

The seconds ticked by. Maggie ran her finger over the dashboard, drawing a squiggly trail through the pale-yellowish dust covering its surface. She smiled, remembering how she used to catch Justine drawing pictures on the condensated windows of the houses where she cleaned. She dotted the dashboard with her fingertip and then erased the marks with the palm of her hand.

It had been Justine's favourite childhood game. It was unlikely she even remembered, now.

'I'm sorry,' Justine murmured.

Maggie knew, then, that she couldn't change her daughter's mind. There was no point arguing, or cajoling, or even threatening. Nothing she said would make any difference. In a strange way, it was almost a relief. At least everything was clear, out in the open.

'You don't want to be like me?' Maggie asked, her voice breaking.

'God, Mum. Do you even want to be like you?'

Maggie glanced down the road. Where was everyone? Why weren't there any cars? 'I never really had much choice . . .'

And then she couldn't speak. Tears welled up in her eyes and she concentrated with all her might on a McDonald's carton which was blowing and tumbling down the middle of the road.

'GOODNESS, MAGGIE,' said Carol. 'Is that a new dress? I barely recognised you.'

Maggie attempted a smile. She had bought the dress a few days before and, although it had been marked down to half sale-price, she felt bad about the purchase. Had Lisa not insisted she buy it, she would not have spent almost fifty dollars on something that would get only one or two wears a year. She didn't even feel particularly comfortable in it. She was conscious, as always, of her flat chest. The dress hung from her shoulders like an old T-shirt pegged on the line to dry. The neckline drooped, showing off far more than was decent, and every time she glanced down, she caught sight of the edge of her bra and the knot she had tied in its elastic – the rough repair job she had carried out on its broken strap. She had only worn the dress because Lisa said she looked good in it. 'Come on, Mum,' she had teased. 'Look, even Bevan has made an effort. You look good . . . sexy. Live a little!' It was the final taunt that had persuaded Maggie. So what if she felt like one of those stunned women who had endured a television makeover? No one would notice, anyway.

Nodding towards the rest of her family, Maggie ushered her children towards the foot of the table. She waited for Storm to get settled, and then kissed her mother, murmuring, 'Happy Mother's Day, Mum. It's nice to see you.' It *was* good to see her mother. And all the others. In fact, seeing everyone gathered together made her feel warm, supported. She was lucky, she guessed. If only Justine and the twins had been there, too.

Maggie placed a small gift-wrapped package on the table: the hand cream she had bought for Elsie at H & J's. Then, turning to her sister, she observed, 'This is nice,' and gestured around the dining area, noticing as she did that it was packed with family groups very much like her own, all celebrating the special day. Two or three people in each party appeared to be talking, but the majority of the diners sat smiling, staring quietly into space. No one looked particularly relaxed but, on the other hand, no one appeared to resent being there.

'Lindsay and I have eaten here a few times,' shrugged Carol. 'It's good. The chef's Australian.'

Maggie couldn't help but notice that the fingers of Carol's right hand kept returning to her left wrist, drawing attention to a fine gold bracelet which dangled loosely around her hand. 'Oh this . . .' Carol murmured once she was sure Maggie was looking. 'It's a Mother's Day gift from Ashley and Gemma. It was such a nice surprise . . .' She was about to say more but Ashley interrupted, 'Not that much of a surprise – considering you got the shop to put it aside.'

Carol laughed with the others but Maggie could tell she was

hurt by the remark. Feeling sorry for her sister, she asked for a closer look. As Carol passed across the bracelet, Maggie was taken aback by the look of gratitude on her sister's face. She had forgotten how vulnerable Carol could be. She was so like Justine.

'It's beautiful,' said Maggie, returning the jewellery. 'It looks expensive . . . Gold suits you.' She smiled at Carol and added, 'I couldn't pull off wearing something like that. It's far too classy for me.' Her remark seemed to please Carol, who replied, 'Those paua earrings suit you, though. I'm glad you've made good use of them. I never liked them against my skin – made it look sallow.' She smiled and held her wrist up, fingering her new bracelet before reaching for the water carafe and filling her glass.

It wasn't important, much less unexpected, but Maggie noticed that Carol had seated herself at the head of the table, whereas Maggie was with the younger children at the foot. It wasn't even as if the settings had been left to chance. Her sister had gone to the trouble of creating place cards. Now that everyone was seated and waiting, Carol fumbled in her bag for Elsie's gift. 'Happy Mother's Day,' she gushed, passing a flat lilac parcel across the table.

Maggie *knew* her sister was not going to mention that the gift was from all of them. Just keep cool, she thought. You don't want a repeat of Storm's party. Let it go. Perhaps Carol was trying to get back at her for buying Elsie some hand cream? But that was hardly a gift – more a thank you for looking after Storm.

Maggie waited a moment longer and then cleared her throat. 'The gift's from Maggie, too,' stammered Carol. 'It's from all of us . . . although I chose it.' Maggie caught sight of her mother and exchanged glances. Nothing gets past her, she thought, relaxing. She watched as Elsie unfolded a silk scarf from its tissue wrapping. That wasn't what they'd agreed to buy. They were meant to give Elsie a leather purse – to replace her old clutch, the one with the broken zip. She glowered at Carol but stopped when she heard her mother murmur, 'Oh, that's lovely. What beautiful colours.' Carol beamed. 'I knew you'd like it. It's the same as mine.'

No one spoke for a moment and then, as if deciding to fill a gap, Murray asked, 'Did your kids get you anything, Maggie?'

'Murray, don't be so rude!' snapped Elsie, prodding him in the ribs.

Murray raised his hands. 'What? What's wrong?'

No one replied. Then, to help him out, Maggie nodded. A look of surprise crossed Carol's face.

As it happened, she stated, she'd been given a new tyre for her car.

As she glanced around, she saw Lisa blush. Her daughter was still worried about the present. She was embarrassed because she didn't think a tyre was a good-enough Mother's Day gift. But Maggie had needed a tyre for so long that she was delighted. Her only concern was the cost.

'How could you afford it?' she'd asked.

Lisa had tried to smile, 'Scott gave us a really good deal. And Dad chipped in, too.' Surprised, yet relieved to discover that Ross had contributed, Maggie hoped her children hadn't spent too much. 'Me and Bevan put in fifteen bucks each,' continued Lisa, 'and Storm gave it a good polish.' Lisa had sighed, even more embarrassed now than before. 'Honestly,' she'd added, 'Dad paid for most of it.'

Murmuring, 'Thanks,' Maggie had smiled at Lisa and taken a step towards her daughter who'd instantly shrugged and shuffled out of the way. 'It's exactly what I needed,' Maggie had added. It was ridiculous but she felt really happy. It was such a weight off her mind. Her kids had no idea.

While Maggie relayed the story to her family, she could see that its meaning was lost on Carol. Her sister smiled and said something about it being a very thoughtful gift but it was clear from the tone in her voice that she would have been outraged if anyone had been foolish enough to give her a tyre. In fact, thought Maggie, it probably proved her sister's point – that it paid to select and put aside your own present.

To Maggie's relief, the waiter approached at that moment and ran through the day's specials. But, before anyone had time to think, Carol chimed in, 'The lamb here is generally quite good . . . and the venison's excellent, isn't it, Lindsay?' Maggie tried to block out the sound of her sister's voice. It was little wonder that Ross had complained that she was bossy. She never stopped. Even now she was busy telling everyone what to order. She wanted them all to choose different dishes, so they could sample from one another's plates. When it came time to order, decided Maggie, she would make a point of asking for the same main as Elsie. That would put Carol in a spin.

Although she'd only been sitting down for ten minutes or so, Maggie felt restless. That was the problem with dining out, she thought. It tied you down, trapped you in one place. It was impossible to wander off and do something useful while you waited for the food to arrive. Even if she had the money, she wouldn't eat out – by choice. It involved too much sitting around. She could never relax in such a situation. She wasn't cut out for it.

Distracted, she looked around the room, her eyes scanning over the other diners. They really did look like they'd made an effort.

Everyone's cellphone was put away, no one was texting. Much to her surprise, even Bevan had turned off his phone. He was actually talking to Murray. She couldn't hear their conversation but it was nice to see Bevan trying so hard to be polite. She hoped he wasn't attempting to wheedle money out of his grandfather.

Twisting in her seat, Maggie noticed that the room was decorated with a number of antique objects. There was an old upright piano shoved up against the wall behind her and an antique Singer sewing machine was on a sideboard next to the door leading to the kitchen. Beside the fireplace was a beautiful copper coal bucket filled with pine cones and next to that was an old-fashioned pitchfork. Everything looked good, but the room itself was too big, too barn-like for a proper restaurant. It was kind of chilly and, now she thought about it, the decorations seemed slightly theatrical, as if put there to camouflage something.

If she took out the tables and rearranged the chairs, the room would be very similar to the chapel where Tim's funeral had been held. Even the flower arrangements were the same. Both places were somehow phoney.

She had put off making the decision to attend Tim's funeral until the last minute and she had been surprised by the number of people already seated at the front of the room when she arrived. She'd got it into her head that he didn't have many friends. Not wishing to draw attention to herself, she had taken a seat at the back of the hall and leafed through a Bible.

Shortly after three, a small group of musicians had walked to the front of the room and started to play. Their faces were familiar, and Maggie realised she had seen them before, depicted in the photograph displayed in Tim's lounge. In the photograph the woman had been young and smiling. Now her hair was sprinkled with grey and her eyes were red-rimmed, from crying.

Maggie had watched as the woman stepped towards the coffin and laid her hand gently on it as she sang. When she'd finished, she'd stood motionless, her fingers resting on the lid. 'Tim and I first met at the Gold Guitars,' she'd murmured. She'd hesitated, as if lost in memory. 'More than twenty years ago. God, I'm getting old.' A few members of the congregation had laughed. 'I won, of course . . . and Tim was the runner-up. He was really pissed off.' The men beside her had nodded, but the woman had appeared thoughtful when she spoke again. 'Tim was a great songwriter, the best. That song – the one we just did – was one of my favourites.' She'd sighed, 'I love that song.' Someone in front of Maggie had applauded, quietly, but she hadn't been able to see who it was. The woman had smiled, nodded and clapped three or four times in appreciation, before continuing. 'From what I've heard, he hasn't written anything for a while now . . .'

Alert, Maggie had sat up straight and watched as the woman had shrugged and lowered her gaze towards the coffin. Although she hadn't been able to hear what the woman said next, she'd seen her lips move. When she looked up again the woman had tried to smile, but her mouth had began to tremble as she'd murmured, 'He was so amazing, so talented . . .' Then she'd raised her hand to her mouth, and it had seemed to Maggie that she might cry. One of the musicians had given her shoulders a squeeze, and together, they'd returned to their seats.

The service had continued for an hour. During that time a number of people had taken to the floor, sharing recollections of Tim. As Maggie had listened, she'd become aware of how little she really knew him. It was clear, from what everyone said, that he had been active in the music scene. A regular at festivals, he had travelled the length of the country performing. He was well known.

He had also been popular with women. Maggie had never pictured him as part of a couple and yet he had had several live-in partners over the years. It was only after becoming ill that he had decided to 'become single'. More than that, some of the speakers hinted that he had become withdrawn, self-absorbed. He hadn't wanted to 'drag anyone down'. It seemed to Maggie that only a few of his oldest acquaintances had managed to maintain a presence in his life. The rest, it seemed, had been scared off.

To her surprise, no one had expressed any anger over what he had done. She found that strange. Not only had he avoided his friends, but he had wasted his musical talent. Maggie had the impression he hadn't valued those things. Thinking about it, she felt cheated.

He should have realised that she would have taken care of him. He could have trusted her. He could have . . . Did it never occur to him that she might miss him? She hadn't even had a chance to say goodbye, or anything. He should have said something, and she could have stopped him from doing what he did. She could have helped. It made her so angry.

He hadn't even allowed her enough time to do a proper job of his song.

'Maggie?'

Maggie started. Her mother was gesturing towards a waiter who stood, hovering behind her, holding a plate.

The waiter edged forward, asking, 'Venison?'

Maggie nodded, and watched as the plate was placed in front of her. The meat looked delicious, but there were no greens on the plate. She swung around, and a second waiter stepped forward, a dish of steaming vegetables in his hands. 'Medley of organic veg,' he said, as he put the bowl of new potatoes, peas and spinach down. A large sprig of mint slipped off, falling on to the tablecloth and he hurriedly retrieved it, stabbing it into the peas. For a second Maggie felt as if everyone was watching and she turned away. From the corner of her eye, she thought she recognised Scott sitting at a table at the far end of the room. His face was partly obscured by a large dried-flower arrangement but taking a closer look, she realised it was him. An old, white-haired woman sat opposite him, and they appeared deep in conversation. Maggie had no idea what they were discussing, but whatever it was, it was making Scott smile. The old woman began to laugh. She laughed so hard that she had to wipe the tears from her eyes with her serviette. They looked so relaxed, so happy – almost a mirror reflection of each other. The old woman must be his mother, Maggie thought. How strange.

'Maggie,' her mother said, 'Would you like to say anything – before we start?'

It was kind of her mother to ask, but Maggie knew better than to say grace in front of the others. It would only irritate Carol. She would think Maggie was trying to make a point, that she was 'better' than everyone else. It wasn't important, anyway. Maggie didn't need to pray out loud.

Maggie shook her head, 'No thanks.'

'You're sure?' asked Elsie.

Maggie registered the puzzled look on her mother's face and nodded, 'It's okay.'

Funnily enough, she had been asked a question similar to her mother's at Tim's funeral. Well, not just her – but everyone. One of his former music students had stood up to read a beautiful, modern poem about stopped clocks and silent pianos and then, when she had stepped down from the microphone, no one had stood to take her place.

Maggie had had the tape in her pocket and for one crazy second she had pictured herself going to the front of the hall and slipping it into the tape machine. She'd imagined telling everyone that Tim *had* continued to write songs. In fact, he had written a song for her. She could even sing it! But she hadn't stood up. Instead, she'd touched the tape, wrapping her fingers around it. The tape was hers, sacred.

After the service, she had stayed a few minutes and had spoken to one or two people. To her surprise, they had heard of her. It seemed that Tim had mentioned her name. At one point, she had been about to leave when a man had walked up and said, 'So, you're the woman who washed Tim's dishes and tidied his house.' He'd spoken so loudly that several people had turned and glanced in their direction, causing Maggie to blush. 'Christ,' the man had continued, 'I've never seen Tim's place so clean before. No wonder he loved you.' Maggie had nodded but felt annoyed. He didn't love me, she'd wanted to correct. It wasn't love. Confused, she wondered what it had been. There had been something between them – but what? Not love, she thought. Not love. It was something more important. Something stronger, more weighty than love. Something she barely recognised. Respect. That was it. Respect.

She'd left shortly afterwards, declining an invitation to attend an impromptu gig which was going to take place later that evening. As she'd walked away, someone had shouted, 'Nice to meet you, Minnie. Pop into the folk club some time. You're always welcome.' But she hadn't turned round so she didn't know who had spoken.

IT WAS LATE when Maggie pulled into the petrol station. From her car, she could make out Scott's figure behind the counter, his face bent over a magazine as he rested his head in his hands. He looked different from usual and it took Maggie a minute to work out why. His white shirt. She smiled and stepped out of the car, walking the short distance across the forecourt to the shop. As she entered the buzzer sounded and Scott looked up, meeting her gaze. She was surprised he didn't say anything by way of greeting but was content to watch as she walked towards him. For a strange moment she felt solemn, as if walking up a church aisle towards a waiting groom. The fact that Scott was wearing his good shirt, the one he had worn at lunch, rather than his familiar work T-shirt, increased her sense of occasion. It was almost as if Scott *had been* waiting for her. The moment passed, and Scott smiled, saying, 'So, you got your tyre, then.'

Maggie nodded.

'Funny Mother's Day present,' continued Scott. 'I don't know what my wife would have said if I . . .' His voice faded and he frowned, rubbing at a small black spot of grease on the back of his hand.

'It's what I wanted,' said Maggie.

She could tell Scott wasn't convinced by her remark.

They stood silently, watching each other. Maggie was unable to explain why she was at the service station. Her petrol tank was full, Lisa was at home with Storm – there was no reason why she should be out so late at night. Nervously, she waited for Scott to ask what she wanted, but as the seconds ticked by she began to think he hadn't noticed anything unusual.

She wondered if she should leave, but Scott offered to make a cup of coffee. As he walked to the machine, she quipped that he should consider managing a café rather than a petrol station. To her relief, he laughed, replying he wouldn't know where to start. It was one thing to push a few buttons but quite another to master the twirly bits made from frothy-milk.

Maggie nodded and looked down, deciding what to say next. Suddenly she remembered Scott's elderly dining companion and asked if she was his mother.

'Agnes?' replied Scott.

Maggie shrugged.

'I've known her since I was three – she was our neighbour. A kind of second mother really.' He explained that he sometimes took her out for dinner but that Mother's Day was their 'special' day. 'Since my own mother died . . .' He hesitated, then continued, 'Agnes is a real character. She grew up on a farm near Dipton. She has a niece who lives there now, and she's great. Nicola. You should meet her . . .' He stopped, appeared embarrassed and mumbled, 'She's about our age.'

Maggie flinched. She wondered if there was something going on between Scott and Nicola. It was none of her business, but she wanted to know, anyway. Silently she waited, but he appeared to have become engrossed in making coffee.

'Does Nicola have children?' she finally asked.

'Yeah, a daughter.'

'She's married, then?'

Scott nodded.

Feeling more relaxed than before, Maggie came closer to where Scott was standing and watched as a thin layer of white froth settled on the top of her drink. In truth, she could imagine him with a large café-style espresso machine, creating small pictures of petrol pumps or cars in milk-froth. She mentioned her idea to Scott, and he smiled. Then, taking a straw, he scored a circle into the cream-coloured foam before offering it to her. 'It's a tyre,' he smiled, joking.

She nodded but was careful when she raised the cup to her lips. She didn't want to destroy the tyre by drinking too quickly.

'Bring your car in tomorrow and I'll get your warrant sorted,' said Scott.

Maggie nodded but her stomach lurched. It was such an old wreck of a car there was bound to be something wrong with it. It was sure to fail. She sighed, impatient with herself for taking the whole warrant business so personally.

She took another sip from her cup and noticed the tyre sink further into the froth. Glancing up, she realised Scott was watching her. He seemed amused by something, but before she could ask him to explain, he said, 'So, what do you think about Lisa?'

'What do you mean?'

'You know, all that stuff about the mysterious universe . . .'

Maggie had no idea what Scott was talking about.

'I reckon it's related to her trip to Christchurch. Ever since she got back she's been going on about that boy, Liam.'

Liam? thought Maggie Wasn't he the son of the teacher she had stayed with? She tried to recall what Lisa had said exactly, but before she could think, Scott added. 'She talks about him all the time. You'd better watch out.'

Maggie took a sip from her cup and saw the tyre break in two. Now she thought about it, Lisa had been acting a little strange lately. She'd been a bit giggly – especially when she was talking on the phone to her school friends. Maggie wondered how old Liam was and, with a sinking heart, she pondered what had gone on between them.

'Did Lisa say how old Liam was?'

'Twenty-four. And he's interested in the environment. Don't you know anything?' There was nothing malicious in Scott's tone, but Maggie felt cross.

'He's a university student,' she snapped. She had reached the limit of her knowledge.

'He's studying to be a cosmologist,' ventured Scott, softly. 'I had to look up the word in the dictionary. I had no idea it was related to astronomy.'

'You mean like zodiacs and stuff?'

Scott shook his head. 'I think it has more to do with physics and maths – like studying the universe.'

Of course, Maggie winced. She knew the difference between astronomy and astrology. She sighed and then mumbled, 'I hate that astrology nonsense.' She glanced around the shop. All the shelves were tidy; everything in its right place. She sighed again. What if

Lisa got it into her head to study cosmology, she thought. Maggie could understand why someone might want to spend a few years studying to become a doctor or lawyer. But a cosmologist?

Niggled, she was confronted by a new thought. Carol would have a field day with this. She could imagine it now . . . 'What a shame Lisa didn't do medicine. How many years has she been unemployed, now? Maybe things will pick up next week.' Meanwhile, her own two children would have risen up through the ranks to become managers, like their father. Maggie groaned. It was all she needed.

'Do you think it might be a phase? I mean, if Liam is twenty-four . . . and she's got a crush . . .'

'I don't know but she's an intelligent girl. Talk to her. Ask her what she wants to do . . .'

'That's all very well,' Maggie grumbled, 'but if you had a teenage daughter of your own, then you'd know it's not that easy . . .' Catching sight of Scott's face, she fell quiet. She took a step towards him. 'I'm sorry. I wasn't thinking. I . . .' Her hands fell slack to her side.

At that moment, the light in the service station struck her as obscenely bright. Neon tubes strung high in the ceiling made the shop appear chilled. The lighting belonged to a freezer or, worse, a morgue. She'd never been in a morgue but she'd seen images of them often enough on television to know what they looked like. Even the living looked slightly greenish, non-human, under their neon lights. She turned away, scanning the shelves, taking note of the confectionery display, the magazine rack and the upright, glass doors of the fridge. Everything looked lifeless – not that shelves of food could look anything but lifeless – but it was kind of creepy, haunted.

She should go. But, even though she wanted to leave, she felt rooted to the spot. She stifled a yawn. What was wrong with her? Scott was watching but, like her, gave the impression of not quite understanding what was going on.

'I'm sorry,' she repeated, but Scott shook his head, brushing aside her remark. 'Do you want another coffee?'

Maggie looked at her empty cup and hesitated. She didn't know. If Scott reached out, took her cup and refilled it, it would be fine. On the other hand, it didn't matter if she went without. Conscious that time was drifting by and that Scott was waiting for an answer, she shook her head. 'No, I won't be able to sleep,' she murmured, adding, 'Not that I seem to get much sleep anyway.' She yawned and glanced at her watch. It was later than she had thought. It was definitely time to go home.

She dropped her cup into the waste bin, watching as the dregs splattered over the pristine white plastic bin-liner. Rubbing the back of her neck with the palm of her hand, she turned to go but the contrast between the well-lit shop and the dark muted-grey beyond the door momentarily disorientated her. She lost her balance. Instinctively, she put out her hand to break her fall but felt Scott's hand take her by the elbow. He supported her only for a second and then stood back, waiting. 'I think it's the coffee,' she explained. 'Or the lights, maybe?' She grimaced, adding, 'I don't know . . . sometimes I have trouble with shiny surfaces and reflections. They seem to throw me off-balance. Stupid, eh?'

Rather than saying goodnight and leaving, she found herself drifting back towards the counter. All of a sudden, she felt so tired that making the decision to go outside, get into her car, and drive home was beyond her. She recalled Storm's movements when he was woken in the night and taken to the toilet, and she was aware of her own body mimicking his dazed passiveness. It was so late. She wished that someone would take her home. If someone could lead her to the passenger door of her car and help her into her seat and then drive. She imagined her sleeping body being carried from the car to the dark safety of her bedroom. She pictured a figure crouched in front of her, unlacing her shoes and then tucking her into bed. She felt her body slump into itself and then the quiet calm of solitude, before drifting off to sleep. It was time to go. Come on, Maggie, she willed herself, get a move on.

In her dream state, she'd forgotten about Scott. Yet there he was, hovering nearby, smiling. Maggie noticed the dark shadows around his eyes. He also looked tired. Surely he could close up for the night and go home. She raised her hand as if to wave goodbye, but let it fall back to her side.

'I heard about your friend,' Scott murmured.

Maggie froze. The light in the shop intensified. Blinking, she felt trapped.

'He was one of my clients,' she shrugged. As she spoke an image of Tim filtered into her head – the expression on his face the last time she had seen him. She had sat next to his bed, her hands resting on his bedspread, as he lay with his back turned to her. When she'd stood to leave the room he'd rolled over and stared at her. His eyes had conveyed an expression of weary despair. There was no fight left in him. He had reached the end.

'I'm sorry, anyway,' Scott continued.

Maggie's body gave a jerk and she found herself nodding – that same automatic gesture she had made at the funeral. She felt her bottom lip begin to tremble and mechanically, she raised her hand to her face, obscuring her mouth. She wished she could figure out what Scott wanted from her. Her brain wouldn't co-operate. She couldn't think.

She heard Scott sigh. In a quiet voice, he said, 'It's hard.' He made a low grunt and shook his head. Maggie watched as he took a step forward, towards her. She didn't know what was going to happen but she thought he might try to touch her again. Unconsciously, she took a step backwards, re-establishing more space between them.

Scott made no further move in her direction; he stood and waited. Maggie noticed that his eyes were very dark, almost black. They made her think of the oily puddles that settled on the ground by the petrol pumps after a downpour of rain. She met his glance and then looked away.

'You get used to it,' said Scott after a moment. His voice sounded so quiet, so flat, that Maggie could barely make out his words. 'You can block it out but it bears down on you anyway, it never really goes away,' he continued, as if speaking to himself. 'It goes on and on and on – and you get used to it.' His voice faded into silence. He sighed, and then murmured, 'You forget that your life wasn't always so painful. You even start to believe that everything is normal . . . but you always feel heavier inside than before . . .' He suddenly looked hard at Maggie, searching her face, she thought, for some sign that she had understood. 'That's life, isn't it?' he finished.

Once more she had the feeling he might reach forward and touch her. She imagined the warmth of his hand as he sought hers. In her mind's eye, she could see herself nestled against him, her body supported by his, and this time she did not retreat. The passing seconds were both awkward and yet reassuring. So, she decided, there's no such thing as closure. Life is open-ended, incomplete.

She caught Scott's eye and smiled. To her relief, he smiled back.

'I want to ask you something – a favour, really,' he murmured.

Maggie flinched, her shoulders tightening in anticipation of what might come next.

'My club's got another of its fundraising events coming up – a karaoke night – and I wondered if you would come with me? You never know, it might be fun to blast out a few tunes.'

Maggie glanced outside and realised that during the past hour the wind had died down. Beyond the forecourt, perched on top of a fence, back-lit by an orange street lamp, was a seagull. It stood quietly, turning its head from side to side, and then, unhurriedly, stretched its wings and flew away, disappearing into the night.

ACKNOWLEDGEMENTS

*T*HIS NOVEL was written while I was the Robert Burns Fellow at the University of Otago, and I am very grateful for the kindness and support extended to me by Greg Waite and the staff of the English Department throughout 2007.

Several Invercargill friends helped me during the writing of this book. In particular I would like to thank Garry Nixon. I would also like to extend my gratitude to the many people I encountered during my frequent journeys south to Winton, Riverton and Invercargill. I want to thank Alison Ballance and Louis le Vaillant who accompanied me on many of my trips.

I am grateful to Stephen Robertson for his friendship and conversation, and for his helpful remarks concerning the Catholic faith. I also want to thank Bernadette Hall for her comments and suggestions. I am indebted to Rodney Keillor, for his patience and grace when describing various eye conditions to me. Thanks to Vanessa McLellan for being such a good sport and agreeing to write a song for the Gold Guitars. And a big thank you to Blair Smith for his frankness and honesty.

Once more I would like to thank Sue Wootton for her friendship and encouragement during the writing of this book – particularly during the editing stages. To my family, Alex, Harry and Wendy, I offer my gratitude and love.

I was fortunate to receive a short residency at Lake Ohau House during the final stages of writing this book. It was a wonderful place to work and I am very grateful to the owners for their generosity.

Finally, I would like to extend my gratitude to everyone at Penguin. Thanks to Harriet Elworthy and Emma Beckett for their patience and hard work. Thank you to Mary Egan for her design work. Most of all, I would like to thank Geoff Walker for his kindness and support.